Tara's World

A Land of Beauty, Danger, and Love

Tom Molnar

Apple Valley Press

This book is a work of fiction. Names, characters, places and incidents are products of the author's imagination or are used fictitiously. Any resemblance to actual events or locales or persons, living or dead, is entirely coincidental.

Copyright © 2014 Tom Molnar

Printed in the United States of America.

ISBN 978-0-9766952-6-4

TARA'S WORLD

PART ONE

An unexpected discovery, two people from different worlds, a dilemma, the enemy, and hope for the future.

PART TWO

PART THREE

A grateful thank you to those who perused this book in getting it ready for publication. Another, for those who reviewed it. Most of all, I would like to thank the important people in my life who provided the inspiration to write this novel.

Tara's World

The star ship moved silently toward the Earth-sized green planet, fourth from its sun. The small, yellow star had long since been catalogued, but like most, its planets had never been explored.

Nick Bartok opened his eyes gingerly; he was not used to the bright sunlight. Suddenly, he jumped out of bed and rushed to the terrestrial energy monitor. Had he seen a momentary blip? He stood there, watching, feeling foolish as he stared at the empty screen. No civilization had evolved on this planet; they knew that, didn't they?

He and his partner, Matthew Kerry, had traveled two months through space to reach this destination, and now their long journey would pay off. He knew that he was being optimistic. In reality, the chance of finding usable crude was always less than fifty percent, and less than that of finding enough oil to be profitable to extract. Still, he, Matt, and the team had studied the charts carefully, had minutely analyzed the spectrographic data, and had applied all the known mathematical formulae and computer analyses to pick out this particular spot in the galaxy. He was proud of their team, and it had been personally hard for him to say goodbye. He thought of Terri, and he remembered how her eyes filled with tears as they kissed their farewell. He thought again of the last thing she whispered. "Please be careful Nick. Come back to me."

* * *

"Oh, that light!" groaned Matt as he wakened, covering his eyes with his hands to shield them from the sun.

Nick pressed the shade activator, saying, "Take a look down there, Matt. Have you ever seen such a lush planet?"

Beneath them, white-capped, majestic clouds framed the emerald green flora of the new world. They could sense already the freshness and the untainted atmosphere of a planet untouched by man.

"It's magnificent," agreed Matt, opening the shades further so he could see clearly. "Let's eat breakfast now, so we'll be ready to leave the ship when we land."

Nick still marveled at the technology that made meal selections so varied. Growing up, his breakfast choice was usually cereal or toast, and often only toast. Milk was frequently not available. "What would you like?" he asked Matt, as he eyed the breakfast menu that appeared on the smooth wall of the restant.

"Croissants, quiche, and tropical fruit," Matt answered.

"What?" said Nick, turning around.

"I'm joking," Matt said, with a grin. "Ham and eggs sounds good to me." He turned back to the orbital tracking readouts.

By the time they finished eating, they had the information needed for landing. The computer provided topographic maps and coordinates specifying initial target areas for oil exploration. Continuing the quiet descent toward the planet, they noted that clouds began to obscure the sun. They dropped the last few hundred yards and felt the unmistakable jolt of landing.

Dawn was just breaking on the planet, and as the light increased, they saw that they had landed in an area with long grasses and scattered trees. Nick opened the hatch and they looked out. The aroma of verdant grassland pervaded the cabin. It was incomparably better than the continuously recycled air they had been breathing for so long.

"Mm! Smell that air," said Matt, inhaling deeply. Stepping to the ground, he moved his arms up and down, turned, and jumped twice to test the gravity. Nick followed; walking out a short distance, he checked the landscape both near and far with a practiced eye.

Despite his training to approach a new environment with caution, he began to feel a sense of giddiness, which he attributed to the high oxygen content of the air. Instead of setting up their instruments, he wanted to explore first-hand their surroundings. The more he thought about it, the more the idea grew on him. "What the hell," he mumbled to himself, thinking about how long they had been cooped up before their arrival.

"Matt, let's take a walk."

"Immediately, before we set up the equipment?"

"That's what I'm thinking. We can pack a lunch, stretch our legs, and see what's out there."

"Fine with me. We can do the setup when we return."

Soon they were on their way, each with a sidearm attached to his belt. They walked away from the ship, through the grass and trees, in the general direction of some low hills in the distance.

They continued quietly for a time, taking note of their surroundings. Nick was the first to speak. "Matt, to me there's something unusual about this place. Not only is it beautiful, but it also seems extremely familiar. It's as if we had landed inadvertently on an unknown and undeveloped place on Earth."

"I know what you mean. There *is* something about it. It's as if we've been here before."

They walked much further, taking a closer look at plant specimens that resembled those they knew from home. They were startled when they fleetingly glimpsed what appeared to be a deer, though it moved too fast for them to positively identify it. Finally,

Matt said, "I'm not used to this much hiking. Let's stop and have lunch."

Nick pointed to a spot where the grass was shorter. They moved there and sat down. Soon, they were enjoying their lunch, and basking in the warm afternoon sun.

"I feel like taking a nap," Matt said, stretching his legs.

"Go ahead." Nick settled himself against a fallen tree trunk. "I'll keep watch, although I don't think we have anything to worry about." He looked toward the nearby pond and wondered lazily what kind of aquatic life it might contain. Soon, he was asleep.

A young woman appeared near some trees at the edge of the pond. She soundlessly disrobed and purposefully walked into the water. She was lovely, of average size, with full curves and a slender waist. Her long dark hair fell down her back, and she stood for a moment in shallow water. Then she turned in Nick's direction, tilted her head as if she saw him, and turned back. She didn't seem at all surprised, if she did indeed see him. She moved again and, with a brief backward glance, walked out into deeper water.

"Nick. Wake up." Nick felt Matt shaking his shoulder. "We've got to get back to the ship before nightfall."

"What? OK." Gradually Nick remembered where he was. "What a dream I had! I saw a gorgeous girl bathing in that pond over there. She undressed first and started walking into the water. Then, she turned and seemed to look right at me. It was as if she was inviting me to join her."

"Nick, we've both been away from women too long."

"It's just that she seemed so real. I'm going over there to see if there's any trace of her."

They walked the short distance to the lake. Near it, they saw something unusual.

"Look at that," exclaimed Matt. "It looks like a road."

Nick pressed his heel into the dark green surface. "Like a road, and yet spongy and yielding."

Kneeling down, Matt rubbed the surface with his fingers. "It appears to be made of some kind of dense vegetative matter."

Nick turned to look along each direction of the roadway. "I wonder where it leads?" he speculated.

"We've definitely found something else here besides oil," Matt asserted, automatically placing his hand on the holster of his pulsar. "I wonder if they know we're here?"

"They might, but I doubt it. Otherwise, they could easily have come to meet us. Or, for that matter, they could have attacked. They must be at a very low level of civilization," Nick continued, "or our energy monitors would have detected spent gases in their atmosphere."

"This road doesn't look very primitive to me."

"No, it doesn't. I'd love to have a mass analyzer here to feed a chunk of this into."

"We'd better get back to the ship right away," said Matt, obviously alarmed.

"Yes. Let's split up and travel about fifty meters apart. That way it would be hard for them to ambush us both, and we can help each other if necessary.

"OK," Matt replied, removing his pulsar from its holster. They cautiously made their way toward the star ship, keeping each other in sight and watching for anything that moved. They had a momentary scare when another of the deer-like creatures jumped out from some bushes, but otherwise they saw nothing unusual.

Back inside the ship, with the perimeter alarm system turned on, they felt less tense. Nightfall settled over the land, and after a satisfying supper, they were ready to make plans for the next day. Realizing that they had not exercised sufficient caution, they were glad there had been no negative consequences. With complex life forms now known to be on the planet, they would have to be careful.

Nick wondered if the girl in his dream was real or had been imagined. Either way, it wouldn't change what they needed to do. They had to find out if there were any aliens living nearby that might be a security concern. The ship's firepower, they knew, would be able to withstand anything except the most powerful attack. Nevertheless, they couldn't proceed with oil exploration if the natives were hostile.

Nick and Matt were prepared to kill any animals that got in their way, but killing aliens was something else. Not only was it not authorized, but to Nick it was not even to be contemplated. Explorers were allowed to bargain with natives within certain limits. However, negotiations often proved difficult, as scientists usually had no special skill in dealing with unknown cultures and had no authorization to offer gifts or royalties. Nick and Matt discussed these considerations until late that evening. When they were ready to turn in, they knew clearly what they needed to do the next day.

After falling asleep, Nick again had a dream. He saw the same girl, who this time appeared to be in a house. She seemed to be trying to tell him something. There was an indistinctness about the vision, although he had the impression that it had something to do with the green road. The last thing that he sensed was a message that said, "Come, there is nothing to fear."

They awoke refreshed in the morning, and the sunshine and wide, undisturbed vista made them feel less apprehensive. After breakfast, their plan was to take their vehicle, the amcar, and drive back to the green road. Once there, they wanted to cut a piece of its surface for analysis, and then follow it to wherever it led. Traveling by car was much safer, as its sensors could be set to detect life forms, and they could speed away if anything threatened. After taking the normal precaution of setting the ship's internal and perimeter protective system, they stepped into their vehicle, and soon were zipping over the grasslands heading back toward the pond.

"I like this little convertible," said Nick. "It may be old, but it maneuvers well, and you still retain a lot of control."

"Yes," agreed Matt. "The newer models are so smooth and automated they make you feel like a passenger in your own car."

"Look, there's the lake," said Nick. "And over there is the road." He switched off the accelerator. They coasted down, landing near the water. They cautiously surveyed the area before getting out of the vehicle. Nick knelt down to examine the road while Matt kept watch. He found the dark green surface hard to extract, but using the sharp side of a rock hammer, he managed to remove a piece from the edge.

"Look at this, Matt. The top is green, but the middle section is creamy white, and the bottom is dark brown. I'm not sure if the surface is something that's sprayed on or if it's a natural part of the substance." He handed it to Matt.

He looked it over carefully. "Unusual. It has the same texture throughout, just different levels of color." He handed it back to Nick, who put it in a compartment in the car.

"Well, what do you think?" asked Nick. "Are you ready to meet the natives?"

"Why not?" Matt answered, taking a deep breath. "It will be very interesting to see what they look like."

They put the top up and slowly drove down the road, staying on high alert since they didn't know what might be waiting for them. They realized that if there were only a few aliens, or if they were friendly, their mission need not be compromised. However, if the inhabitants became scared, and resolved to fight, their stay on the planet would have to be terminated. Hopefully, they could at least do some preliminary testing first to determine if there was enough oil to warrant a return trip. If there were, a diplomatic party would be dispatched to negotiate with the natives. The goal, of course, was to convince them to give up the oil, with gifts and incentives for doing so. Usually that was effective.

If, however, the natives didn't agree, their rights were often usurped. Not by the Worlds' Organization itself, but by pirates who sometimes found undeveloped sites by breaking through encrypted communications. Unfortunately, those thugs cared little for life when the black market oil trade was so lucrative.

They continued down the roadway, and it wasn't long before they saw structures in the distance. As they drew closer, it was clear that the structures were dwellings nestled on the outskirts of a large village. The houses were of unusual architecture with rounded sides and slanting roofs that were all canted in the same direction. They were low lying; in fact, most were at least partially surrounded by earthen embankments. There were open grassy areas between the houses, and a stream flowed along the edge of the town. It was an idyllic scene.

"Look at that," Nick exclaimed. "I don't believe my eyes."

"Neither do I," echoed Matt. "Except for the rounded houses, it looks like a scene from the eighteenth century. I think that may be a mill wheel over there by the stream."

"Of course. They must actually grind their grain there. How picturesque, harnessing water power just like we used to do hundreds of years ago."

"Don't let your guard down too soon, Nick. They may come at us with pitchforks."

"Or worse," Nick agreed. "They may have discovered gunpowder. We need to move the amcar and conceal it well off the road. Then we can investigate further before we attempt communication."

"I hate to leave it behind, but you're right. Chances are it would only scare them. I wonder what form of transportation they use?"

The question was no sooner asked than it was answered. Appearing around a bend in the road, two figures were fast approaching them. They rode large animals that combined a cat-like head on a large, deer-like body. Quickly reaching for their pulsars, they moved to the side. Unfortunately, there was no time to hide. They had already been spotted. They saw that the two riders were women, and in a moment the women were standing before them.

Nick was speechless. The dark-haired girl he had seen in his dream surveyed him from her mount. Her eyes seemed to bore through him. Somehow, he felt she knew what he was thinking.

His own eyes were riveted on hers, so much so that everything else was a blur. In the background, he heard Matt shouting something. Whatever he said, the words didn't register on his consciousness.

The girl dismounted, and now she was standing directly in front of him. She placed her hand on his arm. Immediately, the thoughts he had of fighting or fleeing dissolved. Looking at her, he realized that she was speaking to him. Without words, she was telling him to follow her. Instantly, all the reasons he might have for resisting her wish vanished from his mind. When she remounted, Nick turned to Matt and said, "Let's follow them into town."

"Are you sure?"

"Yes."

As they returned to the amcar Nick explained. "They want to meet us and are welcoming us to come with them to their village."

"OK. I just hope we're not taking any unnecessary chances."

"I believe they can be trusted."

"I'm not so sure, Nick. On the other hand, it seems unlikely that two women and a child would be sent out for what could be a dangerous mission."

"A child?" asked Nick. "Did you say they had a child with them?"

"Yes, didn't you see? The woman on my side of the road had a little girl riding with her. Probably not more than three or four years old."

Nick directed the car to follow the riders at a safe distance. Soon, they reached the first houses. They took the precaution of moving their vehicle to a small copse of trees nearby, and then caught up with and followed the women into one of the houses.

The next few hours went by like minutes for Nick. He spent the whole time with the young woman, whose name, he learned, was Tara. Within the walls of her own house, she seemed even more charming. He guessed her age to be about twenty-two. She wore a soft leather dress that was cinched around her waist with a thong. The garment reached to her knees. She had on a pair of thin brown shoes, also made of leather, and wore no jewelry or other ornamentation. She was several inches shorter than he was, and had an excellent figure and fairly long fingers. She looked as if she could have come from Earth.

Nick didn't understand at first how he seemed to be able to communicate with her. He certainly didn't know the language. Was he somehow reading her thoughts? Her voice was melodic, and she used her hands frequently as she talked.

He concentrated, watching her, and abruptly understood that she was telling him not to focus on the words, but on the meaning. He began to understand what she was saying to him; that communication required emptying his mind of preconceptions, looking directly into her eyes, and letting his consciousness read hers. In time, he got better at it, though he began to realize that he was letting himself become mesmerized by the beauty of her eyes.

"Nick. Nick!" Matt's strident voice broke through his concentration.

"We better leave," Matt said with insistence. "It's getting late."

"OK," he answered. Turning to Tara, he expressed to her that he had to leave and saw that she understood. She followed them to the door, and he held her hand a moment before they went out. He told her that he would return.

They pulled away from Crystal, the name of the town, and Nick was quiet, thinking about Tara. Matt must have had thoughts of his own, because on the short trip back he didn't interrupt his reverie. Once inside the ship, or space module, as it was often called, Nick ordered hot onion soup, bread, and coffee from the synthesizer. He waited until Matt's food was ready and they both sat down to eat. Nick was starting his second cup of coffee when Matt leaned toward him and said, "Nick, we need to talk. I don't understand you. I mean, what is it with the girl? Have you completely forgotten why we're here?"

Nick was surprised. As he looked at Matt, he realized he was serious. "What do you mean?"

"Nick you've been acting like a kid ever since we came to this planet. I admit that I went along with it at first. But today, when you let that girl order you around, and then spent hours looking into her eyes like a lovesick teen, it became obvious to me that something is wrong. Are you remembering that we have a job to do here? Have you forgotten about Terri?"

Nick realized that although Nick had been there with him, he had not experienced what he had. Apparently, Matt had not communicated with them at all. Not knowing where to start, he proceeded to try to explain to him what happened from his perspective. "Matt, you may not understand right away what I have to tell you, but hear me out. First, let me ask you, what did *you* see when we were in the house."

"I saw three aliens, two females and a child. They could have passed for human except that they had rather long fingers. The house we entered was simple, with only basic wooden furniture, cushioned with fabric and animal skin. There was a wood-burning stove in the kitchen, and water was brought in from an outside well. The other female, the one with the child, kept trying to look into my eyes. I looked away, not wanting to be mesmerized as you seemed to be."

"The child with them was cute and playful, and tried to get my attention." He paused to take a drink and then continued. "I wanted to keep a look out for what was going on outside to make sure that no crowds were gathering. At first, everything seemed normal. Some natives passed by, and they didn't stop. Then I saw two of the aliens holding onto another one, apparently taking him somewhere. I didn't know what that was about, but I knew it was time for us to leave."

"That's something I didn't see," Nick reflected. "I'm curious about it."

"I was a lot more than curious," Matt replied, apparently irritated by Nick's speculative manner. "We don't know what these humanoids might be up to. Things with them may not be what they appear to be on the surface."

"Matt, you don't understand. I was able to talk with them. You see, they can communicate in a way that we don't. That's why the woman was trying to make eye contact with you. They converse by thought transference, similar to mental telepathy. It wasn't easy, but with Tara's help, I was able to do it too. The process requires eye-to-eye contact. I wasn't just staring into her eyes; I was actually talking to her."

"Really? And what exactly were you talking about?" asked Matt with irony in his voice.

"Different things. She told me that her name is Tara, and that she teaches, and also works at a medical facility. She told me about their culture. I learned, for example, why our sensors couldn't pick up any signs of energy. They are solar powered. That's why all the house roofs slant in one direction, toward the sun. They have rock storage systems built under their floors that radiate heat when the sun doesn't shine. Their climate is moderate, with no extremely cold or hot weather. During warm weather they use sliding shutters to the block the sun's rays."

"As for their economy, it's rustic and unsophisticated. They fish at the stream and at a nearby lake. They raise sheep-like animals for food and use their wool and skins to make clothing. They also plant vegetable crops and harvest cereal grains that they grind and make into bread. They even raise a crop that's similar to cotton. For the most part, they have the same kind of crafts that have been known since at least the days of the Roman Empire. There's a blacksmith, shoemakers, a milliner, instructors, butchers, potters, carpenters, a cooper, and, of course, a brewer."

"Tara explained that the children, and even some adults, can't speak by thought transference. Most, however, begin to acquire the ability by the time they reach their middle to late teens. It's important to remove any preconceptions from one's consciousness so that another's thoughts can be perceived. I think the process came easier for me because I was attracted to Tara from the beginning."

"You certainly were. That was obvious. Unfortunately, it may also be the problem. These aliens have some mental powers that we know little about. Do you realize the danger we are in if they are able to control our conscious thoughts? It's possible that the whole scene in front of us may only be a figment of our imagination, an idyllic world created out of our own cultural memories. Remember how we both noted how similar their world is to ours, including almost identical grass and trees? If they can do that, they can also make our minds think that they look just like humans."

"That's crazy. The way you're talking, I wouldn't be surprised to hear you say that Tara is really a scorpion in disguise! Really Matt, I think you've been reading too much science fantasy. I've read stories like that myself, but we and our predecessors have explored thousands of worlds, and found hundreds with advanced life forms. Nowhere have we found anything other than what we perceived it to be."

"Are you sure about that? What about the third planet of Borigidor?" Scientists still don't know what's there because each team of experts sent to investigate it comes back with different observations."

"Yes, I've heard of the planet. The anomaly appears to be caused somehow by the constant mists and its multiple suns. I definitely believe, and all the historical data supports me, that what we're seeing now is really here, and that what I touch and feel is reality."

"Don't you see," insisted Matt, "that we are here on an important mission to find oil for the eastern half of the galaxy, which desperately needs it. Despite that, you've suddenly lost interest. That's not like you. Our company has a lot of money invested in this mission. They don't expect us to be sidelined by the native girls."

Stung by Matt's remarks, Nick walked out of the cabin and stepped outside. He gazed at the grass and the trees within range of the perimeter lights surrounding the module. Going a little further, he pulled up some blades of grass, and rolled their stems between his thumb and fingers. He came to a tree, leaned against it, and felt its solid mass. Then, he looked back at the ship and thought about the two month voyage that brought them here. Somehow, it seemed like a long time ago.

Right now, he felt like walking, walking through the night, continuing, until he found the road that would take him back to the village, back to Tara. "Wait. What am I thinking?" he asked himself. "Why am I suddenly having these feelings for a woman I've met once?" He began to wonder if he was indeed being manipulated. On further consideration, he realized that he really didn't know. He still thought Matt was wrong about things not being what they seemed. However, he was right about one thing. No matter how he felt about Tara, it was time to get to work. He returned to the ship and entered the cabin. Matt was there, looking over some charts. He said to him, "Better get some sleep, Matt. We've got a lot of work to do tomorrow."

Chapter Two

The days that followed were filled with exploration and analysis of the data generated by their instrumentation. They took the amcar to several more distant sites to study geological formations of porous and impermeable rock. The place where their ship landed was in a former sedimentary basin, which eons ago had been under a swampy sea. The vegetation that had grown there for millions of years gradually dropped to the bottom as it died. The water level had risen, and in time, all the accumulated vegetation was covered over and compressed by layers of silt, which in time became rock.

Eventually, the tremendous pressure of the silt, rock and water caused the decayed vegetation to turn into oil and gas. The same thing happened on Earth and on other planets with sufficient warmth, vegetation, and oxygen. Man's voracious appetite for this "black gold" to power his machinery and heat his dwellings had created a demand unequal to the supply.

There had been warnings of shortages as far back as the twentieth century, when the Arabians briefly cornered the market. For a time, nuclear power was seen as a viable alternative until there were a series of accidents leading to the disastrous total meltdown in Botswana. It was estimated at the time that the explosion killed over two million people instantly, and that tens of millions more suffered an agonizing and slow death.

The dark winds that blew from the ashes infected the rest of the world, causing cancer rates to escalate around the globe for the next fifty years. Botswana itself was uninhabitable for a hundred years, and parts of Africa, and even Madagascar had to be evacuated for twenty years. Of course, there were foolish inhabitants who refused to be moved. They paid with their lives for their intransigence.

That was a long time ago, and for over two hundred years since then nations and planets had relied on oil and gas, with the expectation that the new worlds brought into the supply nexus would always meet the demand. Unfortunately, that assumption was unproven, and as virgin oil fields seemed harder and harder to find, the cries for conservation and even a return to nuclear energy were again being heard. Scientists were hard at work trying to find substitute forms of energy, but as yet, no inexpensive energy source had been developed.

That's why Nick and Matt were here, on this distant planet of another star, many light years from home. Highly paid geologists, they had to give up months of their lives in tedious space travel to make the round trip to this destination. The reward, however, was such that one good oil strike would make them well known and financially independent for the rest of their lives.

Nick had already been in deep space four times and had found nothing. He promised himself that this was his last trip. He had enjoyed seeing other worlds and the cosmopolitan ambiance of the space centers, but he realized now that he was ready to settle down. He thought about Terri, whom he knew would be awaiting his return. Matt interrupted his reverie.

"Nick, what do you want to do tomorrow on our day off?"

"I don't know. I've thought about it, but nothing interesting comes to mind. How about you?"

"Yeah, I don't know either. I'm not sure if I want to see another movie or play a simgame or both. I do plan to relax with my favorite drink."

"I'm getting tired of everything simulated," Nick answered. "Maybe I'll just read a book and take a walk. Are you ready to wrap it up for today?"

"We might as well. There's not much more we can do before it gets dark. Next week I think we'll be ready to take some core samples and analyze them. The preliminary findings in sectors 31 and 38 definitely look promising."

They packed up their equipment, dusted off their clothes, got into the car, and headed back to the ship.

It had long become standard practice in the oil industry, even in the outposts, to take one day a week off. Without a day to rest, tensions could build to the detriment of the work and the team relationships. All modern ships took the need for recreation into account. Most had digital libraries, movies, and play and game simulators that recreated the originals with satisfying authenticity. With the sport simulator, for example, one could participate in almost any sport, and even experience specific muscle and tendon injuries, like "tennis elbow" if overdone. In the library, memory banks provided the literature of the world, and in seconds, a selection could be downloaded to a pocket reader.

Although starships, through computerization, carried the world with them, there remained one major deficiency. Other than one's partner, there were no real people with which to interact. Nick missed that companionship more and more. In fact, he was not far from admitting to himself that he was lonely. At twenty-seven, he knew that he wanted someone real, warm, and affectionate to be part of his life.

* * *

The morning dawned bright and cool, with the prospect of temperatures rising during the day. Matt slept in. Nick ate breakfast and attended a short, recorded service. He stretched his legs and decided to take a long hike. He enjoyed walking. It helped him to take his mind off the job, and it was good exercise.

He began striding toward the morning sun but turned left as another thought entered his mind. In less than an hour he found the green road. He smiled and continued walking. Now, he knew exactly where he was going.

What was it about her that attracted him so much? He tried to analyze it. Was it only the loneliness of too many long trips away from home? No, that wasn't it, he assured himself. There was something about her that affected him as no one else had, not even Terri. He had recognized that when they were together at the house. Now, he had to go back to find out more about her.

Soon, the town stretched out in front of him as he stood on a rise in the road. Then, to his surprise, he saw her. She was walking across his line of view, slowly, with her hands clasped together in front of her as if in a reverie. He called her name. She looked toward him, and instantly he felt a warm message of welcome. They moved quickly to each other, and as they met he instinctively put his arms around her, drawing her close. She looked up into his eyes, her long, silky hair framing her face, and asked why he hadn't come sooner. He realized that she had missed him. He laughed softly at the intensity of her feelings and felt a tenderness toward her that was new to him. He proceeded to explain to her the importance of his work and how he had to fight to ignore his thoughts of her during the week. Now that he was in her presence again, he felt happier, with a lightheartedness he hadn't experienced for a long time. He liked the lilting richness of her voice and the way the words seemed to flow musically together. She gestured often with her hands for emphasis, and though Nick didn't understand everything she said, he got the main ideas.

As they continued walking, she talked about her family and mentioned that her parents had both died. She was anxious for him to meet her grandfather, who lived nearby, and to get to know her sister and her daughter. She wanted to learn more about him, how he had come from another world, and what it was like on Earth. She asked about his family, and wondered what women on Earth were like.

She had so many questions. Nick started by telling her how they had spent two long months in space navigating to the planet by means of their galactic starship. She was amazed to learn that he had come so far, from a distant sun, and had difficulty conceiving of a vehicle that could travel for so long a distance through the dark and cold in the complete absence of air. She was childlike in her total lack of knowledge of space and other worlds.

Nick told her about Earth and its huge cities with skyscrapers over a thousand feet tall, and of its underground highways and towns. He described the teaming multitudes of people in the large cities and the relative sparseness that remained in some parts of the land. He related to her how the Worlds' Organization had acted to quash major wars between nations and how long ago it had banned all major weapons systems. He acknowledged that conflicts still broke out from time to time, usually over old disputes or unsettled boundaries.

Nick told her it was deplorable that nations still hadn't really learned to live together, but he was glad that at least dissident nations no longer had the power to destroy entire populations. The Worlds' Court schedule was always full, and the one hundred men and women from all the major planets and countries who sat on it made some unpopular decisions, but Nick felt that it was the best alternative to internecine warfare.

Tara seemed much more interested when he talked, at her request, about the women of Earth. She was astonished when he described some of the fashions that were currently in vogue, including the way women coiffure their hair. Nick could see how Tara was trying to visualize herself wearing the styles he was describing, and he knew she would like to see them.

"Someday I'll take you to the ship, and you can see for yourself on EV." He tried to explain briefly how that worked, and ended up saying, "I really like the way you look now, nothing artificial."

"Now, yes. But people get tired of the same thing after awhile."

" I wouldn't."

"I know what," she said. "I could dye my hair ochre and wear it up on my head, like this."

He laughed as she piled her dark hair on top of her head and grinned at him. "Maybe I won't show you those films," he said half seriously. "I don't want to corrupt you."

Abruptly, she made a mock pouting face.

"OK, I'll show you some films, but first I should introduce you to my partner, Matt. He'll want to get acquainted with you before we do anything at the ship."

Just then, they were interrupted by a call. A middle-aged woman, coming from the gristmill, recognized Tara and hailed her. She waved, and while still approaching, began speaking animatedly. Then she paused, looked into Nick's eyes, and extended her hand. Nick read her clearly. She said, "Pleased to meet you." Nick grasped her hand and mentally said, "My pleasure." She took his hand, and instead of shaking up and down, she drew it back and forth, in a sawing motion. Then she turned to talk some more with Tara. After chatting a short while, she again looked at Nick and said, "Goodbye."

"That was Mrs. Marferti," said Tara. "She's an old friend of my mother. She doesn't have any children of her own and has always been close to Shari and me, especially since mother died."

"What did she die of?" he asked, as they walked toward her house.

"The same thing most people die of."

"What is that?" he asked.

"Her heart. Isn't it the same on Earth?"

"No, not at all. On Earth, people die from many different things. Besides heart attacks, there are strokes, pneumonia, emphysema, various diseases, and even cancer."

"Really. Do they have to suffer then at the end?"

"Yes, they often do, and sometimes for a long while. Fortunately, most can be helped with medication so that it goes a lot easier. How is it for people here?"

"Most of the time it comes suddenly, with heart pain. At other times, it goes on for a few days or even weeks. Both my mother and father died suddenly."

"I'm sorry."

"Thank you. Much has happened since then. At first, I missed them terribly, but I've gotten over it, and it helps to know I'll eventually see them again." She waved to a neighbor as they reached the door of her sister's house. When they entered, Shari greeted them at the door, and her little girl, Neena, ran in from the kitchen to meet them.

"Hi, Neena. How's my big ampasso?" asked Tara, as she lifted the girl into her arms. Neena began chattering excitedly as they walked further into the house.

The room they entered was large, with a high ceiling, and was illuminated mostly by big windows on two sides. A candelabrum, centered in the middle of the table, lit the place settings.

"You're just in time for dinner," said Shari, as she tended some crocks at the stove.

"Did I hear dinner announced?" a deep voice responded from another room.

"Yes, grandpa, you might as well come now," Shari answered. "We have a guest who will be eating with us today."

"You *will* stay for dinner, won't you?" asked Tara, turning to look at Nick.

"I'd be happy to. I haven't eaten real, unprocessed food for a long time."

"Hello, young man," said Tara's grandfather, extending his hand to Nick as he entered the room. He was tall, husky, and white-haired, with a friendly demeanor. As Nick looked at him, thoughts in the nature of, "Glad to meet you," registered in his consciousness. They shook hands and Nick replied similarly, "Glad to meet you, sir."

The mind connection seemed to be working because he answered, "Just call me Ruskin. I've heard you've come from another planet far away from here." He hesitated a moment. "It's so hard to believe that it's really possible," he said, with evident astonishment.

"You can talk to him about it later, grandpa," said Tara. "I think Shari's ready with dinner."

Nick watched as they bowed their heads and then passed the steaming bowls around the table. Tara sat at Nick's right and told him about the different dishes as they came to them. The contents of two of the bowls looked familiar; one of them looked liked potatoes, and the other could have been carrots. All the food was hot, and most of it was delicious although one salad dish had an unusual taste that he didn't savor.

Ruskin tended to monopolize the conversation, keen as he was to learn all about the space trip, life on other worlds, and their project on the planet. Nick had some trouble at first understanding what the older man was saying, but Tara helped, and he got better at it after a while. He learned that Ruskin was one of two herbalists in the town, and that he grew and prepared extracts for medicinal purposes. Nick had had a passing interest in biology years before entering the space program, which helped him to understand what he was saying, although Tara frequently needed to interpret. At length she said, "It's getting late already, and it's dangerous to travel after dark at this time of year. Would you stay over with us until morning?"

Nick looked at his chronograph. "No thank you," he answered. "I'd like to, but Matt would be worried if I didn't come back tonight. Why do you think traveling at night is dangerous?"

She explained to him that the mating season of the Great Thorns begins at about this time every year. "It's the time when the male birds set out on extended flights far from their cliff-side rookeries. They travel silently in the night, searching for large prey. When they find it, they swoop down, plunge their long sword-like beak into the unfortunate creature, and carry it back to their lair. Their quest is driven not by hunger, but by their eagerness to prove their prowess to a female. At the height of the mating season they will sometimes hunt even during the day."

"Don't worry about me, Tara," Nick was quick to assert. "No bird would stand a chance against my pulsar."

"If you must go, I'll walk you to the end of town." She thought a moment. "I know. You could take my forc."

Nick thought about the animal that he had seen her riding. "Thank you, but I'd rather walk," he said.

"Then I'll go with you a short distance."

They went quietly along the stream that bordered the village.

"What do you think of my grandfather?"

"He's an interesting person. I was surprised at how much he knows about natural medicine. If he had modern Laboratory equipment, who knows what kind of breakthroughs he might make."

"Oh, he does have a Laboratory. I'm sure he'd like to show it to you sometime."

They came to the outskirts of town all too fast, and it was time to say goodbye. He kissed her, and she returned the kiss. As they parted, she asked when she would see him again. "Soon," he answered.

He proceeded down the green road away from her, and when he came to a bend, he turned to see her still standing there. He waved, and then continued on. Suddenly, he fell to the ground. He wasn't hurt, but his head felt like it was turning without his body and he could scarcely move his limbs. It was the last thing he remembered.

Chapter Three

At the starship, Matt paced back and forth. It was after eleven p.m. by synchronized Earth time, and there was still no sign of Nick. Matt's earlier irritation was now changing to fear. He had guessed that Nick might have gone to visit Tara, but it was unlike him not to be back by now.

Midnight. Still no sign of him. He began to fear the worst. He imagined that Nick had been deluded by their mental deception, and now he was hurt or captured. Maybe they had even taken control of his mind. If he wasn't hurt, could he be trusted? Matt turned up the sensitivity of the ships perimeter protection system. One a.m. He thought seriously of alerting the Space Patrol. Though they might never respond this far away from their rounds, at least there would be a record in case he didn't make it back. One thirty. He sent the message to alert the Patrol. Then he realized how foolish that was. Even if they got the report, it would take them over a month to respond. At this distance, they simply wouldn't do anything except record it until an outer boundary ship happened along.

Two a.m. *Wait*, he thought to himself. *They don't know anything about the firepower I have on this ship. They apparently don't even have guns. With two hand pulsars, I could stand off a hundred of them.* He began to take courage. It was obvious to him that the aliens could win only by mental deception, and now he was alert to it.

Matt knew that his next step was to find out what happened to Nick. He coolly resolved that if they had killed him they would pay dearly for it. If, instead, they had captured him, he felt certain that he could rescue him by force of arms. Even if Nick's consciousness was under their control, Matt thought that if he could bring him back to the ship, he could get him out of their power.

He decided that he would wait until early dawn to attack. In the interim, he tried sleeping, but it was no use. His consciousness was alerted, and almost automatically, it projected him into different scenarios so that he could decide how to react, regardless of the situation. Finally, he saw the first faint light of day through the window. He munched on an energy bar while strapping on two pulsars. Then he got into the amcar and pressed the accelerator. He was traveling over the trees at high speed, and soon the town appeared in view. He slowed down to look for the house and quickly found it. Then he parked the car in a nearby thicket.

The day was just dawning, and it was still dusky in the town. No one seemed to be about. As he silently approached the house, he steeled his mind so as not to come under their influence. He held a pulsar in each hand. An animal made a low sound that startled him. It was one of those strange creatures that they use for transport. He reached the door and found it unlocked. He quietly pushed in. Entering, he found that he was in the dining area. He heard nothing. He crossed the room and stopped, listening intently for the slightest sound, snoring, breathing, anything. Then, from an upper room, he heard something indecipherable. It sounded like a shudder, followed immediately by a gasp.

He hesitated a moment, then bounded up the stairs with pulsars ready. The sight he saw in the candlelight he would never forget. Nick was lying on his back in the bed, his face bloated and swollen almost beyond recognition. And there, beside him, were Tara and an old man who was trying to force something between Nick's clenched teeth. "Stop!" he yelled. "What are you doing to him?" He resisted an impulse to kill them on the spot. The old man was startled. Tara quickly stood up. In the half-light, she saw the two pulsars trained on her. She saw the menace in Matt's eyes and gestured helplessly toward Nick lying unconscious in the bed. She silently appealed to Matt with her eyes, telling him, "Nick is terribly sick. Can you help him?"

Matt studied her and understood. He saw her haggard appearance and the worried look in her eyes. He realized that she had been up with Nick all night. For a moment, he sensed her sorrow, and he had an impulse to comfort her. Then, abruptly, he remembered his resolve not to allow himself to be manipulated by the all too human appearing aliens. He turned from her and focused on Nick's swollen face. Training his pulsars on the two of them, he gestured threateningly for them to back themselves out through the other door. As they exited, he closed it then bent down and managed to hoist Nick's limp body over his shoulder.

Still holding a pulsar in his left hand, he was able to get down the stairs and through the house. Not seeing anyone, he opened the outside door and then stumbled down the two steps leading from the porch. Getting up off his knees, he made it to the amcar and was able to get Nick's limp body inside. Lurching forward, he turned the car and headed toward the space module. A huge winged bird flew across his path as he accelerated into overdrive.

Almost immediately, he was flying high over the treetops. Suddenly he saw another enormous creature diving toward him on a collision course. He maneuvered his craft wildly, somehow managing to avoid impact. "Whew! That was close," he exclaimed. He sat tensely at the controls, wondering what else they might unleash against him.

The rest of the short trip back to the ship was uneventful. He took the precaution of circling the module a few times and could see no sign that anything had disturbed the area. He landed near the entrance, stepped out with pulsars drawn, and entered the ship. Everything appeared to be normal.

Going back to the amcar, he lifted Nick out, dragged him inside, and laid him on his bed. Nick didn't look good. His face remained so swollen that he probably couldn't have opened his eyes if he wanted to. On further examination, he didn't appear to be bruised or have any broken limbs. Opening the medical kit, Matt took a sample of Nick's blood and put it into the bioanalyzer. The results took longer than normal to read out. They showed an extremely high white blood cell count caused by the invasion of an unknown bacterial strain. Matt punched its genetic code into the analyzer for an antibody and waited. He waited for what seemed like a long time. Finally the answer came. There was none. The type of bacteria infecting Nick had never before been encountered. Matt took a deep breath. Suddenly he felt very tired. Although he had done all he could for Nick, the lack of a remedy could prove fatal. Frustrated, he fixed himself a drink and said a prayer. He lay down, and after awhile, fell into a fitful sleep.

Several hours later, he was wakened by the perimeter alarms. Jumping out of bed, he reached for his pulsar and looked out the window. It was Tara. She was approaching the entrance. Looking up, she saw him at the window. He pointed the pulsar at her and motioned her to go back. She lowered her head, ignoring the threat, and continued forward until she stood beneath the window. She looked up into his eyes, and he returned her gaze, looking at her closely for the first time. She was a slender young woman who seemed sad and tired, hardly anyone to be feared. He sensed that she was terribly concerned about Nick. He struggled within himself, trying hard not to show any compassion toward her. Feeling rather insensitive, he turned away and closed the window shade.

Time passed. The planet's yellowish orange sun rose high in the sky.

"Oh, God! Oh, my head!" Nick cried out, in intense pain.

Matt got up from the chair where he had been catnapping and rushed over to him. Nicked moaned, holding his head in his hands, as he twisted in agony. "Help me Matt. Please help me."

Matt hurried over to the dispensary, fumbled for a painkiller, and returning to Nick, pressed the nozzle into the base of his neck. For a while longer, Nick writhed in agony until gradually the medication began working. Then, he lay quiet and unmoving.

Matt paced back and forth in the cabin, not knowing what else to do for him. Eventually, Nick wakened. Lifting his head he asked, "What happened to me?"

Matt approached the side of the bed. "Glad you're better, Nick. Early this morning, when I brought you back here, your face was so swollen, you couldn't have talked if you wanted to. Do you have any memory of that?"

"No. I don't. The last thing I remember, I was walking away from Tara's house, and then I lost control of my legs and fell down. I don't remember anything after that until I woke up here."

"How do you feel now?"

"Like I've been drugged, and I'm just coming out of it. Extremely tired."

"No wonder. When I found you last night you were in a bed at her house. You looked like you were dying. In fact, I didn't know if you would survive. I'll tell you more about all that later, but for now, you need to get some more rest. Do you want anything to eat?"

"No, thanks."

"Here, I'll give you another dose of the pain killer. Hopefully when you wake up again you'll feel better."

A few hours later, Nick again opened his eyes. This time he felt OK. His headache was gone, and he had an appetite. He tried moving his legs. Although his body felt rigid, he was able to roll out of bed, get up on his feet, and walk stiffly over to the food synthesizer. Noticing that the window was dark, he deactivated the shade to let in more light. Then he saw Tara. She was bent over, lying against the side of the landing gear. He opened the door and gingerly stepped down. She lifted her head at his approach and smiled at him. He stiffly extended his hand to help her up.

"How long have you been here?"

"Since morning."

"Really? Why didn't you come in?"

"I think Matt was afraid to open the door."

"Why? That doesn't make sense. Why would he do that?"

She proceeded to tell him about what happened after he fell down on the road. How Matt had come early in the morning to "rescue" him. "I believe he thinks I poisoned you," she concluded.

"Damn! What's with him? Why can't he forget those paranoid ideas of his?" He took her hand, and walking directly into the module, he confronted Matt.

Nick began sarcastically. "Thanks for saving me from Tara. Do you know she's been waiting outside all day because you wouldn't let her in?"

"I'm sorry Nick. I was afraid you'd been poisoned, and I didn't. . ."

Just then, the perimeter alarm sounded. Looking out the window, Nick saw Tara's grandfather dismounting from his forc. Walking cautiously to the ship, he knocked on the door.

Nick opened it, saying, "Come in."

The older man looked past him. "Tara!" he said with relief. "We've been looking all over for you." Then he focused on Matt and Nick. Turning to Nick, he said, "I'm glad to see you've recovered, young man."

"Thanks. I still feel weak, but I'm glad to be alive after last night. Mr. Ruskin, this is my friend and partner, Matt." The two reluctantly shook hands. Nick could see that Ruskin was uncomfortable in Matt's presence.

"I won't hurt you," Matt said. He looked at Ruskin to see if he comprehended what he said. "I know I imagined the worst, especially when I saw Nick's face so badly swollen."

Ruskin nodded. "You think of us as different, Matt, but if you get to know us you'll find we're just as sentient as you are." He turned to face them all. "It just occurred to me that Nick's sudden sickness must have been caused by an allergic reaction to something in the food he ate at our house."

Nick looked to Tara, verifying what he thought Ruskin said. "That sounds plausible," he answered. "A delayed reaction. Probably something you have a natural immunity for that we haven't acquired."

"If we can isolate the substance we can analyze it and possibly develop an antidote," Matt added. "If not, we will definitely avoid it."

"Then all we need to do is find out everything Shari used in yesterday's dinner," declared Tara.

"Yes, if we bring it here, we can isolate it in the bioanalyzer and see if it reacts with samples of Nick's blood."

"Can you really do it that simply?" asked Ruskin.

"Oh, yes," Matt replied, finding that he was able to decipher more of the conversation himself. "The equipment we have on board will do a lot, though it's not like having a complete laboratory. It should be able to show us the causative element."

Although Ruskin must have surprised at the advanced technology, he didn't overtly show it. "If it's that easy," he said, "let's get to it. I brought your forc, Tara. We can talk to Shari, get samples of everything, and come back here in the morning."

Tara looked at Nick, then turned back to her grandfather. "Yes, I guess we should leave before dark, especially at this time of year."

Nick moved to be next to her and said, "I'll look forward to seeing you tomorrow." Then she and Ruskin were off, riding with surprising swiftness.

* * *

The next day dawned bright and clear with a slight chill in the air. Nick waved when he saw Tara and Ruskin returning.

"How do you feel today?" asked Tara, her eyes expressing concern.

"Just fine," he replied. "I'm loose and limber and ready for anything today." He flexed his arms to demonstrate.

Tara laughed and said, "I don't think anything could keep you down for long."

"You're probably right. By the way, is that some of the native fare that you're bringing for us to eat today?"

"Yes, that's what it is," she replied, catching the spirit of his banter. "We feel it's our duty to share with the less fortunate."

"Well, thank you kindly, miss." He took the small, wrapped package from her and added. "I'll tell my partner that the natives here seem to be friendly. Hey Matt, here's the food samples."

"OK., bring them in. I've got the analyzer set up."

"Could I see how it works?" asked Ruskin.

"Sure. Go right in," replied Nick. "And take these samples in with you. Matt can show you how the tests are run."

Tara backed up to let her grandfather by and found herself captured in Nick's arms. She looked up over her shoulder at him. "Is this the way spacemen treat girls on other planets?" she said coquettishly.

"Of course. We try to make a lasting impression with all the girls. That way when we come back, we're always welcome. Matt and I have girls on all the planets we've been to, Yaltum, Bircolae, Shantun, and Firesta."

"Really?" She slipped out of his arms and turned to face him. Seeing his smile, she said, "I don't believe it." But she appeared uncertain, and stepped out of his reach when he tried to hold her again.

"I was only kidding," Nick said. "Didn't you know that?"

Tara looked up at him, her eyes seeming to flash a mixture of hurt and relief. "Well, it's not the way to talk to someone you care about."

Just then, the ship's door opened and Ruskin stepped out. "All findings are negative so far, but I have an idea. Tara, would you join us inside for a minute? I have a hunch I'd like to check out."

"Sure. I'm glad to help any way I can." Still sulking, she walked past Nick without a glance and stepped inside. Within ten minutes, she came back out. Matt and Ruskin appeared at the door. Both of them were smiling. Tara walked over to Nick, looked him straight in the eyes and said, "I'm afraid what you're allergic to is me."

"I don't believe it," Nick exclaimed. He thought a moment. "That kiss on the trail, before we parted?"

"I think that was it," she said. "I'm so sorry. I didn't mean to hurt you."

"Hurting isn't what concerns me now," he said, drawing her close. "I was just getting to know you," he said softly so the others couldn't hear him. "I don't want that to end."

"I know, Nick," she replied, barely audible, as she nestled in his arms. "I don't want it to end either."

"There has to be a way to overcome this, and we're going to find it."

"Yes, she agreed, seeming to take heart. My grandfather may be able to help. He knows a lot about herbal medicine. I think he can find a cure."

Matt said, "I can go through the computer's medical journals. Maybe we can develop a vaccine."

Then for a short time, no one said anything. Tara broke the silence. "I need to get back to the center. They've been backing me up, but I need to return to work now. She faced Nick squarely, her countenance expressing the sadness she felt. Though she didn't speak, Nick read her concern. Was she going to lose him now? Did it really mean enough to him to try? What if finding a cure was difficult? What if there was no cure? She looked at him steadily and then stepped forward to give him a parting hug. "Please be careful. The month of Ravidian has started. Watch out for the Thorns, especially early in the morning and just after sunset. Promise me you'll be careful."

Nick told her he would take precautions, and Tara and Ruskin said goodbye and rode away, leaving only the paw marks of their mounts. Nick felt dejected. He looked out at the savanna in front of him then turned and stepped back into the ship. He was tired. Matt had already left to go somewhere with the car. Nick got a glass of water and sat down to think. Why did he feel the way he did? There were lots of girls in the galaxy. He had always believed that. Why was this one affecting him so much? Certainly, there wasn't anyone like her. But then again, how well did he really know her? His thoughts were disorganized. Finally, he went to the computer, selected an old movie, sat in front of the EV, and waited for Matt to return.

After the short film ended, Nick looked outside and saw Matt getting out of the amcar.

"Where'd you go?" he asked, opening the door.

"Nick, I just got back from taking another look at sector 38. I thought it might be worth further testing, so I took the equipment over there. I made some inferences based on our earlier samples and sent the probe down. When I sent it down this time, I had a hunch it might be the right spot. Look." He lifted the probe onto the table and pointed out the oily film clinging to its sides.

"Oh, yes. Yes!" Nick exclaimed. "You found it!" The two of them whooped, high fived, and punched each other in their excitement. When their fervor subsided a bit, Matt fingered the lock to open catch door number seven of the automatic probe. As the door opened, thick, black oil oozed out.

"Whoa! That's what we've been looking for," said Nick. He collected some in a small vial and lifted it to his nose. "Mm, I like that smell. Were you able to find out if it's very extensive?"

"Not yet. The field doesn't appear to rise very high, but it could run deep. As for area, I don't know yet."

During supper they speculated extensively on how much oil they might find and planned the locations where they would sink the next probes. It was particularly exciting work for Matt, who had never been involved in a find. Nick had helped discover an oil site once before, but it had unfortunately been deemed "Not economically feasible to remove, using current technology." Still, he knew that this time could very well be different, and with a major discovery, they would quickly become wealthy and famous.

The excitement stimulated them, and they worked far into the night planning for the next day.

In the morning after a hasty breakfast, they were back in the car, heading for their first site. As they approached it, they saw two huge birds take wing. Matt whistled in amazement. "Look at the size of those creatures!

"No wonder the townspeople are afraid of them. Their beaks must be almost a yard long."

Nick guided the car down to the site. The Thorns, however, instead of flying off as expected, began a wide turn at low altitude around the amcar.

Nick pointed south. "Look. They haven't left. See them over the treetops there?"

"They look like they're circling us."

"Obviously we didn't scare them off."

"Maybe we had better wait in the car for awhile. Tara said they will attack people at this time of year."

They stayed inside for another half-hour until the birds flew out of sight. When they left the ship they remained on high alert, pulsars ready, in case they returned. Not seeing any more of them, they went back to drilling and found an abundance of oil. Almost every time they sank the probe into the ground, it returned holding more of the precious black crude.

As the evening sun was setting on the horizon, they finished packing and congratulated themselves as they headed back to the ship.

"What a day!" exclaimed Matt, wiping his brow. "This is the stuff of dreams."

"Like a special fishing spot where you catch a big one every time you cast," Nick agreed.

"I can't wait to get all this data into the computer so we can see the whole picture."

"Right. We definitely have quite a concentration. How extensive it is we will soon find out."

When they returned to the ship, they didn't even think about eating. Quickly finishing the graphs, they entered the data and let the computer make the analyses. They didn't have long to wait.

"Look at this," said Matt, practically pulling the analagram from the printer. "We've got major concentrations in all the areas surrounding sector 38."

"Yes," Nick concurred, as he stood up to examine the analagram. "But notice, Matt, how it begins to thin out as we move further along the edges."

"Like a deep lake with a shallow shoreline."

"I hope that's not what we're seeing here. I saw that on Bircolae. A pocket of oil hemmed in by a range of nonporous rock."

"So, in other words, we've got oil but we still don't know if it's worthwhile?"

"It's worth something. We just don't know yet if there's enough to come this far to extract."

The perimeter alarm sounded, and within moments, they heard sharp knocking on the door. "Tara," said Nick, as he opened the door. "What's the matter?"

She quickly came inside, obviously very upset. "The Thorns," she uttered between breaths. "They killed Petra! It was horrible! She stopped again to breathe. "One of those, those. . .creatures, tried to carry him back. He was still alive and struggling. It was taking him away, but he fought it and fell from its grasp. We found his body in the woods. His neck was broken." She bowed her head and sobbed.

Nick moved to her and held her close. He didn't know what to say, but he held her until she stopped shaking. She looked up at him, and returning his embrace, put her head on his chest and closed her eyes tightly, as if trying to block out the memory of what she had seen.

"I'm sorry, Tara," Nick spoke softly. "Was he one of yours?"

She nodded, lifting her head. "One of the best." Again, the tears welled up in her eyes.

"If there's anything we can do to help, we will," he said.

Matt seconded him, "Yes, we would like to do something."

Tara looked at them and said gratefully, "Thank you so much. You could come to the funeral. I would appreciate that. That is, if you have time."

"Of course," Nick answered. "When is it?"

"Normally it's done at night, but during this month everything is done during the day because of the Thorns. It will be tomorrow afternoon."

* * *

The wake was held at the youth's house. All the family, relatives, and most of the neighbors attended. In fact, it was hard to get in. Nick and Matt had not planned to stay long. While there, they met a number of the townspeople, many of whom seemed curious about them. Some even asked who they were and what they were doing. Tara helped with introductions whenever she was nearby. Nick caught parts of conversations, and sensed that the majority of people there were quite concerned and worried about the Thorns. Already, a house-to-house sentry program had been started. If one of the creatures was seen, sentries would ring a warning bell, so everyone would know to run home or to the nearest shelter. Nick learned that people stayed inside at night, making only the most furtive trips from one house to another, and then, only if it was necessary.

The fear was tangible. What was even worse, from Nick's perspective, was the general perception that it would be foolhardy to fight back. He learned that many of the townspeople believed that if they did manage to kill one of the creatures, the whole colony would attack in force. Matt heard the same thing, and when they had a moment to discuss it between themselves, they both felt that it was an irrational fear. At one point, Matt, who was becoming irritated by all the anxious talk, told one of the guests that if a Thorn came close to him, he would shoot it out of the sky. He was apparently understood well enough, because word began circulating that they had lethal weapons.

As they were getting ready to leave, they learned that those who came for the wake were also expected to attend the funeral, which had been scheduled for the next morning. Tara had already made accommodation for them at her house, and it was only after much discourse that Nick was able to convince her that it would be safe for them to return overnight to the ship.

Actually, Nick would have stayed, but he knew that Matt was anxious to return to the comfort and security of the space module. Nick appreciated that Matt had given up his time to come to the wake and that he was willing to go to the funeral tomorrow. So, after saying goodbye and receiving insistent admonitions to be careful, they walked back to the amcar. After all the talk, they were tense as they pulled away from the town, quickly reaching cruising speed above the treetops. Soon they were back at the module, where they felt safe in their familiar surroundings.

The next morning dawned bright with thin hazy clouds. Matt agreed to go to the funeral only if they left immediately afterwards. They were both anxious to get back to the oil fields. As they prepared to leave, Nick looked out the window and saw one of the huge flying creatures. This time, it was much closer. "We have company," he whispered, as if the bird could hear through the insulation of the ship.

"Look at the size of it," Matt replied, in a hushed voice. The creature was on the ground, less than one hundred yards away. Partially hidden by a low tree, it appeared to stand about fifteen feet tall. Through the branches, they could see its eyes. It appeared to be stalking them.

"This one is going to be in for a surprise," whispered Nick, as he got out his pulsar and charged it to full strength. Matt did the same. They stepped outside. The Thorn immediately spread its huge wings and climbed into the air. Rapidly it bridged the distance between them, its murderous pointed beak aimed right at them. A low hum emitted from the two pulsars. The bird crashed to the ground, dead, forty feet in front of them. Another one, apparently its partner, emerged from behind the ship and flew swiftly away over the treetops. Matt walked over and kicked the dead body, saying, "This dumb bird won't bother anyone again."

At the funeral service, they sat with Tara, Ruskin, Shari, and her daughter. Before the opening hymn, Nick mentioned to them that they had killed one of the birds. Ruskin was aghast.

"Don't you realize that if you kill one, the whole colony will return to avenge their dead?" He continued to talk, in a very agitated manner, asking them more questions about the incident. Tara, too, appeared to be frightened for them, but she was able to calm herself, and even her grandfather, before the service started.

After the ceremony, both Ruskin and Tara spoke with Nick and Matt about the consequences of killing a Thorn. When they learned that there was a second one that got away, they were even more appalled. It was not long before the news reached the people who remained after the service, and soon everyone was talking about it. Tara insisted that Nick and Matt not go back to the ship. Others informed them that there could be thousands of Thorns nested in their rocky cliff dwellings, many miles away.

Nick and Matt were definitely going to return to the space module. They were more concerned about the need to protect it from damage than anything else. Breaking away from their well-meaning friends, they returned to the amcar and headed back.

"What do you think?" asked Nick, as he guided the vehicle over the trees. "Do you think the Thorns will come back?"

"I doubt it. Maybe it *has* happened before, but my impression is that it must have been in the distant past, if at all. I have to admit though, they were all certainly scared."

"Yes, that was evident. I agree with your analysis. The retaliation story may be a legend that's been handed down for generations. They're so afraid of the creatures to begin with, something like that could be blown way out of proportion."

"Still, if there's any truth at all to it, I want to be prepared. That ship is our trip home."

* * *

Back at the star module, they went to work cutting down some small trees. Their plan was to make a barrier of scaffolding around the ship using poles spaced several feet apart and tied together at right angles. That way, none of the birds would be able to get through to land on the ship. They were hard at work, sawing logs the old fashioned way, to conserve pulsar power, when they were surprised to see people approaching. The visitors came in pairs, riding forcs, each two carrying a long log between their mounts. Among the early arrivals were Tara and Ruskin. Tara dismounted, walked toward Nick and said, "They all wanted to help, Nick."

Nick looked past her to see Ruskin in the background, already directing the positioning of the poles. "You really do think they're going to attack, don't you, Tara." He put down his saw and hugged her. He noted the concern and fear in her eyes. "You don't have to worry, Tara. We're going to be all right. See this." He withdrew his pulsar and showed it to her. "This is instant death for those creatures. If they dare to come close, they'll regret it."

She placed her hand on top of the pulsar, felt the hard molded polymer, and sensed the power of it. "Do you have any more of these?" she asked.

"Yes, we each have a spare."

"Is it hard to use?"

"Not at all," he answered, beginning to discern where the conversation was leading.

"Then I want to stay with you to help when they attack."

"No, Tara. I appreciate your wanting to help. If they do come back, this could be a very dangerous place to be. You know I care about you. I sure don't want to take a chance that you could be hurt. Besides, if it happens, it's our battle."

"It's our battle too, Nick," she insisted, her eyes flashing. "It was one of us who was killed by those creatures. It was my neighbor's son who died. We are the ones who have to live in fear of them. Don't you see? The battle may be fought at your ship, but it will be fought on our soil. We are the ones who win if the Thorns are killed."

Nick couldn't dispute her logic, as much as he wanted to. "OK," he replied, putting a hand on her shoulder. "If you feel that strongly about it, you can stay with us. We will prepare for combat.

I will teach you how to shoot this, and if they come, you can shoot them out of the sky. Is that what you want to do?"

Tara nodded and looked up at him, tears glistening in her eyes, but smiling at the same time.

"What are you crying about?" Nick asked, mystified.

"I don't know. I guess I'm just happy to be here with you. I wish I could kiss you."

"Yes, that is a problem," he acknowledged. "I've been thinking about that and have an idea about how it can be solved."

"Really?" she asked, enthusiastically.

"Well, it's a process that might take awhile. I'll tell you about it when we have more time."

"Great! I would like to show you how we in Crystal kiss."

"Sounds interesting. I'll definitely have to show you how North Amis kiss.

"Hi, Tara," said Matt. "Nick, can you give me a hand with this log?"

The work of building the fortifications proceeded. Most of the long poles the townspeople had brought were now in place, and viewing them from the spaceship, Nick and Matt could see how the tall posts would prevent the Thorns, with their long wingspans, from getting through. The two of them, along with Tara, continued work on building the smaller structure of logs and branches surrounding the module. As evening approached, they stood back and surveyed the battlements. Around them for forty yards in every direction, stood poles about five inches thick, thirty feet high and twelve feet apart. Across the ship itself, struts were positioned about six feet apart, with a patchwork of thick branches tied five feet above the top of the ship.

"I think we're about done," said Ruskin. He walked over to say a few words to the last of the townspeople who had finished erecting a pole. Then he walked back to the ship.

"Thanks so much for all your help," said Nick. "I'm still hoping we won't need all this."

"You're perfectly welcome," answered Ruskin. You know we're all pulling for you boys. You will do us a real favor if you can kill some of those horrid creatures. My prayer is that all these posts will keep them from getting through to you."

"They should certainly help," Matt replied.

"Tara, we had better be leaving, before it gets too late," Ruskin said.

"I'm staying here tonight, grandpa."

Ruskin looked surprised but didn't answer. Instead, his eyes locked steadily on hers. Finally, he turned and said to all of them, "I'm staying here too. Do you have an extra cot for an old man? And, an extra pulsar?"

That evening they practiced using the pulsars. Tara quickly learned to shoot with remarkable accuracy. Ruskin had a harder time getting used to the handgun; though with practice, he too, was able to do OK.

None of the Thorns appeared while they were practicing, and as darkness fell without a sign of them, they began to feel more relaxed. Nick ordered some delicious food from the restant, and after eating an excellent supper, they thought that if the Thorns didn't come, they might as well enjoy the evening together. First, however, they spent time working on strategy, in order to be prepared for any eventualities. Tara quickly grew tired of that. She went to the other side of the cabin and leaned back in a chair, obviously bored.

After awhile, Nick noticed her there. He got up, turned on some music, and asked her to dance. She smiled, stood up, and was quickly in his arms. He turned up the volume and held her close. It was surprising to him how well she followed his lead. Then, faster paced music began playing, and they separated. For a minute, she watched him dance alone. Then she joined him. Nick laughed as she tried to follow his movements, adding her own variations. She smiled when she looked up and saw Ruskin and Matt watching her.

On the next song Matt joined them and, after a warm-up, started his inimitable fast step style. Nick sat down and saw Tara attempt to follow Matt. She couldn't keep up with him, and started to laugh. At first, she tried to hide it by putting her hand over her mouth, but she couldn't keep it in. Matt hardly noticed, he was so much into the music.

When the song ended, Nick and Ruskin applauded them. Matt theatrically bowed and then took Tara in his arms as a slower melody began. Matt was a good dancer, Nick had to admit, as he and Tara swirled around the cabin. He glanced at Ruskin who was watching them dance with what looked like amused contentment. Nick and Matt continued dancing a while longer, taking turns with Tara.

Eventually, Ruskin stood up and told them he was ready to go to bed. They all thought it was a good idea as it was already getting late and they didn't know what tomorrow would bring. Matt offered his bed to Ruskin, who insisted on taking the cot instead. Nick offered his to Tara, who tried lying on it and remarked how comfortable it was. Nick prepared for bed, and when he returned to the sleeping quarters, he found Tara already under the blankets. For a moment, he forgot and started to kiss her goodnight, until they both remembered at the same time and instead hugged briefly.

As he started to leave, Tara looked up at him and said, "When I was a little girl my mother would tuck me in and kiss me goodnight. Then my father would come in and give me a big hug before blowing out the candle. Since they died, I've missed that, but somehow you make me feel cared for like they did."

"I don't know exactly why," he said, "but I'm very comfortable with you, too. I feel that you're genuine and unpretentious, and it pleases me that you're so open to try new things. Like the dance steps you picked up so quickly tonight. And more important, how you seem to have accepted me, a stranger from a world you know so little about."

She patted the bed, inviting him to sit down. "I know what you're saying. From the first time I saw you, I sensed a gentleness in you that makes me feel special. I feel I can trust you, and it makes me lose my reserve.

Nick looked into her eyes, and stroked the inside of her arm. He smiled down at her. Squeezing her hand in his, he got up, saying, "I hope we get to know each other very well." He gently blew her a kiss and turned off the light.

Chapter Four

In the morning, they woke to see the birds—not as many as they feared, just a few circling above languidly. Nick speculated that they were surveying the fortifications.

"These few will give us no trouble," stated Matt, who seemed anxious to begin the fray.

"Maybe they'll just go, and leave us alone," Tara said, hopefully.

"I hope you're right," Nick replied. "Just so they're not the scouting party."

"Unfortunately, that's a distinct possibility," said Ruskin.

As they watched, their fears were realized. Advancing from the west, a rapidly moving dark cloud appeared. As it came closer, they could see that it was made up of a multitude of flapping wings.

"Look at that!" said Nick in awe.

They watched in horror as the huge cloud approached until the birds were directly above them, circling, screeching, and making short dives in their direction. Without speaking, Tara turned to look at Nick. Nick looked back at her and then at Matt and at Ruskin. Wordlessly they resolved that, whatever the odds, they would stand and fight.

Nick and Matt spoke briefly with each other. They were concerned that the perimeter shields might use up too much energy trying to withstand such a massive onslaught. As they conferred, a Thorn crashed into the shield, and then another and another. Although individual Thorns were stopped by it, the rest didn't stop coming. A check of the energy monitors showed that the system was approaching overload. "I'm shutting down the perimeter shield," announced Nick. "Ready your pulsars."

"Look!" yelled Tara, pointing out the window. "They're landing over there by the poles." The men left their positions at the other windows to watch the huge birds alighting on the ground just outside the line of defense. There were seven of them, and as they watched from inside the ship, the creatures began attacking the shafts with their powerful beaks.

"I don't think those poles can withstand that long," Ruskin asserted. Already they could see splinters flying under the attack. Then, the first pole went down.

"We shouldn't wait any longer," Matt declared.

"No," answered Nick. "Let's get them!" He slid the window open. The pulsars hummed their lethal power, and four of the Thorns dropped. Two were motionless while the other two still quivered. The others started to take flight, and one was hit in mid air, falling with a thud to the ground.

Overcoming the immediate threat, they were elated, until they looked out the window on the other side. Massed there were at least a dozen more of them. They had already started to attack the outer poles, and the wood was breaking apart. Two of the logs crashed to the ground. As the pulsars discharged again, more Thorns fell sprawling to their deaths. Nevertheless, huge numbers of them continued to land around the outer poles. Now they were coming from every direction.

Though the birds were easy targets, they began coming in so fast that they were able to break down the shafts before they could be killed. The defenders soon became aware of another concern. They weren't able to recharge the guns fast enough, even though Tara was now working the charger full time. If the onslaught continued, it would only be a matter of time before they would be landing outside the doors. The bodies of the fallen Thorns were heaping up along the outer logs, but those that had not been shot hopped over the dead ones and continued battering the posts. It was strange, Nick thought, that they kept coming, as if programmed. Even imminent death didn't deter them. The poles kept crashing down.

Abruptly, the noise stopped. As they watched, the Thorns on the ground stretched their wings and rose up to join the ones still circling above. Then only the flapping of wings was heard as the whole assemblage began moving away from the ship. One bird, larger and blacker than the others, flew high in front of the rest, seeming to lead the way. The huge cloud passed over them and moved back to the west. In a few minutes, they were out of sight.

"I do hope they've given up," voiced Tara.

It was a sentiment they all felt. Around the outer area of the fortifications stood the remnants of shattered poles and the bodies of lifeless birds. They covered an area forty or more feet wide and up to ten feet high. Though it was a horrible sight, somehow the defenders couldn't take their eyes off it. At last, they looked away from the carnage and realized how hungry they were. It was already nearing noon, and they hadn't eaten anything. Tara, with Nick's help, made lunch. As they sat tired and quiet at the table, they silently gave thanks for their survival. Not one of them believed that the Thorns wouldn't return.

Ruskin left the main room to take a nap, and Nick and Matt went outside to look at the full extent of the damage. They wanted to see what repairs could be made to the fortifications. Tara stayed inside for a while and then came out. However, the sight and the smell of all the dead birds repulsed her, and she soon went back in.

She looked at the cabin, trying to imagine what it would be like to live there for a two-month space trip. She glanced out the window and saw Nick and Matt alongside one of the poles, tying on a crossbeam for added protection. Out of the corner of her eye, she caught sight of something moving in the sky. In a moment, she knew what it was. She hastened to open the door and call out to Nick and Matt. The Thorns were back.

By the time they were all inside the cabin, the creatures were already closing in, and rising high above the others was the great lead Thorn. As they watched, it turned to one side, appearing to look down on them. Although it was still far up in the sky, Nick had the distinct impression that its eyes were red. He pointed it out to Matt.

"See that one there, above all the rest? If it comes in range, let's try to knock it down." Their view of it was almost immediately obscured however, as the Thorns started circling in a huge black cloud directly above the ship. They readied their pulsars in preparation for another attack on the remaining poles. But it didn't come, and the Thorns continued to fly in a large circle above the ship. They waited, wondering what would happen next.

As they watched, a bird dropped out of the sky toward the ship.

"Shoot!" yelled Nick, touching open the window. The Thorn's head went limp, but its body hurtled toward them like a rock. It landed a few feet from the ship with a loud thud, shattering a pole as it fell.

"That was close." Matt yelled. A second bird dropped from the sky. "Get it!" he shouted. It was on Ruskin's side, and he shot three times before it folded and dropped its head. The creature's dead body fell like a brick, landing inches from the ship.

"I'm going outside!" shouted Nick. "We've got to hit them immediately when they start their dive or it's going to be too late."

When the Thorns saw Nick, they went into a frenzy, diving toward him rather than at the ship. Like bombs, they began dropping from the sky. Nick held on to his pulsar with both hands, firing at the fiendish creatures diving at him from out of the swirling maelstrom. He pivoted around in a circle, trying to keep ahead of the Thorns coming down at him from every direction. As his pulsar found its targets, their heads drooped, their wings folded, and they fell, sometimes knocking down logs as they crashed to the ground.

"Look out!" shouted Tara. Nick spun around, firing a late shot at one that came from behind. The bird died a quick death, but its body snapped a pole, which landed on Nick's thigh. He fell down. Tara gasped, and Matt sprinted from the cabin, firing as the Thorns continued to dive-bomb them. Nick pushed the log off his leg, got up, and the two of them, standing back to back, fired at the unrelenting Thorns. Nick yelled to Tara that his pulsar power was weakening. She threw him a recharged one, and he tossed the spent one back to her.

The battle continued. It went on for a long time, until the whole area was littered with shattered poles and dead Thorns. There didn't appear to be any end to them. Then, as if by signal, the screeching stopped. In silence, they continued to circle above, until, as if called by a mysterious signal, they again began moving to the west. Despite all the birds left on the ground, the number above seemed only slightly diminished. As they flew off, Nick could once again see the large black bird flying above all the rest, leading them home.

The four of them were exhausted, not only by the activity, but also by all the tension they had been under. Words were few. Tara wanted Nick to lie down so that she could look at his injured thigh. She was glad to see that although it was dark and swollen, there were no open wounds or lacerations. Matt went to the restant to order a meal, which they ate stoically. The pulsars were again recharged up to their maximum.

They went about their few activities woodenly. Around the ship, the view was desolate. Thorn bodies were everywhere among the splintered logs, and a few were impaled on the poles. Despite the scene of overall destruction, the logs and bracketing immediately surrounding the ship remained intact. By virtue of Nick and Matt's skillful shooting and luck, none of the creatures had landed on the framework. That structure remained, their last line of defense. How much longer would it hold? The unspoken question was on all of their minds. Nick and Matt went outside to add some bracing to reinforce it. As darkness fell, they returned inside to join Ruskin and Tara.

Tara was talking to Ruskin at the table. She looked up as they entered and asked, "How does it look?"

"Not bad, considering," Nick answered. "Our main barrier around the ship is intact, and we added some timber to make it stronger."

"Can I fix you both something to drink?"

"Not for me, thanks," Matt replied. "I just want to lie down."

"I'd have a cup of chocolate with you," Nick answered.

"No thanks for me," said Ruskin. "I'm going to bed too."

Tara had already learned how to operate the restant. She came back to the table with two cups of the piping hot brew. She studied Nick for a moment and set the cups on the table. She could see his weariness.

"You should go to bed too, Nick. You've been working so hard out there."

"I know," he said, reaching for her hand across the table. "They just don't seem to want to give up. This whole thing is a terrible nightmare."

"Yes," she said, caressing his hand. "I know you and Matt have been doing all you can. You need to rest now. Try to put it out of your mind for awhile."

"I wish I could."

She got up and, bending down, hugged him around the neck. "You're so tense. Let me give you a massage. Turn your back to me." As she worked with firm hands on his tightened neck and back muscles, Nick could feel some of the tension leaving his body.

"Thank you. That feels much better."

They parted to go to their beds, and after a short time, all four of them were asleep. But the Thorns fought on in their dreams, as they had during the day.

Long before daybreak, Nick woke up. He thought he heard something coming from above. Listening attentively, he was sure of it. A look out the window confirmed his worst fears. Without touching on any of the lights, he roused the others. They gathered together in the darkness. Then they heard loud scratching sounds overhead. Nick stood on a chair to open the hatch in order to see what was going on. What he saw made his hair stand on end. The creatures were landing on the bracketing, scarcely six feet above him.

Matt yelled, "Hurry! They're piling up on top of the framework. With all their weight they're going to break it down!"

He and Matt began firing through the hatch into the massing bodies. The blood of the wounded birds drained down through the opening, drenching them. Ruskin grabbed his pulsar and a chair and joined them while Tara returned to the job of recharging the pulsars. So much blood was streaming down, that all three of the men soon looked like they were mortally wounded. Outside, the carcasses were piling up around the module, as they fell from the top. Then they heard a sharp crack, followed immediately by loud pounding that rocked the ship. The birds had broken through the barrier. They were swarming on top the module!

Inside, they could hear beaks pecking and claws scratching, trying to force a way in. Nick glanced at Matt and then rushed out the door, slamming it behind him. He clambered over the bodies and began shooting at the horde that was still coming down from the sky and landing on the ship. Intent on the module, they didn't at first notice him. Nick began to feel a sense of hopelessness as he realized that there were just too many of them. If the attack continued, they would burst through long before they could all be killed. He had an idea. His eyes searched the sky high above him, hoping to glimpse in the pale moonlight the huge black Thorn with the red eyes.

It was no use. There were just too many of them flying about, blocking his view. There was a clearing, and peering through it, Nick recognized the huge Thorn, still flying high above the others. He steadied his hands and fired carefully, once, twice, three times. On the third shot, he thought he saw the creature shudder, but his view was again obscured.

He continued to watch for several more seconds. Again, there was another clearing, but it showed nothing of the huge Thorn he was looking for. Had he shot it down? And, if so, did it make any difference at all? Apparently not, he decided, as the Thorns continued unabated their onslaught against the ship. He fired repeatedly at the Thorns landing there, but his pulsar was beginning to lose power. He heard Tara scream at him through the open door of the module, and he turned to see a gigantic Thorn with blood red eyes bearing down on him. He tried to jump out of its path, but was knocked to the ground. He felt the sharp stab of its beak in his left side.

Suddenly he felt extremely weak and thirsty, and he realized he was in danger of passing out. Managing somehow to deal with the pain, he tightened his grip on the pulsar. Then he saw Tara climbing up over the dead Thorns as she rushed toward him. "Go back," he tried to shout, but in his weakened condition, his voice sounded feeble, even to himself. She kept on coming.

He saw the Thorn returning to finish him off. As the creature zeroed in on him, he raised his pulsar for one last shot. At the last moment, the giant bird saw Tara and altered its course. Nick saw it turn toward her. As it closed in on her, he fired once and then again. His pulsar was spent, but the bird's terrible eyes closed, and its body trembled. Its momentum carried it forward, and it crashed to the ground between Nick and Tara, covering them with its still outstretched wings. It didn't move.

"Nick!" screamed Tara. "Are you alright?"

"Yes," he lied. "Are you OK?"

"Yes," he heard her answer.

Then, from underneath the outstretched wings of the Thorn, came a sound like heavy drops of rain. Next, from the direction of the ship he heard yelling. It sounded like cheering. *Why were they cheering?* Nick wondered dimly as he lapsed into unconsciousness.

Chapter Five

The first thing Nick saw when he opened his eyes, was Tara bending over his bed. She was attending to the wound on his left side and she looked so anxious that he smiled weakly at her and said, "Surely it can't be that bad."

"Nick," she cried, the sadness immediately leaving her face. "You were badly hurt, Nick. I'm so glad you've come out of it." She moved closer and took his hand in hers. "How do you feel?"

Nick's health gradually improved, and he learned more about what had happened at the end of the battle. Apparently, the Thorn that attacked him was the one that he had seen leading the others, because when it was killed, the others withdrew in disorganized haste, passing water as they flew.

Then, for a long time, the defenders waited, fearing their return. But they didn't come back. Before long, the dead bodies surrounding the space module created such a stench that the ship had to be moved. Matt, with the help of Ruskin and Tara, dismantled what remained of the broken defense barrier and selected a site closer to the oil fields. The new location was on higher ground, not far from the old site, and was situated at the base of a small hill covered with mixed grassland and small trees. Matt, with some help from Tara, whom he taught to check the coordinates, had eased the module up and over to the new location.

Nick began to enjoy the days of his recuperation. While Matt spent much of his time away, exploring for more oil, Tara became a regular visitor. She came each day after work, and she often stayed to make supper for him and Matt. Frequently she would bring in meals she had prepared herself. Nick and Matt grew to appreciate the native food and began to look forward to it. Tara, in turn, learned some of their card games, and more than once, Ruskin joined them for dinner and cards to make a foursome.

Nick delighted in having Tara around. Her cheerful demeanor and ready sense of humor made the cabin feel lived in and more homelike. She talked about goings on in the town, about some of the children she taught, and about Ruskin's extensive Laboratory and pharmacopoeia. She described the three doctors who worked there and explained how they prescribed curatives for all types of ailments and injuries. Twelve others worked in the lab, which besides the medicinal facilities, also had sections dedicated to agricultural and biological studies.

What interested Nick most was an upcoming trip that Ruskin had planned for the purpose of harvesting wild medicinal plants. Nick was interested, not only because he had taken courses in biology and botany in college. He had learned that Ruskin was also going to be on the lookout for herbs that might decrease his allergic reaction to Tara. When Nick told Tara that he might like to go with them, she was enthused. She told him they would be leaving during her break from teaching, and as part of an apprenticeship program, two students would also be going along.

Nick talked to Matt about it later that night. As he expected, Matt didn't like the idea. He had been on the planet long enough and wanted to finish the job so he could go home. Nick understood his point of view but reasoned that since Matt had been doing most of the work already, and there wasn't that much left to do, having two in the field wouldn't speed things up that much. Since they had only one car, they could only work one site at a time anyway. In the end, Matt stopped disagreeing. He knew, of course, that Nick was attracted to Tara, and he was good-natured enough that he could accord him some time off for "an affair of the heart" if necessary. He asked one question.

"Will you stay here with her if you do find a cure?"

"I don't know," Nick answered truthfully.

Later that night, as he lay in his bed, he thought again about Matt's question. What *did* he really want to do? The idea of leaving her forever was difficult to contemplate. Would he instead want to take her back with him, assuming she would be willing to go? Did he want to stay with her in Crystal? He mulled the possibilities for a long time, deciding finally that he just didn't know the answer. In time, he might know, but time was one thing he didn't have. He knew he couldn't keep Matt waiting much longer.

The next day he went with Tara to see the Laboratory for himself. He was feeling much better by now and knew that walking would be good for him. After seeing the lab, he was impressed. Although they were unaccomplished in industrial processes and transportation, the community had made strides in biology and chemistry. Inside the "lab," as they called it, he was invited to look at different organic cultures through surprisingly powerful hand crafted microscopes. He saw diatomic algae being propagated for the relief of sore throat, and he met some of the technicians, learning a little about their current projects. Although much of the work was of a routine nature, such as preparing specific antidotes at designated potencies, research was also being conducted.

Nick enjoyed talking with the people there and was pleased that he was able to understand much of what they were saying. Tara showed him around the Laboratory with obvious pride in her grandfather's life work. Nick could tell she was gratified that he didn't think it primitive. On the contrary, he assured her, it wasn't. He talked with Ruskin, who was, in an orderly and systematic way, making preparations for the trip. Ruskin discussed it briefly and, in answer to Nick's question, explained how his allergy to Tara might be suppressed. When Nick asked if he could come along, Ruskin genuinely welcomed him, saying, "You can learn a lot on this trip, if you're interested in herbal medicine."

Over the next several days, Nick and Matt worked together in the oil fields taking samples and recording data to try to quantify the full extent of their find. It was dull, repetitious work, but it had to be done. Now that they had indeed found oil, they needed to complete all the necessary paperwork and fill in the numbers, so that the statisticians could make their feasibility determinations. Then, if they gave the go-ahead, a subsidiary of the Worlds' Bank would authorize a loan to cover the huge cost of sending ships and equipment to extract the oil and bring it back for refining. Nothing happened unless the managers in the big offices gave their OK, and unless the paperwork was completed *their* way, chances are nothing would happen.

Nick often thought of Tara as he worked. Wanting to help Matt get as much done as possible before leaving, he had not visited her since returning to the job, and he found it harder than he realized to be away from her. The day of the expedition finally arrived, and early that morning Matt dropped him off at the house.

It was a beautiful day. The sun was just rising, and there was a fragrant quality to the air. Many of the trees had a fresh growth of pale green leaves, and after a gentle rain in the night, everything seemed to glisten in the light of the morning sun. Spring had arrived.

Tara looked up from attending to the forcs, saw Nick coming, and ran to meet him. Nick quickened his pace, and they embraced as they met. The tension he had felt over the past few days melted in her presence. As they walked together, hand in hand, she introduced him to the two young apprentices, Jon and Erik. Jon, who was fourteen, was the more slender and the taller of the two. Erik was twelve, comparatively husky, with reddish brown hair. Tara told Nick that they were two of her better trainees and that they were quite interested in learning more about medicine.

Ruskin came out of the house and wished them all a good morning as he sauntered down the steps, carrying an assortment of gear, which he handed to the boys. "Fine day," he said, and he looked around to check that everything was in order.

Altogether, they made up a fair-sized entourage. Seven forcs were at ready, one for each of the travelers and two more that were saddled with provisions and gear. Ruskin gathered everyone together and said, "As you know, this is an important mission that we're beginning today." He looked toward the two youth. "We can enjoy each other's company and have some fun, but for you apprentices, these days should be mainly a learning experience. Tara has told me you both want to become practitioners. She has recommended you to me, and, as you know, not many have the chance you have to go on an expedition like this. The significance of our mission, however, is more important than that. People here are depending on us. Their health is at stake. That's why you must follow our directions precisely. As for the trip itself, it will be long and at times arduous. You have been told all this already." He glanced from the boys to Nick and Tara, and then, getting on his steed and raising his hand, he said, "Let's go."

They quickly mounted and were off, with Ruskin in the lead followed by Tara and Nick, Jon and Erik, and the two pack animals in the rear. As they traveled along, Tara frequently rode up to talk to Ruskin, and Nick often talked with the boys. Although the youths were not yet very good at thought transference, Nick had already learned enough language that he could understand and make himself understood by them most of the time. He was impressed that, despite their ages, they were quite intent and serious about the trip. This was especially true of Jon. Nick sensed that for him the journey was truly a personal mission, and that he was ready and willing to do anything that might be asked of him.

Erik, on the other hand, although committed, was fundamentally more fun loving and more easily distracted. As for Nick himself, he knew why he was going, or did he? Certainly, he liked being in Tara's company. Besides that, he decided he would learn what he could and enjoy the trip. As they emerged from some trees, she pointed out an escarpment rising to the left and said they would encounter territory that was more mountainous and eventually would have to dismount. The excursion was longer than it needed to be because they had decided to circle around the nesting area of the Thorns, even though they were assumed to be dangerous only during the month of Ravidian.

As the expedition continued through the day, the terrain became more scenic and wooded. Outcroppings of rock appeared on the hills, and when they reached the higher elevations they looked down on small lakes and streams that meandered across the countryside. The air, borne by southerly breezes, was warm and fresh and carried the scent of pines and other heady smells he could not identify.

Although they had not yet reached any mountains, it was apparent they were gradually gaining altitude, though at times they seemed to descend from their generally upward trek. With an hour still left before sunset, Ruskin signaled a halt. They were situated on one side of a meadowland that sloped down to a valley of short, thick grass, ending in a small stream. Above, a sizeable cliff jutted out of the grass, and on top of the hill, short trees swayed in the breeze.

"Let's stop here," said Ruskin. "We'll have time to put up the tent and find some vegetables before the sun goes down. Jon, Erik, help me get the tent set up. Tara would you and Nick find some greens and gather some firewood?"

As they dismounted, Tara beckoned Nick to follow her. They set off, going up the side of the hill toward the cliff near the top. When they reached it, they were both breathing heavily. She took his hand, and they looked out over the beautiful valley and surrounding plain beneath them. Then they turned to the sparse woods that began behind the rocks of the cliff.

Tara led the way, holding his hand, and before long she stopped to show him a broad leafed, serrated edged plant called "rashanks," which she said was crispy and delicious. Next, with some difficulty, she pulled from the ground a waist-high plant with deeply lobed bluish green leaves. Turning it over, she showed him how to remove the orangish outer covering from the rootstock. The creamy white inner root looked much like a carrot. "This is panga," she said, breaking off a piece and handing it to him. "I think you'll like it."

He took it from her and cautiously bit off the tip and chewed it. He smiled and took another bite. "It's very good. I hope we can find more of it."

"There's more over there," she answered, pointing toward the right, about fifty feet ahead. "You can help me get them out." They walked over to the bluish-green plants, and soon they had pulled a dozen nice-size stalks. They spent more time gathering food and then picked up some wood for the fire. With arms full, they returned to the campsite. The large tent was erected, and the boys were running, stopping, and then running again, playing a game with a ball they had brought with them. Ruskin was coming from the creek carrying a small pail of water, and he waved when he saw them approaching.

Soon they had the fire going, and smoked venison was boiling in a pot as darkness settled around them. By this time, they were all hungry, and they chatted as they lined up for the delicious smelling hot venison and steamed vegetables that Tara was serving. Nick sat down and waited for her to join him. Ruskin gave thanks for the food, and they ate heartily as the last traces of light left the sky. The utter darkness was relieved only by the flickering of the campfire and the points of light glowing in the night sky.

Relaxing by the embers, they discussed the trip in general, what tomorrow would bring, and the kinds of plants they would be looking for. After awhile, the boys went into the tent to go to bed. Ruskin grew silent, puffing contentedly on a lit stem, while staring into the fire. Who knew what thoughts were going through his head? Soon he too said goodnight and disappeared into the tent. Tara was sitting next to Nick, and she leaned toward him. He put his arms around her, and they watched together the glow from the fire and the resplendent twinkling of the stars that filled the sky above them. "Can you tell which sun is yours," she asked, as she languidly lay back in his arms.

"Yes. It's the small star over there, down from the bright bluish one."

"That little one there?" she asked, pointing to it.

"Yes, that's the one."

"Does our sun look that small too?"

"Oh, yes. Just as small as ours at this distance."

"Amazing," she concluded, as she nestled in his arms. Then she sat up straight. "We better get some sleep. As soon as daylight breaks, grandpa will want to get going."

They entered the tent together and in the darkness could barely make out the sleeping arrangements. As their eyes adapted, they could tell that the boys were on one side of the tent and Ruskin was in the middle, lightly snoring. Nick and Tara's bedding was already laid out on the other side.

Nick went to the edge of the tent, removed his shoes and outer clothes, and tucked himself in. Tara waited briefly before coming to bed. Nick was tired, and his sleeping bag was surprisingly comfortable, so he didn't think he would have any trouble falling asleep. Nevertheless, he did, and as time passed, he found himself staring wide-awake at the top of the tent. Hearing Tara turn in her bed, he whispered, "are you still awake?"

"Yes, I can't sleep," she answered.

He rolled over and found himself at her side. Placing his arm around her, he felt the narrowness of her waist. He experienced a rush of tenderness toward her and whispered, "I wish I could kiss you."

"Me too," she answered, stretching her arms out to hold him.

"I've wanted to hold you like this ever since I left you that first night at your house," he said.

"I've been dreaming of you holding me," she whispered, her body trembling slightly.

"Are you cold?"

"No," she said, smiling, her body relaxing more in his arms. "I've never been held by anyone like this before. It makes me feel so good to be in your arms."

"Yes," he replied, as he pondered the mystery of a girl so beautiful who had experienced so little. He touched her face and bent down to kiss her underneath her chin, near the nape of her neck. He felt her soft breathing and the rise and fall of her breast. She held him closer and closed her eyes. Then, suddenly letting go of him, she whispered, "Let's go outside."

"Why?"

"Just come," she said softly.

Nick felt around for his clothes and shoes, put them on, and finding his way to the tent entrance, met Tara there and took her hand.

"Let's go up there on the knoll," she said, pointing toward the hill that was barely visible in the darkness. The night was still warm, and a quiet breeze moved the air around them. They reached the top of the knoll and sat down together. The valley was spread out beneath them, and the stars shimmered above. "Have you made any plans for the future?" she asked.

He put his arm around her waist, and answered, "Yes, I've thought a lot about the future. I was planning to make a lot of money, settle down, raise a family, and travel with them all over the universe. Lately I've been rethinking some of my plans. I don't think that making a lot of money is so important anymore."

"I understand that you need it to travel," she interjected. "Wouldn't you miss that?"

"No, I don't think so. Not anymore. You see," he continued, looking into her eyes, "I had a girl when I left Earth several months ago. Now I can scarcely remember her features. Someone else has replaced her image in my mind. I think you know who that is." He embraced her, and she spontaneously returned his embrace, but then abruptly turned away again.

"When you get to the next planet will you forget about me too?"

"I don't think so," he said, noncommittally. "How could I ever forget you? Besides, maybe I won't leave."

"Really?" she exclaimed, thrilled by the revelation. "Wouldn't you miss everyone back at your home town?"

"Tara, if we can cure my allergy problem, would you marry me?" he asked.

She tilted her head to face him directly, and in the starlight he could see tears glistening in her eyes. "That would make me so happy, Nick, if I could really be your bride. The thing is, here we marry until death, and that is the only way I would want to marry you. I understand that on your world people often wed for a time. Nick, I couldn't do that. It would break my heart."

Nick saw tears run down her cheeks. "I know, it's true; many on Earth do that. "Tara," he said emphatically, "I would never want to leave you. By my God and yours, I swear that I would never leave you. I want to love you till we're both old and gray."

"Then I will love you that long, too," she replied, taking his hands in hers and holding them tightly in her lap.

Nick leaned over to kiss her.

"No. You can't!" she said quickly.

"Damn! I forgot." He took her hand; they got up and walked together down the hill back to the tent.

Chapter Six

When Nick wakened the next morning, it wasn't just the dawning of a new day. He was elated and found it difficult to calmly eat breakfast, chatting casually, when he felt like making an announcement to the universe about the two of them. Furthermore, what he really wanted to do was to take her away with him, to a place where he could hold her and love her. If only he could be sure there was a cure for his allergy. There must be one! At the moment, Ruskin's relaxed and ordinarily stimulating conversation held little interest for him, as there was so much he wanted to talk about with Tara. Still, everything hinged on the problem. He told himself to calm down and be patient. There was nothing that could be done about it now. They would have to wait until the expedition was finished before any cure could be attempted. In the meantime, he would have to live one day at a time while hoping for the best.

He listened as Ruskin talked about the territory they would reach today and the types of plants and minerals they would be looking for. Nick had come to admire his low-key, knowledgeable style. Quietly enthusiastic about his subject, he was always ready to answer questions and to explain the uses of the herbs and succulents that they were collecting.

They finished breakfast, packed up their equipment, and started leaving the campsite. Just then, an unlikely looking trio appeared from the other side of the nearby hill. Three large men, dressed in dark brown robes, ambled toward them. They had an expectant look on their faces. Nick glanced at Tara, who smiled and said, "They're mendicants."

Ruskin stopped, and they watched as the three lined up in front of them, bowed deeply, and in unison rubbed their hands together. Then the one in the middle, who was also the largest, raised his head and intoned in a deep, soulful voice; "We are the Brothers of Midian, who have unfortunately fallen on hard times. Although you can see the coarseness of our garb and the sorrowfulness of our demeanor, we are too proud to beg."

"Sirs, if you have need of food, we will give you some. However, we don't have a lot to share as we still have a long way to go," said Ruskin.

"Oh no, kind sir," spoke the one on the right, the smallest. "Although verily, we are hungry, we cannot take from your stores without giving you some measure of recompense." So saying, he picked up the provisions that Ruskin had already unpacked for them.

"All right," Ruskin replied, dismounting, though obviously impatient to get underway. "We will stop for a short time if you insist."

The rest of them also dismounted and sat down at the base of the small hill to their right. The three men huddled together, heads bent down, as if deciding what they were going to do. Suddenly, they separated and started yelling at the top of their lungs, running and zigzagging in every direction. Abruptly, they stopped. The boys thought their short spectacle was hilarious, and they shouted, "More! More!"

The three looked up and acknowledged their audience with a bow. Then they sprang into action again, turning cartwheels, jumping over each other's backs, doing flips and pirouettes, all while yelling like madmen. Their agility was amazing, especially for such heavy men. Judging by the perspiration on their faces, they definitely put everything into their performance.

Ludicrous as their presentation was, Nick began to feel admiration for them. They weren't done yet. Looking around for a podium, they found a large rock and rolled it into place. The largest mendicant climbed on top while the other two stood on each side facing their audience. He addressed them:

> "We are the men of Mendax,
>
> the strangers in your midst.
>
> We come from many miles away,
>
> To please you is our wish.

> And if our crazy antics,
>
> Make your spirits glow,
>
> Our mission is accomplished,
>
> and we are free to go.

> We thank you for your patronage,
>
> and thank you for your bread,
>
> and now we must be moving on,
>
> glad to be well fed."

After saying this, he jumped down from the rock, and the three of them marched in single file to the east, humming a tune. Stunned, their audience continued to sit there watching them go until Nick broke the silence. "What a show!"

"They must have done it for the boys. I've never seen them go on like that," enthused Tara.

"Then you know them?" Nick asked.

"We've seen them before, but we don't really know them," answered Ruskin. "I think they come from a small settlement a long way from here."

"I've seen them twice before, but this is the first time they did acrobatics," added Tara.

"Yes, any time they've been around in the past, they've recited poetry or given little speeches. Looks like they've broadened their act," said Ruskin.

"It was so unexpected to see such heavy men tumbling," Nick remarked. "For me, that's what made it so funny."

"I don't think any of us will forget that act," reflected Tara.

Ruskin mounted his forc, and, following his lead, the small group started out again. As they traveled on, the sun rose high above them, and the terrain became rough and mountainous. They were definitely gaining altitude. The sky was a bright blue with white clouds that drifted by. The air grew cooler and breezier, the trees were sparser, and rocks appeared more frequently. Whenever they had steep hills to climb, they dismounted and led the animals along the trail, a precaution they took to keep them from slipping and possibly breaking a leg. It was slow going, and when they stopped for an afternoon lunch break, they were glad to rest.

Nick was amazed at Ruskin's endurance. He appeared to be no more breathless than anyone else. While the adults took their time eating, Jon and Erik finished quickly and scampered up a steep hill. Soon they had disappeared. When they were ready to leave, Tara called out to them, but the boys didn't answer. Nick started up the hill to look for them, and Tara joined him. As they neared the top, they saw a terrible sight in the sky above them. Flying, about one hundred feet overhead, was a large Thorn.

Nick and Tara exchanged anxious glances and hurried the rest of the way up. From their high vantage point, they anxiously scanned the area, trying to spot the boys. They were nowhere to be seen. Not knowing how the Thorns would react closer to their own territory, they were reluctant to draw attention to themselves by calling out, and yet they were becoming increasingly worried about Jon and Erik.

"If you go down that way, I'll check this way," said Nick, pointing out directions. "But let's not get too far apart."

He started descending the right side of the hill and saw Tara a moment before she disappeared through the trees on his left. Rather suddenly, it became much darker, as a cloud covered the sun, and Nick entered a dense, forested area. Surprisingly, the wind seemed to be blowing stronger and cooler through the valley, and he began to wonder if his imagination was playing tricks on him. He surveyed the area around him through the tree trunks and still saw no sign of the boys or of anything else out of the ordinary. Then he heard Tara's faint cry in the distance. He answered her call, not knowing if she heard him, and advanced quickly in the direction of her voice. Soon, he saw her through the bushes. She was with Jon and Erik. "Are you all right?" he asked.

"We're fine," she replied. "Jon and Erik have something to show you."

"Look at that!" said Erik with excitement, as he lifted his jacket off a large, white object. To Nick's astonishment, there, lying on the ground, was a huge egg. It must have been almost a foot and a half long and a foot thick.

"Oh, no. Is that what I think it is?" he asked, looking at Tara.

"I think so," she replied. "I'm surprised it hasn't hatched by now."

"Where did you find this?" he asked, speaking to Jon and Erik.

"Over there," they answered in unison, and Erik pointed to a hill about two hundred feet away from them.

"It was near the bottom of that hill," added Jon. "Maybe it rolled down from the top."

"We better leave," declared Tara, apprehensively glancing upwards. "Look!" she said, pointing to the sky where a Thorn circled lazily overhead.

"Into the woods!" Nick whispered. They all rushed toward the protection of the trees. From beneath the branches, they tried to follow the Thorns movements. Soon, it was out of sight, and they could breathe easier.

After climbing back up the hill, they went down the other side to where they had left Ruskin. They anticipated that he would be worried about them. Instead, they found him sleeping peacefully in the sunlight.

"Grandpa," said Tara softly, putting her hand on his shoulder. He woke with a start, slowly looked around him and then up at Tara. He seemed slightly chagrined to have been found sleeping, and Tara smiled at him saying, "We're ready to go now, grandpa."

As they continued along their route, they filled him in on their adventure. He was concerned, and wanted to know everything about it. He concluded, however, that he didn't think the Thorns would be much of a threat during any other month than Ravidian.

The trail was rougher now. They climbed over hills and down valleys and forded small streams. Now, more often than not, they had to dismount and lead their forcs behind them. The scenery was spectacular; but their muscles were sore, and their breathing was heavy. Finally, Ruskin stopped and said, "Let's camp here tonight." It was earlier in the evening than usual.

After supper they felt reinvigorated. There was a small lake nearby, and Jon and Erik were anxious to go swimming. Nick wanted to bathe, and together he and the boys walked over to the lake. The water was cool though not cold, and soon they had undressed and were all splashing in the nude. The boys found a small ridge overlooking the lake, climbed it, and jumped in. Enjoying the leap immensely, they returned again and again to the cliff, and Nick began tossing their ball toward them as they jumped. It was great fun for them to try to catch it out of the air as they fell. They were having such a good time, Nick tried it also. As he came up from his dive, he caught sight of Ruskin bathing about two hundred yards away. Then he heard Tara call out, "When are you boys going to be finished?"

"Where are you?" he asked, still not able to see her.

"Over here," she answered. "I'd like to bathe, too, when you're done."

"Come join us," he invited.

"No. No thank you," she replied. "I'm not coming in till you're gone."

"Boys, I think we've had enough swimming for today," said Nick.

"Aw," complained Erik. "I want to play some more. Just a little longer, please?"

"Let them play awhile longer," said Tara. "I'll wait." She still was not visible to Nick through the bushes.

"Where are you?" he asked again, trying to get a glimpse of her.

"I'll tell you when you're dressed," she answered.

Nick climbed out of the water, dried off, and began putting his clothes on. Before he had his shirt on, he heard branches rustling, and Tara stepped out of the bushes. She openly admired his muscular upper body.

"Did you really expect me to come in with you?" she asked.

"It would have been nice," he nonchalantly answered, as he pulled on his shirt.

"Jon. Erik." he called out. "Let's get out now."

"Thanks," she said, stepping forward to give him a quick hug.

The next day they slept a little later, and after a quick breakfast, soon were hiking swiftly toward the sea. They all were enthusiastic because today, if they pressed on, they would finally reach their destination. Tara had been there once, many years before. Only Ruskin was perfectly sure of the way, and he led on relentlessly.

"Hey! Wait for me," Erik cried out from behind the pack animals.

"Yes, Grandpa, don't you think we should take a rest?" asked Tara.

"Of course we can," Ruskin replied. "I guess I get a little excited when we get this close. Yes, let's stop for lunch. I'm ready to eat. How about the rest of you?"

They ate together in the lower level of a mountain whose summit they had climbed earlier, and the cool sea breezes rippled through their hair. They didn't want to lose too much time, and soon they were on the way again. By early afternoon, they had reached the crest of a hill where they could see the inlet of the sea. "There it is, down there," Ruskin pointed out triumphantly.

The rest of them shaded their eyes from the sun and looked out. "Oh, I see it." yelled Tara, as she stood on her tiptoes. "See it, over there," she pointed it out to Nick.

"OK. I see it now," he said. "It's still a long way off."

"Well, it's a downhill trip from here," said Ruskin. "We'll be there before nightfall."

It turned out to be a very long trek down to the lagoon, and as the five weary travelers set up the tent and prepared a late evening meal, they knew everything would have to wait until tomorrow.

That night, after they had eaten, and the others had gone to bed, Nick and Tara spread a blanket on the ground and sat looking out over the landscape and up at the stars. Tara snuggled next to Nick to keep warm. "Tell me about the stars, Nick. It's a very different world out there, isn't it?"

"Many different worlds. Some, like the one I come from, are densely populated and very automated. Others, like that blue star there," he pointed to it, "has a habitable planet, but few people live there because the weather is hot all the time. Many of the stars have celestial bodies circling them, but few of those have habitable conditions where people could live without building major life support systems. Still, there are more than enough livable places out there to satisfy population needs. The problem in recent decades has been a lack of enough energy resources to support the growing number of inhabitants. See that large red star up there?" He pointed it out.

"The one that forms a triangle with the bright yellow stars?"

"Yes, that's the one. Its name is Antares, and it's where the oil freighters have been most active. It has a smaller star in a distant orbit around it and several planets, two of which have supplied almost thirty percent of the oil needs used by the eastern half of the galaxy for the past fifty years."

"That sounds like a lot."

"It definitely is," he agreed. "Unfortunately, the oil fields there are gradually being depleted, and with scarcity there's more of a chance that a war might be fought over the limited supply.

"Are there many worlds that are being supplied with oil?"

"Oh, yes. Thirty-seven to be exact, although some of those have only minimal need"

"If you could go anywhere, to any of the worlds, where would you go?"

"Well, I haven't been to all that many, but for a vacation Olanda looks the nicest on EV. It's a tropical paradise with floating islands drifting in a warm sea. There are all kinds of fruit trees ready to be plucked, and I understand the natives are very hospitable."

"That sounds beautiful. You mean the islands are actually drifting in the sea?"

"Yes, from what I've heard, they are only a few feet thick in most places, and they actually float."

"Amazing. I'd like to go there too."

"I'd love to take you there, but it might not be possible unless they come to extract the oil we found here. I'm not so sure I would want that anymore. It might bring too many changes to your beautiful planet."

"Our beautiful planet," she corrected him, as she leaned toward him.

"Yes. *Our* beautiful planet," he repeated, as he held her close.

When the sun rose the next morning, Nick was the first to stir. He quietly slipped on his shoes and jacket, and stepped out of the tent. He walked to the edge of the lagoon to see what it looked like in daylight. To his surprise, it was dry. Instead of water, the surface was covered with sparse grass that erupted in various places with short, strange looking plants of many shades and colors.

He cautiously stepped down onto the flat, brownish surface. It supported him, and he could feel the buoyancy of the water underneath. He took a few steps and felt the surface sway beneath his feet. It was one of the strangest sensations he had ever experienced. He was afraid to go out much further before finding out if it was safe. He carefully walked back to the edge and was glad to be back on solid ground again.

Back at the campsite, Tara was preparing breakfast, and Ruskin was busily at work preparing vials and adding labels to most of them.

"Where'd you go?" she asked, looking up from her cooking.

"Just over to the lagoon," he answered as he came up and stood behind her. "Smells delicious," he said, nuzzling her with his chin.

"What, me or the food?" she replied, her hands occupied with cooking.

"Both. Say, did you know the lagoon is covered with plants? I mean, you can't even see the water."

"Of course. It's always that way," she replied, seeming surprised that he would mention it.

"I've never experienced anything like it. Is it safe to walk on?"

"It's fairly safe, but you have to be careful, especially where the plants come up. In places where there is a lot of vegetation, they weaken the surface of the mat. Also, you have to be careful not to walk too far toward the center of the lagoon because there the mat thins out until it's all open water."

"Unusual. What is it made of?"

"It's just matted vegetation and humus that floats up on top.

"You mean you don't have anything like it on Earth?"

"Not that I'm aware of. At least not so thick that it can be walked on. The whole basin must be filled with nutrients to support vegetation that thick."

"I never really thought much about it," she replied. "There is a stream that feeds the lagoon and empties into the sea through the coral reef. Ruskin says that it's the mix of fresh water and seawater that produces the great variety of plants in the pond. On this side there are mostly freshwater plants, but toward the reef there are plants that have adapted to seawater."

"I can see why this is such a botanical gold mine."

"Gold? What is that?"

"I'll tell you about it at breakfast. Will it be ready soon?"

As they ate, Nick told Tara about the precious metal, and then Ruskin briefed them on what they would be collecting. He urged them to be careful, pointing out the dangers, and took special pains to talk to Erik and Jon about safety. As always, he instructed them on what to look for and whether to harvest the roots, stem, leaves, blossoms, or fruit of the plant. He emphasized that they should be on the lookout for certain rare plants and for others that were especially beneficial.

Then, as an extra precaution, he told Jon and Erik to stay together at all times while on the lagoon's surface. With that, they loaded up their specimen bags, vials, and drying nets.

Dividing the area into sections, Ruskin assigned one to the boys, adjacent ones to Nick and Tara, and an area for himself. As Nick and Tara walked together to their areas, she showed him that there was little to fear from walking on the floating vegetation, and as they continued over its surface, he lost his sense of unsteadiness and instead marveled at the softness with which the underlying water cushioned his step.

By the time they separated, he was eager to begin collecting. He was impressed at the variety of vegetation to be found in one place. Soon, he was absorbed in wandering from one plant to the next, selecting nice specimens, pruning, marking, and dropping them in his bags. He glanced at Tara from time to time, to see that he didn't get too far away from her, and could see that she was also engrossed in the work. It was a calm, peaceful day under a mostly sunny sky, and he was content to spend the whole day there.

Then, a loud shout broke through the early afternoon stillness. It was Jon, and he frantically called out to them. All three of them started running toward him, though from their distance he appeared as just a small figure on the horizon. After running swiftly for over a minute, Nick arrived to find Jon crying, hysterically pointing at a large hole in the floating mat. "Erik's under there!" he shouted.

By the time Tara and Ruskin arrived breathless on the scene, Nick was poised to jump in after Erik.

"Wait!" shouted Ruskin. "Here, hold on to this rope so you'll be able to find your way back to the opening." Nick grabbed the rope, took a deep breath, and dove in. The water was so black he couldn't see a thing. He circled around near the top, frequently bumping his head on the bushy bottom of the mat surface. He was beginning to run out of air when he nudged something soft and solid. It was Erik. Grabbing his arm, he jerked on the rope with his free hand and felt himself being drawn rapidly toward the hole in the mat. He pushed Erik's lifeless body up onto the surface and gasped for air. With his knees pressed against the sod, he took Ruskin's hand and climbed out of the water.

Quickly, he turned Erik over, and taking one look at his blue, lifeless body, he knelt down and started mouth-to-mouth resuscitation. For what seemed like a long time, nothing happened. Then Erik drew his legs up and simultaneously coughed and threw up. He opened his eyes and looked at them vacantly. Nick helped him to sit up and thumped him solidly on the back. Erik coughed up some more water and began breathing normally.

Tara, seeing that he was all right, sat down beside him and caressed him. "Oh, Erik, we're so glad you're OK. We were so worried about you. How do you feel?"

"I feel sick," he answered.

Ruskin approached Nick and in a low, awed voice said, "Nick, that boy was dead. What kind of power do you have? You breathed life into a dead body."

Nick took a step back. "Ruskin, it's not supernatural. It's mouth-to-mouth resuscitation, something we practice in training back on Earth. Erik wasn't dead, only unconscious from lack of air.

What I did was get air back into his lungs. When it's done in time, anyone, just like Erik, may regain consciousness and start breathing on their own again."

"Well, that's simply amazing. We should definitely learn how to do that," he said to Tara. "In fact, everyone in the lab should be taught it. Nick, this is too good not to pass on. Will you teach us the technique and all the parameters for using it when we get back?"

"Yes, of course. This method is much better than the one that they used to use on Earth centuries ago. It will work even if a lung is partially collapsed. Once I'm cured of my allergy to your granddaughter, she and I can demonstrate it at the Lab." Turning to Tara, who was still comforting Erik, he spoke a little louder, "Tara, you'll help me demonstrate mouth-to-mouth resuscitation won't you?" She looked up from Erik and smiled, without saying a word.

For the next two days, they gathered specimens, then brought them back to the camp to be catalogued and packaged. Ruskin stayed up late at night tallying the results of the day's collection. He was very pleased with the quality and quantity of their procurements and congratulated them heartily. "You have all done a terrific job," he told them on the eve of their departure. "We can stock the Laboratory for at least two years with all the specimens you have obtained. Jon, Erik, I congratulate you and welcome you to the lab when you finish your studies."

Chapter Seven

Over the next several days, they proceeded to make the long trip home. Nick and Tara continued to meet late in the evening after the others had settled in. They looked forward to these times when they could be alone and talk. They discussed many things, the customs of Earth, versus those of Crystal, and their own ideas about life and love. They agreed that they would marry if the allergic condition could be overcome. The "if" was troubling them, however, and just as troubling to Tara was her suspicion that the treatment itself would be dangerous for Nick.

At last, they arrived back in Crystal and went directly to the Laboratory. There everyone enthusiastically welcomed the tired travelers. Entering the main lab room, they were glad to remove their heavy packs and sit down to drink big glasses of fresh guava. The staff was happy to see them back, and they crowded around them. Most were also very interested in seeing all that they had collected. Ruskin sat down on a stool and talked about the trip and about the various rare plants they had found. He spoke in general terms, promising he would make a complete report later.

One man, whose name was Range, asked if they had seen any Thorns. Ruskin motioned to Nick, who got up from his chair to tell them about the incident with the Thorn and the egg. Range questioned him further and was quite interested in anything Nick could tell him about the Thorns. The two of them agreed to meet at another time to talk more about them.

More time passed, and Nick was ready to leave, but he could see that Tara was engrossed in conversation with a sandy-haired, intelligent looking man, so he waited for her. A young, pretty girl remained with him after the others had left. She regarded him candidly and asked if he was tired after the long trip. Nick admitted he was and with a look of concern, she offered to get him more to drink. She told him she wished that she also could have gone on the trip. Nick learned that her name was Trila and that though she was only seventeen, she was already a receptionist and lab assistant. She said that she knew something about him already from her cousin, Tara. Nick got the impression that the dark-haired girl had somehow acquired a very high opinion of him, and he looked around somewhat uncomfortably to see if Tara was finished talking. As she caught his eye, he excused himself from Trila and went over to her.

"Can you come with me back to the house now?" she asked.

"Yes," he answered, unable to tell what she had in mind.

Upon leaving the lab, and walking with Tara in the cool night air, he quickly felt refreshed. "Who was that man you were talking with so intently," he asked, trying to make sure he didn't betray the tinge of jealously he felt.

"Why, that's Dr. Gefert," she replied. "He's our best allergy specialist. In fact, he's the one who will be your doctor."

"I'd like to begin the treatment as soon as possible."

"I'm afraid it's not going to be easy for you. Are you sure you want to do this?"

"Yes, whatever it takes," he answered quickly. "I can't say I'm good with pain, but being without you would be worse."

"I'm worried, Nick. Dr. Gefert believes that what he proposes to do will work, but even he's not certain. What scares me is that there is a chance the treatment could seriously hurt you. I mean what if the medicine triggers some kind of unexpected reaction in your body that our doctors aren't prepared for? What if. . ."

"Tara, please stop worrying. You're scaring me too. We've talked about this many times, and we know there is some risk. The risk is worth it to me. Isn't it worth it to you?"

"Yes, yes! It is, Nick. I'm sorry. You know it's what I want, too. I just don't know what I would do if . . ." She wiped the tears from her eyes.

"Don't worry, darling. Everything will be all right. I'm strong and healthy, and with God's help, we're going to start a new generation, just the two of us. The best of both worlds."

Tara looked up at him and smiled through her tears. "Yes, my Earthman, you're right. We're going to do it together. We're going to be a family. We're going to conquer this thing and nothing's going to keep us apart." She stopped and appeared to think for a moment. Then, she spoke in a slower pace. "Before there are any children, there has to be a lot of love. That's very important." She looked back at him.

"Don't you know yet how much I love you?" he asked as he drew her closer to him.

"Yes," she replied simply, smiling as she nestled in his embrace.

Nick slept overnight on a cot at Tara's house, and early the next morning he left to go back to the ship. He arrived to find Matt eating breakfast. They were glad to see each other again. Nick ordered some breakfast for himself from the restant, and sitting down together, they talked at length about all that happened since they had last seen each other.

Nick told Matt about his growing relationship with Tara and his plans for a future with her, if he could overcome his reaction. He told him about the trip for medicinal plants and of saving Erik's life when he almost drowned.

Matt told Nick about the progress he had made in oil exploration and how, despite all his work, he still didn't know if the corporate office would consider the site large enough for commercial drilling. He showed Nick the trove of samples he had collected to take back for analysis and the wealth of data accumulated.

Nick was impressed. Matt had indeed worked assiduously in his absence. The delicate part Nick saved for last. He told Matt that he definitely planned to marry Tara, *if* the treatment, scheduled to start the next day, was successful. When Matt learned that there was some danger that Nick could be hurt by the therapy, he was concerned. In the end, since he couldn't get Nick to reconsider, he agreed to stay on for up to a week and a half. By that time they would know whether there would be a wedding or if Nick would need treatment, perhaps at a hospital on Earth.

Early the next morning Nick arrived as scheduled at the Laboratory. Dr. Gefert was attentive in his usual officious manner, and Tara was sweet and meek as a lamb, as she listened intently to everything the doctor said. In its details, it was a complex procedure that he described to them; but, in general, the plan called for a steady progression in the dosage of the allergen until immunity was obtained. Once that was achieved, boosters could be administered every two years as a protective measure.

The doctor explained rather mechanically, how an extreme dilution of Tara's saliva, in a specifically selected herbal solution, would be used as the initial dose. He handed Nick the vial. Nick took it carefully in his hand, looked into Tara's eyes, and then quickly emptied the contents into his mouth and swallowed.

"I feel fine," he said as he leaned back on the bed. He didn't feel that way long. In a moment, his head began swimming and his vision began losing clarity.

"Nick! Are you all right?" entreated Tara as she bent over his supine body, sensing that something was wrong.

"I feel dizzy. My head feels like it's spinning," he said with difficulty.

"We were expecting some disorientation and other physical manifestations at the outset," said Dr. Gefert.

Nick moaned as increasing pain rushed through his body.

"Doctor! Can't you do something?" cried Tara.

"No need to," he answered, completely unperturbed. He put his hands on Nick's head and neck and concentrated on what he felt there. Then he spoke again to Tara. "I expected this. When he comes out of it he will be on the way to overcoming the initial dosage."

"But surely it's not going to be necessary to knock him out with each dose!" she said heatedly.

"Do you want him cured?" he asked.

Tara nodded yes and tried to keep herself under control.

"Then we'll do it my way," he continued. "There is no easy way; you should know that. If we take things one step at a time, I'm confident he's going to make it. Cheer up, girl. He's a strong young man."

Tara took some heart in what Dr. Gefert said. She caressed Nick's limp body and waited, praying silently. She waited at his side for what seemed like a long time. Finally, she felt Nick's arm move. Then he shuddered and opened his eyes.

"Tara?" he whispered, in the darkened room.

"Yes, it's me," she responded eagerly. "How do you feel?"

"Terrible. I have a splitting headache, and I feel so cold."

"Here," she said, folding a thick blanket around him. "You've been unconscious for hours. Dr. Gefert predicted as much. He wants me to tell him when you wake up."

"I had such a strange dream," he continued, shaking off his grogginess. "A space cruiser was either coming or leaving, I don't know which. Anyway, as it reached the dark side of the planet, it exploded in a blinding flash of light. The fragments of the space vessel rained down on your world, making brilliant arcs in the night sky. Then, and this is the odd part, the children of Crystal came out to gather up the chunks of melted fragments. They put them together in a pile and danced around them."

"That's eerie," she whispered. Getting up from the bed, she lit two wall sconces and said, "I better let Dr. Gefert know that you're awake." As she walked out, Nick tried to fathom what his strange dream might mean.

Soon the doctor returned with Tara at his side. "How do you feel?" he asked pleasantly.

"Not so good," Nick answered, turning his head from side to side. "My head feels like it was hit by a log."

"I'm not surprised. No nausea? That's good. Maybe I can do something for your headache. Here, bend over toward me." His skilled hands tapped on Nick's forehead then moved back, applying steady pressure back and forth along the top and sides of his cranium. "There," he said as he finished. "Does that feel any better?"

"A lot better."

"Now, don't get overanxious or exert yourself in any way," he cautioned. "You're going to need rest to get ready for the next concentration." Turning to Tara he said, "Please make sure he gets plenty of sleep and remains calm. If he's ready, we can continue tomorrow."

Nick didn't remember anything about the rest of the night. When he awoke, he could see through the gaps in the blinds that it was already bright outside. Tara was gone, and so was Dr. Gefert.

A girl entered carrying a tray. She opened the window slats, and sunlight splashed into the room. It was Trila, the young Lab assistant.

"Good morning," she said brightly. "I hope you're ready for breakfast."

"Definitely," he answered, returning her smile. "It seems like two days since I've eaten."

"If you sit up, I'll put a pillow behind your back, and then rest this on your lap, Mr. Bartok."

"Mr. Bartok. Where did you get the mister from? I haven't heard mister in front of my name since I left Earth."

"Well," she said, hesitating. "My cousin told me that on Earth people are addressed as Mr. or Mrs. or Ms. I hope I didn't use it in the wrong way."

"Not that you misapplied it, Trila, it just seems so foreign to me here. On Earth, mister is used for correspondence or when people don't know each other well. I'd like it if you just called me Nick."

"Oh, sure, I'd be happy too," she answered, seemingly glad to do without formalities.

"Tell me, what else has Tara been telling you about me?"

"Lots. How you piloted a huge ship between the stars. How you gave up wealth and family on Earth to find oil to warm the houses. How you fought valiantly to defeat the Thorns, and . . ."

"Wait a minute," he protested. "It seems you've been getting a rather idealistic picture of me."

"Well it's only the truth," said Tara, entering the room. "Trila and I are cousins and we also sometimes work together in the Lab. I couldn't keep quiet about you."

"I just hope you haven't deluded her into thinking that I'm some kind of hero," Nick replied.

Dr. Gefert strode into the room and, in his businesslike manner, said hello to Tara and Trila. "How do you feel today, Nick?"

"Much better, doctor. The headache is completely gone, and I feel fit and well rested."

"In that case we might as well go on to the next step. Why don't you take a few minutes and get some fresh air first. It's a fine day."

"That's a good idea," Nick replied, glad for a chance to get out.

Nick and Tara walked together through the door and into the bright sunlight. They hadn't been outside long when Range hailed them.

"How's it going with the treatments, Nick?" he asked as he came up to them.

"So far, I've only had one, and it's definitely not been fun," he answered. "Tara is already planning for our wedding however, which you could take as a good sign that I'll pull through."

"Sure he will," she asserted spiritedly, leaning against Nick. "It's just a matter of time."

"Glad to hear that, Nick. I've been thinking a lot about those Thorns. They've been getting more aggressive in recent years, and after the attack you fought off last Ravidian, I'm afraid of what might happen next year."

"You think they might be even more ferocious?" asked Tara.

"Yes I do, and, frankly, I don't like the idea of just waiting for them to come back. I think we should go after them on their own grounds and exterminate them."

Tara gasped. "That would be suicide!"

"Not if we have a plan and some pulsars. What do you think, Nick?"

"I like the idea," Nick reflected. "But it could backfire. I don't think that in the past the birds have thought that man was their natural enemy. Unfortunately, that could be changing. My concern is that if an attack failed, they might retaliate by attacking the town."

"My worry is that they might do that regardless," said Range.

"You may be right. In any event, we should make some plans. Want to work on it together?"

"Definitely," he answered, slapping him on the back so hard that Nick almost stumbled. "Count on me."

"Nick, we better go back to the clinic," broke in Tara. As soon as they were far enough away from Range, she stopped and faced him. "You're not really thinking of fighting the Thorns again?" she asked heatedly.

"Not immediately," he answered, squeezing her hand. "I think we need to be prepared though. Don't worry. I really don't want to take any unnecessary chances."

"I think you should just leave them alone," she said emphatically, shaking her head.

"Take it easy," he said, putting an arm around her shoulders. "If they leave us alone, we'll leave them alone. OK?"

"Do you promise?" she asked, concerned.

"I promise," he answered, giving her a hug. "We better go back. Dr. Gefert is probably waiting."

Nick reacted similarly to the next treatment as he had to the first. He blacked out, regaining consciousness with a splitting headache. In the days that followed, however, the dosage was gradually increased, while his reaction to it gradually decreased. Yet, whenever Nick or Tara asked Dr. Gefert about his progress, he seemed reluctant to talk about it. At last, in frustration, Tara asked him directly. "When will he be done with all this, doctor?"

"At this point, the only way you can be certain that our allergy desensitization program has achieved its objective is to test it in a natural setting without any Laboratory controls."

"Do you mean we're done?" asked Tara.

"I think so. I'm going to give you these three vials just in case. Take one immediately with water if you notice any discomfort following contact. Let me know how it goes."

"We will be glad to try it out, doctor," said Nick, smiling as he placed his left arm around Tara. Extending his free hand, he added, "We want to thank you so much for everything you've done and want to invite you to the wedding."

"I shall be happy to join you." They shook hands.

Nick and Tara strolled out of the clinic, and turned to kiss on the doorstep.

"I don't feel a thing," said Nick, after their long kiss.

"I do," she said, looking at him attentively. "Are you sure you don't feel anything?"

"Yes. Really, I don't feel anything at all."

She turned to kiss him again, a long, ardent kiss. Some passersby turned to stare at them. As they parted, she gazed dreamily into his eyes. "Do you feel anything now?" she whispered.

"Yes," he responded huskily, pulling her tighter to him. "I definitely feel it."

"Nick!" A loud voice pierced their absorption with each other.

"Matt," they echoed as he quickly joined them.

"I want to congratulate you and Tara before I leave. I heard you've made good progress in overcoming the allergy."

"Thank you. We sure owe a lot to Dr. Gefert and the Lab team. You don't have to leave right away, do you Matt?

"Yes, unfortunately. I received new coordinates from a long-range galaxy transcender today. There's been a disturbance in the gravitational resonance synchronization between this sector and Earth. It's important that the ship leave as soon as possible to minimize transduction problems."

"What's causing it?" asked Nick with heightened concern.

"They either don't know or aren't saying," answered Matt. "I hope it's not more trouble. Anyway, I wanted to say goodbye to you both and to wish you the best for the future."

"Thank you, Matt," said Nick. "I'm sorry you won't be able to join us at the wedding. We will miss you very much."

"Yes, I'm sorry I won't be able to be there. Maybe I'll come back someday and see you and you're children. Wouldn't that be a surprise?"

"Matt, you'll always be welcome at our house," said Tara, giving him a parting hug.

The two partners stood facing each other for a moment, and then they hugged warmly, realizing that it might be the last time they would ever see each other.

That afternoon, Nick, Tara, Ruskin, Trila, Range, Dr. Gefert, Erik, Jon, and many of the townspeople went to the site of the space module to say goodbye to Matt. He enthusiastically mingled with the crowd and personally said farewell to them all. Then he stepped up into the spaceship and, from a window, waved back to them.

The ensuing blastoff was relatively quiet, and Nick raised his arm in salute as the ship gradually disappeared from sight. Tara looked into his eyes and could see a tear silently trickle down his cheek. She knew he had given up much to stay with her.

Chapter Eight

It was a simple church wedding with only relatives and close friends present. Vows were exchanged, and celebrant's words were poignant and terse:

"Love one another always, even in sickness, and raise children a credit to our community and to God."

The reception, by contrast, was exhilarating. It was held in a special reception hall where drinks and music flowed freely. Glittering arrays of candelabra lit the hall with a soft, intimate brightness, and the musicians plied their instruments with gusto and finesse. People sat at the tables or danced in the open area, as their mood inclined. Tara was on the floor a lot as many younger as well as older men asked her to dance. She saved most of the slow ones for Nick, as he had learned the steps, and when she didn't, Trila and Tes often sought him for a partner. Tes was Range's wife, and a good friend of Tara's. Range, Ruskin, and others made toasts in honor of the newly married couple. Nick and Tara sometimes kissed when dancing or at the table; it was expected, and whenever they did, the crowd signaled their delight by clapping. He asked her during a lull in the music how much longer the night would last.

"Not much longer for us," she mysteriously replied, looking into his eyes.

Sensing that there was more she wasn't saying, he tried to discern what it was and asked, "What is it? What happens next?"

Before she could reply, the music changed to a soft but upbeat melody of very distinctive style. The people on the floor stopped dancing, and everyone began clapping slowly in a cadenced tempo.

"It's time for us to leave," she spoke softly. "Just follow me."

Tara led the way with a graceful, swaying movement toward the back of the hall as Nick followed. Then she ascended a narrow staircase while the crowd whistled, cheered, and increased the tempo of their clapping.

At the top of the stairs, there was a little veranda, and from there Tara blew kisses to the guests and motioned Nick to do the same. The noise level of the crowd rose in response, and Tara turned to Nick and embraced him. Then she threw her head back and looked up at him with such tenderness that he bent down to kiss her, forgetting momentarily all the people beneath them. Tara slowly backed away from him and slipped out of his embrace. She turned to the crowd and waved, then pushed open the door behind them. She led him into the room and closed the door, shutting out much of the sounds from below. From behind the door they faintly heard the musicians change tempo again to a mellow serenade.

They stood there for a moment in darkness. Tara squeezed his hands and left him briefly to light two candles. In the soft light of the candles, Nick felt that Tara had never looked more beautiful. Her eyes sparkled, and he could see that there were tears in them. He asked if there was anything wrong. She told him that she was so happy. He embraced her tenderly, kissing her full lips softly. She melted into his arms and whispered something in his ear. He held her tight and they kissed, and for a time the universe stood still.

In the morning, the sunlight that streamed into the room through the blinds found them lying side by side, arms entwined around each other. Tara awakened first, and for a while, she watched Nick sleep. When he opened his eyes, she snuggled closer. "I love you so much, my Earthman."

"I love you too, my darling."

"I wonder what our future will be like?" she thought out loud, raising her head.

"We'll find that out, together."

"Together," she echoed, drawing closer.

Chapter Nine

(Six months later)

In the six months since his marriage to Tara, Nick has been working as an apprentice at the Lab and in his spare time completing their house near the stream. The exterior had been erected by the men of the neighborhood, and was finished a few days after their wedding. Just now, Nick was looking at the area that Tara wanted to make into a nursery. She had already bought some decorative fabric, and had accumulated so much gear that Nick wondered if they would have enough room for the baby. That's what he planned to do today, make some storage space.

It was Saturday, the sun was shining, and Tara was at the market buying supplies. He lingered awhile over his hot guava, thinking about how his life had changed. Looking out the window, his view took in the land and garden that he and Tara had worked together. He glanced languidly at the tall pine tree that marked the back boundary of their property. He saw something black flying in the sky and felt a chill as he remembered the battle with the

Thorns. He blinked and looked again, not really believing what he was seeing.

As he stood up and stared out the window, he realized that it was not his imagination. They were back! With horror, he thought of Tara at the open market. He ran to the back of the house, grabbed his pulsar, and rushed to the market square. It was a three-block run, and as he raced there, the Thorns were already darkening the sky above. He was afraid he was going to be too late.

Reaching the market stalls, he saw customers scattering in every direction. Frantically, he looked for Tara. Then, in the adjacent playground, he saw a woman rushing away from the square, heading toward the circling birds. Suddenly, he realized it was Tara. She was running toward a small child who remained in the field. He yelled but she didn't hear him.

Above, the din of the flapping wings and screeching Thorns drowned out everything except the screams. Running as fast as he could, he bridged the distance to her and then stopped short. Two hundred feet ahead, a Thorn swooped down to seize the last of the children in the playground. Tara screamed. Nick lifted his pulsar and fired. Too late. The creature was gone in an instant, disappearing over the trees. When he reached Tara, she buried her face in his chest, sobbing uncontrollably.

For a moment he stood there, too stunned to move. Then he raised his arm and angrily shook his pulsar at the remaining Thorns still flying high overhead. He realized the futility of trying to shoot them down so far above them. Grabbing Tara he shouted over their screeching, "Let's get out of here!" She looked back at the now deserted field, and ran with him to the Town Hall, the nearest shelter. The place was filled with people, and punctuated with the wailing and sobbing of mothers who had lost their children to the Thorns. Nick looked out the window. The last of the birds were moving away from the town. Soon, the sky was clear.

Nick and Tara slowly walked the short distance to their house. When they arrived, Ruskin, Shari and her little girl, Neena, were there. Ruskin came over to Nick and spoke with him in a low voice while Tara and her sister embraced sadly. Tears still in her eyes, Tara knelt down and tightly held Neena in her arms.

"How's my big girl?" she said, moving her to arms length to take a good look at her.

"I'm good," said Neena matter-of-factly. "Chalka hurt her knee when we came to your house."

"Your dolly hurt her knee?" said Tara in a concerned voice. "That's too bad. Here, let me kiss it to make it feel better." She bent down to kiss the doll's knee.

"Chalka feel better now, Aunt Tara," said Neena.

There was a knock on the door and Range stepped in. After greeting the women, he went straight to Nick and Ruskin. In a quiet but intense voice he said, "We've got to do something about them."

"Yes," replied Nick bitterly. "Let's go outside where we can talk."

They excused themselves from the women, saying they wanted to get some fresh air. Once on the porch they spoke in earnest.

"Those demons got six of our children today, three boys and three girls," said Range between gritted teeth. "We've got to exterminate them!"

"But how?" asked Ruskin, "There must be at least a thousand of them."

"Yes," Nick replied, "we would need to recruit and equip a small army."

"I know we can get enough men together," said Range. "I've already talked to Charl and Loader. Both of them lost children to those monsters."

"O.K.," said Nick. "We've got people angry enough to fight, but what are they going to fight with?"

"They'll fight with clubs if they have to," said Range.

"We can do better than that," said Ruskin. "Don't forget, we can make bows and arrows."

"That's right," said Range. "I used one when I was a boy."

"Do you think that bows and arrows could stop those birds?" asked Nick.

"I don't know," answered Ruskin. We've never used them for much except small game and target shooting. We would have to make them sturdy."

Nick looked down, thinking. Then he raised his head. "How about crossbows?"

"Crossbows? What are they?" asked Range.

"It's a bow design that increases power," Nick answered. "On earth they were used in the Middle Ages to fire a shaft with enough force to penetrate a coat of mail."

"Would it take a lot of strength to handle it?" asked Range.

"No, not at all," Nick answered. "That's the beauty of it. It takes a good pull to load it, but once loaded just about anyone can shoot it."

"I would be very interested in seeing how it works," said Ruskin. "Do you think it would have the power to stop a Thorn?"

"I wouldn't have much doubt about that," Nick answered.

"It sounds like what we need," said Range. I'll spread the word that we're going to fight those creatures. We'll have plenty of help making those crossbows." He shook hands firmly with Nick and Ruskin, and mounting his forc, rode off to spread the news.

Nick and Ruskin regarded each other and saw that they were totally in agreement on the mission. Then they walked back inside.

"What were you men talking about so intently outside?" asked Tara.

"Let's talk about it tomorrow," Nick answered. "We've been through so much already today."

Tara stared at him. Nick looked away.

Late that night, after Ruskin, Shari and Neena had gone home, Nick wearily undressed for bed. Tara came into the room. Despite his tiredness, he admired her beauty by the single candlelight that still flickered on the wall. When she came to bed, he reached for her. Without speaking, they held each other close.

Chapter Ten

Tara was up first, as usual, and she was already preparing breakfast. The early morning sun was streaming through the windows. As Nick came to the table, she eyed him from across the kitchen.

"So, you're going to go after them," she said.

"How did you know?" he answered, looking up from the table.

"Don't you know yet that I can read your mind?"

"Usually," he admitted, "you can."

"Nick, don't you realize that there are thousands of them, and your three pulsars won't mean anything against so many!"

"I know that, darling, but we have some plans as well as other weapons we will be able to use against them. Believe me, we won't take any unnecessary risks."

"You won't take any unnecessary risks! Do you think they're going to let you start shooting at them without fighting back? What are you to hide behind that they couldn't break through? Nick, if they could break through your spaceship they could get through anything that we have. And how many other men will you take with you? Nick, we've lost enough people already to these, these,– creatures. Leave them alone and maybe they'll leave us alone."

"Tara, we can't go around in constant fear. They have a taste for people now, for our children. We have to destroy them."

"Nick, I'm so afraid." She moved toward him. "I'm afraid for you and for me too. I don't want to lose you. Hold me. Promise that you won't fight unless you can protect yourself and the others."

Nick took her in his arms, and promised her what she asked, although he didn't yet know how he was going to do it.

The next day he met again with Range and Ruskin, and also with Cord, the town cooper. He showed them his drawings of crossbows, including a two shot bow he reinvented, which enabled an arrow to be fired from each side of the bow, one at a time.

"The main thing we need," he said to Cord, "is a type of wood that's strong enough, and springy enough to supply power without being too heavy."

Cord thought for a moment and said, "I think I know just what we need–samoth. Range, you work with wood. What do you think?"

"I've tried it on wagon wheels, and it's not sturdy enough for that. It definitely is springy."

"Yes," said Cord. "Unless I bend it, and leave it for hours in boiling water, it keeps trying to return to its original shape. What I can do is make a bow on the design of your drawing and then we can try it out. That's the only way we'll know for sure if it will work."

"Good," said Range. "How much time do you need?"

"Give me two or three days and I'll have a model ready for you."

* * *

"Tes," said Tara, slightly breathless after her fast walk from town. Her friend lived on the western outskirts of the community. "I've got to talk to you."

"Come on in," said Tes. "I'm so glad you dropped by. But where's your forc? You didn't walk all the way here did you?"

"Yes, I came straight from the Center. Tell me, how are Rimmi and Brad?"

"Rimmi's looking forward to going to school. In fact she's playing school with Brad right now." She lowered her voice and motioned for Tara to follow. "Just look in. See how she has him sitting at his little desk."

"Oh, Tes, that's so cute. Hi, Rimmi. How's your student doing?"

"He's just starting to learn, Aunt Tara."

"With a good teacher like you, I'm sure he'll learn a lot," said Tara, smiling.

The two women went back to the kitchen.

"Would you like some guava?" asked Tes.

"Sure, thank you," said Tara, sitting down at the table.

Tes brought two cups of steaming guava to the table and sat down next to Tara.

"Tes, has Range talked to you about an expedition to go after the Thorns?"

"Well, he did say something about it right after that terrible afternoon. Everybody was so upset then, I didn't really think he meant it. Going after them would be foolhardy."

"I know," said Tara, "but that's what Nick's planning to do."

"I don't believe it. It would be suicide. Tara, surely you can talk him out of it."

"I've tried to talk to him, but he just doesn't listen to me. He thinks we have to go after them so they won't come back again.

"I can understand that, but there are just too many of them. I have an idea. I'll talk to Range about Nick's plans right away. He can talk to him. If necessary we'll get some of the town leaders to speak with Nick."

"I do hope that will get him to change his mind," said Tara, gratefully.

"Yes, it really would be much too dangerous. Don't worry; I'm sure Range will be able to convince him. I hate to even think about it." She got up to get more guava. Changing the subject, she asked, "How have you been, Tara?"

"Good. Nick and I have been doing a lot of finishing work on the house. We're just now beginning to work on a small nursery area."

"Oh, really?" said Tes. She turned to face Tara directly.

"Yes," said Tara, with all the casualness she could muster. "We're going to have a baby in Darmarten."

"Wonderful!" said Tes with a broad smile as she set down the kettle and came back to the table. "Darmarten. Let's see, you must be five months pregnant already. Well, I wouldn't have known. You hardly show at all. We must put together a party for you."

* * *

That same evening, unknown to Tara, Nick, Range, and Ruskin went to Cord's place, next to the stream. Cord proudly showed them the crossbow he had made.

"This is it, gentlemen," he said, holding it up for their inspection. "I just finished it this morning. I had a chance to shoot it, and was impressed."

"It looks quite serviceable," said Ruskin.

"What do you think, Nick?" asked Range.

"It looks to be the right size and shape," said Nick, reaching for the bow. He checked its weight and balance and then put it down on the ground. Taking an arrow from the table, he placed his feet on the bow, and using both hands pulled back on the bowstring to secure an arrow in its notch. Then, turning the bow over, he positioned a second arrow the same way.

"So that's how you do it," said Cord, surprise registering on his face. "I had a heck of a time trying to load an arrow."

"Let's try it out," said Nick. They exited Cord's shop and Nick lifted the bow, aimed at a small tree twenty yards away and released the arrow. It flew to the right of the tree and went into the grass. "I need practice," he said with a grin. Then he turned the bow over, aimed, and shot the second arrow. With a "whap" it stuck solidly in the tree.

"Good shot," said Range as they walked to the arrow.

"That's really in there deep," said Ruskin.

"Yeah, I can't even pull it out," said Range, as he tried unsuccessfully to remove the arrow.

"It must be in three inches," said Cord.

"Cord, you did a great job on this," said Nick, patting him on the back. "This has the power we need and it's surprisingly light."

"Thank you," he replied. "Actually, it wasn't that hard to make. I just worked from the excellent designs you gave me."

"Now," said Range, "we need to think about how many men we can outfit. Also, we'll have to get some help for Cord, to make enough crossbows."

"Once they're made, we'll need to schedule some practice time so that everyone learns how to shoot them well," said Ruskin.

"One thing worries me," said Cord. "How do we protect ourselves from being overrun by them once we attack."

"I've thought about that," said Nick. I've been told there are forests surrounding the cliffs where they live. If we need to retreat, we could move through the trees. They couldn't fly down on us there, with their wide wingspans.

"Then what we should do," concluded Range, "is get our men together, make these crossbows, and prepare for battle."

"Yes." said "Ruskin. "The spring harvest will be finished in a month, and then there will be more men available to go with us."

"Cord, I'll pass the word that you need help making these crossbows, and we'll also pay you for your time and material," said Range.

"Yes," agreed Ruskin. "Every man should pay for his own crossbow, with either work or money."

"Nick, after we have enough bows and plenty of arrows, you will need to train us in their use," said Range.

"Right," replied Nick. "Cord, with help, will make the bows, you get the volunteers, and I'll do the training. Ruskin, will you help me with that?"

"Agreed," said Ruskin, "once I learn how to use the bow myself. Let me try loading the arrows while you watch, Nick."

Late that evening Nick approached his house and his thoughts turned from fighting Thorns, to thinking about Tara and their child to be. It concerned him that Tara might not understand the need to attack.

"I'm home," he said cheerily, on entering the door.

"Where have you been?" she asked, appearing somewhat flushed.

"At Cord's place."

"Really? Did you buy a new storage container for us?"

"Not exactly."

"So darling," she said, facing him squarely, "What were you doing there?"

"Making plans," he answered, without elaboration.

"Plans for what, dear?"

"Tara, you know I can't lie to you. Range, Cord, Ruskin and I are making plans to attack the Thorns."

"Range and Ruskin too!" she replied, shocked. "I just talked to Tes today. She didn't know anything about it. Why are all you men keeping this a secret from us?"

Nick moved to hold her but Tara backed away. "I didn't want to worry you. I had an idea on how we might be able to go after the Thorns, but I didn't know if it was practical. Now that we've tested it, and know it will work, we're ready to go ahead."

"I can't believe you wouldn't tell me," she said, her voice expressing a mixture of hurt and anger.

"Darling, you know I love you more than anything," said Nick, trying to soothe her. Tara backed farther away, and taking one more look at him, she opened the door and ran outside into the darkness.

She didn't know where she was going, she just ran. When she stopped, she put her head down and quietly cried. Warm, copious tears flowed down her cheeks, and for a moment, her body shook. Gaining control of herself, she wiped away the tears, and walked toward her sister's house.

Nick remained alone in the house. He was extremely upset by Tara's behavior, and many thoughts were going through his mind. He wondered if he had made the right choice in staying on this planet. He had done it for love of Tara, and if she no longer loved him, nothing else mattered. True, he liked the people he had come to know here, but without Tara, all the rest left him feeling empty. He looked around at the home they had spent so much time working on together. He realized he would have done none of it without her. Why couldn't she understand that he was willing to risk his life for her and for their child to be? Where was she?

Two hours later Tara returned. She didn't look at Nick, didn't say a word. She went to the bedroom and got ready for sleep. After awhile, Nick followed her there. As it was late, he too prepared for bed. He could see that Tara's eyes were closed, but he didn't think she was asleep. He reached for her. There was no response. He whispered her name. There was no answer. After a long time he finally went to sleep.

Chapter Eleven

The next several weeks were busy ones. Nick spent his spare time at Cord's, helping him with the assembly of the crossbows. They were making good progress with them, and they had made some modifications that improved their performance even more. It was time for Nick to think about training the volunteers.

Instead, he found himself thinking about Tara and himself. Since that night when she ran out of the house, she remained distant and aloof from him. He wasn't happy, and he knew that she wasn't either. What was their problem? Was it just a simple difference of opinion, or was there more to it? Their first few months together had been so wonderful. Now, the joy in their relationship was gone. It seemed as if they were both just going through the motions. Yet, when she was with other people, he observed that she seemed as friendly as ever to them. How could she be warm with them and not with him? He resolved to talk to her again. That night, as they were silently putting away the supper dishes, he asked, "Tara, is it only our difference of opinion about fighting the Thorns, or is there something else that is bothering you?"

She looked at him, sighed, and then looked away. It seemed to Nick that she was ready to cry. He felt a strong tenderness for her.

"Nick, you know I don't want you to go. You know I don't want to lose you. Unfortunately, I believe there's more to it than that. I really do think there is. I don't know if you want to hear it."

"Tara, you know that you can tell me anything. Especially if it will help me to understand why you feel the way you do."

"Well, sit down," she said, seating herself at the table. "Nick, I've been doing a lot of thinking about us since you announced you wanted to fight the Thorns. I wonder if I made a bad mistake, falling in love with an Earthman. You see, Nick, we're from two very different cultures."

"Yes, I know that," he replied.

Tara continued. "Do you remember how you used to tell me how much you loved it here in Crystal? How peaceful it is, compared to where you came from?

"Sure," he answered, surprised that she would mention it. "I still feel that way."

"Well," she said, looking again into his eyes, "I believe you when you say that."

"Of course I do."

"Anyway," she continued, her voice expressing her deep feeling. "You've told me enough about your world for me to know that there's always been a problem there with wars, murder, and violence."

"That's true, but what's that got to do with us?"

"Don't you see," she said, bursting into tears. "It's in your blood! You think of it as bravery, and it means more to you than anything else, including me." She ran crying into the bedroom.

Nick was taken aback. With one exception, everything she said was true. There was nothing he could disagree with except his feeling for her. On his world, bravery *was* a virtue. It's something he learned early in life. On the other hand, he had learned not to take unnecessary chances. Nevertheless, fighting for what you believed in was not an evil—not when the cause was right. This cause was certainly right. Besides, they would be killing birds, not people. Why couldn't she understand that?

* * *

The days were filled with activity for Nick and the men who prepared to fight the Thorns. Altogether, there were twenty-four of them, and Cord had finished making twenty-seven crossbows. All were the same size, except one that was much larger, which required a threaded device to load it. Cord was proud of that crossbow, and believed it might send a bolt a half mile away. Nick and Range were quite intrigued with it, and they began thinking about how they might be able to use it in battle. At Nick's on the front side of each bow, so that they could easily be armed while standing by placing a foot in the strap, while pulling back on the bowstring.

Plainly, this was a civilian force. The men came every day after work to practice using the new equipment. Cord had set out old barrels in the field near the stream, about fifty yards away. After a few days of practice, all the volunteers were at least able to hit the casks. When they were proficient at that, they advanced to positions along the length of the field, where they practiced shooting at different distances parallel to the stream. In time, they learned to estimate the bow inclination needed for the arrows to hit the targets. After several days of this, some of the men were regularly able to hit barrels almost a hundred yards away.

When they had been meeting for three weeks Nick and Range realized that they needed to formulate some battle strategy. For that, they would need leadership. It was agreed that Nick and Ruskin would head one group of ten, and that Range and Cord would lead the other group. The four of them stayed late that night to discuss their progress so far. It was obvious that marksmanship skills had dramatically increased. However, they knew that the birds would not be waiting on the ground for them. What they really needed was a method of preparing themselves for what they would face once the attack began. Cord suggested that they might place light, flat sheets of wood high up in the trees, so they could practice shooting them down.

The next day they tried doing that but it wasn't very successful as the boards were either shaken down by the wind, or more frequently, remained in the trees even after being struck by arrows.

Next, they came up with the idea of screwing hooks onto wood planks and attaching long ropes so they could start them gliding down from the trees. Although it was fairly labor intensive to get the flat sheets up in the trees, it definitely gave them all good practice hitting moving targets. It also helped them to develop speed in reloading their crossbows.

One clear spring-like afternoon, Tara left from school and walked the considerable distance to the practice field. She spotted Nick and waved to him. He immediately left the field and came to join her.

"Hi. I'm surprised to see you here."

"I was just taking a walk," she replied. "I can see the men are really getting quite good at shooting." She looked across the field and waved to an old friend who waved back to her. "Could I try it?"

"Of course. Take mine. I'll load it for you." He bent down to pull back the bowstrings. Carefully handing it to her, he showed her the trigger. "Just sight along the arrow and aim for that barrel over there."

She did as he said and pulled the trigger. The arrow flew straight toward the barrel and skidded in front of it.

"You need to add just a little elevation to allow for the drop of the arrow over the distance. Try it again with the second arrow."

Tara aimed and pulled the trigger. This time, the arrow flew to the target, striking it with a crack, near the top. "That wasn't hard," she said smiling.

Nick saw her smile, the first time he had seen it for a long time, and couldn't help smiling back at her.

"Show me again how you load it," she said.

He took her hands, showed her how to position her feet, and how to mount the arrows. Her joining him like this felt like the old, happy times they shared and Nick felt a spontaneous tenderness toward her and the child she carried. He spent the next half-hour coaching her on how to shoot with accuracy. He didn't dare to ask her why she was interested in learning. He admired her spunk in handling the heavy draw needed to load the bow, and was surprised at how quickly she learned to improve her accuracy.

"I'm going home to make supper," she said suddenly, handing him the crossbow and arrows.

"Thanks for coming by."

"I enjoyed being with you," she answered.

Nick regretted that he couldn't get home for supper that night, but it was important that the four leaders meet to make plans for going after the Thorns.

"We may have to induce them to attack," stated Range.

"They will," said Ruskin, "once you start firing arrows into their lair."

"We need to get them out in the open, where our shots will be effective," said Nick.

"But we can't ask our men to be decoys," said Cord.

"Not without protection," Nick replied. "Why not make shields to protect them when they're not in the safety of the woods?

"That might work," said Ruskin.

"What size shields do you have in mind?" asked Cord.

"I think we need large, full body shields like the Romans used," Nick answered.

"Roman shields? What do you mean?" asked Range.

"Sorry, I should explain," Nick continued. "The Romans were the most powerful country on Earth for almost a thousand years. They maintained their power by using large rectangular shields that allowed them to advance or hold a position simply by joining their shields together in the face of their enemies. Even the middle of the phalanx could be protected from overhead arrows by holding the shields aloft"

"I see what you mean," said Range with enthusiasm. "With shields like that we could form a moving, protective box around our men."

"It definitely sounds like a good idea," added Ruskin. "We should do anything we can to protect ourselves."

"What you're describing appears to be the height and width of my largest barrel," said Cord.

"Yes," affirmed Nick. "That size, but straighter, with a large handle on the inside."

"How many would we need," asked Cord.

"I think we need at least ten or twelve.

"Wait," said Range. "The way I figure it, if we had three men on two sides, with two each on the short sides, we would need three in the middle to protect the top from attack. A total of thirteen."

"Yes," said Nick. "It's feasible do it with less than thirteen if we had only two men on a side but we might need the extra shields."

"Well, give me the plans and I'll make them," said Cord. "They'll need to be reinforced to withstand those sharp beaks."

"We'll help you," said Ruskin.

"Why don't we ask everyone to work on them," said Range." It would be a break from bow practice, and with all of us helping it won't take long."

They agreed.

Making the thirteen shields didn't take long at all, with everyone working together on them. They were heavy, weighing about sixty pounds each—not what anyone would want to carry for very long. They practiced using them, learning to stand close together to form rigid barriers with the shields, which they might very well need when battling the Thorns. When they were satisfied with their skill, they returned to practicing with the crossbows.

As Nick watched, he could see the dramatic improvement in their skills. He could also see that the men had an intensity about them that they channeled into mastering their weapons. He knew that many of the volunteers had lost a child to the Thorns that terrible afternoon, and they wanted vengeance. Range walked up to him as he was contemplating.

"They look good, don't they, Nick?"

"That's just what I was thinking, Range."

"We can't hold them back much longer, Nick. They are ready to fight."

"I know. How much time do you think we'll need to get everything else ready to go?"

"No more than two or three days, sooner if necessary," answered Range. "School will be out in two days. Why not leave in three days, early in the morning?"

"I can be ready then, if it's enough time for Ruskin and Cord."

"There they are," said Range, signaling to Cord and Ruskin, who were just walking out of the shop. The four agreed that they would set off on the third day.

Chapter Twelve

In the pale stillness of the morning on the third day, they began assembling at Cord's place. Wives came with their husbands, bringing their children to see them off. As they loaded the supplies on the forcs, more and more of the townspeople gathered around them. Soon everything was loaded and the shields were balanced, two to an animal. Tension rose, as they readied their mounts. Men and women embraced and kissed each other goodbye, and children were given one last hug. Nick kept looking out into the crowd for Tara, but she was nowhere to be seen. He walked his forc over to Ruskin.

"It isn't like her not to be here," said Ruskin who seemed puzzled himself.

"I sure do miss her," said Nick.

Ruskin looked up at him but didn't reply.

"We better get started," said Range as he rode up to them both.

"Sound the horn, Thad," said Nick. "We're ready to go."

Thad, the youngest of the group, was caught in the arms and kisses of his girlfriend, Frecka, who didn't want to let go. He was able to lift his horn with one hand to give one good blow before Frecka again kissed him on the mouth.

"I have to go now, Frecka," he told her.

"I love you, darling," she said, as she at last relinquished her grip on him.

"I know. I'll be back."

"I'll be waiting for you."

Thad backed up toward his forc, blew her a kiss, and mounting it turned to join the rest of the men coming up behind Range. Range looked back at him and deadpanned, "I think she likes you, Thad."

Thad looked slightly embarrassed, but answered with a big smile, "And she's not afraid to show it either."

They traveled swiftly, slowed only by the pack animals. By the end of the second day they reached the hill country where the going was considerably more difficult and the heavily laden animals sometimes balked. They called a halt, set up the tents, ate a nourishing supper, and retired as darkness closed over them. Ruskin sat outside his tent a little longer, smoking his calandula pipe. When he came inside the two-man tent, Nick asked him what he was smoking.

"Currosh." "It's an invigorating smoke to increase one's energy and endurance. Not that I need it," he added with a smile. "Try some, you might like it."

"No thanks, maybe another time"

"Well, so far, so good," said Ruskin. "I hope the pack animals settle down. I can see why they complain though, carrying are equipment and those heavy shields."

"Soon we'll be walking along with them, as I recall," Nick replied.

"Yes, a few more hours travel and the terrain will be too rough to ride."

The next day was just as difficult as they had expected. By noon, they had to get off their mounts and pull the reluctant animals along. Slowly, they led the forcs over the increasingly rocky trail. The going was so rough that during a pause, they agreed to set up camp early. Traveling for another hour or so, they came to a place Ruskin knew was a good campsite. It was situated in a large level plain, nestled between hills, and overlooking a stream on one side. There they stopped.

After supper, an hour remained before sunset, and many of the party took the opportunity to go down to the stream to bathe. Afterward, as twilight began to descend on the encampment, the men sat or lay around in circles discussing what might happen on the next day when they reached the territory of the Thorns. Then someone noticed that three men, wearing long robes, appeared in the distance on the hillside. Everyone looked in that direction, surprised to see anyone in the vicinity.

Nick and Ruskin recognized who they were immediately—the three Brothers of Midian, the men from Mendax who had entertained them on their previous trip. This time the Brothers of Midian didn't seem so friendly. In fact, they didn't even acknowledge shouts to get their attention. Instead, they hurried along as if they wished they hadn't been seen. Soon they were out of sight on the other side of the hill, heading, it appeared, toward the land of the Thorns. Nick and Ruskin glanced at each other without speaking. They were both thinking the same thing. Could there be some connection between the big Brothers of Midian and the Thorns? It didn't seem plausible. Were they just getting edgy? As they bedded down for the night, Nick tried to dismiss his apprehensions but was unable to overcome a strange feeling of uneasiness.

The next day's journey was just as tough. They climbed up the sides of boulder strewn hills and on the other side had to carefully pick their way through rocky rubble to avoid tripping. Overall, they were gaining altitude, and the thin air was becoming cooler. They caught occasional glimpses of Thorns winging through the air far in the distance. As none came close, they held their fire.

The plan was to try to reach a point on the forth day close enough to be within easy striking distance but far enough away that the birds would not attack first. Their intention was to settle in the forest and rest after their arduous trip and then attack before dusk while the Thorns were still in their nests. The element of surprise was important.

Later that day they neared the territory of the Thorns and stopped, still two miles away from the nesting area. From there, Nick and Range set out to scout the territory leading toward the enemy. They wanted to find a place on the other side of the rookery where dense growths of trees might offer some protection. The two traveled together for a while until they located a suitable campsite. Then Range went back to bring the contingent forward while Nick pushed forward to scout out a good place to begin the attack.

As he approached the steep valley separating them from the Thorns, he discovered a ridge directly across from the nesting site that overlooked a steep drop toward a small stream. Moving quietly along the ridge and keeping behind the trees, he could glimpse Thorns in the sky going back and forth above him. He crept as close as he could to the drop off without being seen.

Looking across a steep grassy valley, he saw the rocky cliffs that rose up on the other side. Taking a deep breath, he watched in awe as the huge birds landed or spread their great wings to lift off from the jagged cliffs. From the relative safety of his position behind a fallen log, he scanned the area around the valley. He was looking for a piece of higher ground where they might more easily send arrows down to their nests. He saw a spot to his left, but it looked too narrow to provide footing for more than a few archers. Furthermore, he couldn't tell how well it could be defended, as there were not many trees around it. He saw one other possible vantage point. It was hard to tell in the fading light, but it appeared that there was a hill behind the cliffs of the rookery. If so, they might be able to send men around the open valley area and across the woods, in order to reach higher ground behind the Thorns and attack them from the rear.

Nick had seen enough. He wanted to get back to the campsite before dark. As he turned away from the ridge, he sensed that he was not alone. He had the distinct feeling that he was being watched. Alert for any sound or movement, he quietly crept away from the ridge of the valley and moved to the left, keeping low to the ground.

The light from the sky was fading but it was still much brighter than the surrounding trees. He strained his eyes and still couldn't see anything. Then he heard a twig snap ahead of him. His skin crawled, and he removed his pulsar from its holster. He caught sight of a movement in the forest in front of him. He knelt behind a tree and waited. There was definitely something in the woods with him. As it came closer, he realized it wasn't a bird. The glimpse he saw of its outline showed something smaller than a Thorn. He relaxed a little but kept his position behind the tree. As it came closer, he saw that it was a person, not an animal. He called out quietly, "Who is it?"

"It's me," answered Tara.

"Tara! What are you doing here?" he asked in a hushed voice.

"I was looking for you."

Coming to her side, he whispered softly "do you know how close we are to the Thorns?"

"I don't care," she answered, facing him. "I don't want to be away from you any more. When you fight the Thorns I want to be with you."

"But you're seven months pregnant. You shouldn't. . ."

Her lips pressing on his smothered the rest of what he was going to say. He put his arms around her and held her close. As their bodies came together, he felt the fullness of her stomach against his and then he felt a kick. He smiled and looked into her eyes. "Our son is glad to see me too," he chuckled.

"Or it may be your daughter, glad to hear her Daddy's voice. I sure am glad to be back in your arms."

"Yes, we belong together. But we better get back to the camp," he added. "It's not safe here." He put his arm around her and together they walked back. Nick led her to the tent that he and Ruskin shared. Ruskin wasn't around.

"I'll just straighten it up a little while you look for him," she said.

Nick found him, in Range and Cord's tent. Standing, he told them what he had learned about the Thorn nesting site before he took a seat. The four of them began formulating a plan of attack. Several hours later, he and Ruskin walked back to their tent. Inside, in the darkness, he made out the still form of Tara lying near the edge. She appeared to be asleep. Taking off his boots, he lay down next to his wife and put his arm around her. "I love you," he whispered in her ear. She mumbled indistinctly, "I love you too," sounding more asleep than awake. Nick curled his body around her sleeping form. "Thank you, God," he whispered, glad that he and Tara were together once again. Soon, he was asleep.

Chapter Thirteen

Morning came too early for Nick, but like everyone else, he quickly shook off his sleepiness in anticipation of the battle. Tara was awake and was already outside helping to serve a quick breakfast. They didn't know when they would have time for their next meal. They soon finished eating and they reloaded the forcs and put on their battle gear. As they were ready to depart, Nick handed Tara one of his pulsars. He cautioned her to use it only if necessary, as it couldn't be recharged. She had brought a bag with her that he knew contained medicine. He hoped it wouldn't be needed.

They set off quickly through the woods toward the nesting place of the Thorns. It took longer than anticipated for them to travel in the faint predawn light but in less than an hour, they reached the steep drop off across from the Thorns. Nick pointed out the high spot to the left overlooking the nest, and Cord and five other men made their way toward it. They carried his great crossbow, which had been outfitted with a huge sling like pouch, so that it could fire a volley of either arrows or rocks at the same time.

Range positioned himself and five men a short distance to the right of Cord. From there Range could direct firepower to assist Cord, or toward the nests of the Thorns. Nick stationed the remaining twelve men, Ruskin and himself included, and Tara further to the right on the ridge overlooking the drop off, facing the Thorns. Once the contingent was in position, and the crossbows were readied, he left to join Range to watch the slow ascent of Cord and his men up the steep side of the hill leading to the high cliff. Range pointed them out to him. Barely visible in the predawn darkness, they were already above their level and had only a short distance to go to reach the top.

Nick stayed with Range for a while longer until they could see that Cord had made it to the top and had begun to set up the large crossbow. Then the two clasped hands tightly and wordlessly before he went back to his men to alert them that the battle was about to begin.

They waited in silence. When the signal was given, they sprang into action, releasing the first volley of arrows at the enemy. Suddenly, the mountainside across from them erupted in noise and motion as thousands of Thorns began screeching and took to the air. The sky became filled with them and the archers took aim and fired repeatedly. The cries of the wounded Thorns soon drowned out even the screeching of those flying above. Hundreds of the killed or wounded creatures began dropping from the sky to land in the valley. Then, the birds began to circle in a definite pattern, rising ever higher in the sky so that they were beginning to get outside of arrow range. Nick signaled a halt to the shooting.

In the valley the cries of the wounded Thorns continued to fill the air with their clamor, while above, the Thorns were already so high that their screeching was muted by distance. The attackers wondered what the flying horde would do next, and took advantage of the break in the action to lay out more arrows and cock their bows. Fearing a frontal assault, they sheltered themselves as best they could behind trees and bushes. For what seemed like an eternity, the creatures circled high above them, effortlessly gliding with no sign of coming back down. From their vantage point on the edge of the cliff, the attackers waited impatiently for the creatures' next move. They were becoming tenser by the minute. For two more hours, they waited.

In the interim, two of the men went back to the pack animals, to get provisions for lunch. The small company sat down to eat, while keeping an anxious eye on the Thorns. Suddenly, the birds began diving out of the sky. They swooped down so rapidly there was no chance to aim or shoot at them. When the creatures reached a level just above the archers, they broke from their dive and swept quickly toward their attackers. Without warning, the platoon was quickly besieged, as hurtling black bodies and wings crashed into their defenses. They hardly had time to grab their arrows and flee as the birds swarmed in on them.

"Retreat!" yelled Nick.

"What about Cord and his men?" yelled Tara above the din.

Nick looked through the trees toward the point where Cord had been. He saw only Thorns. "There's nothing we can do," he shouted to her. "Get back!"

It was not an organized retreat. In panic, they ran through the forest in the general direction of the pack animals. The Thorns were able to knock down some of the smaller trees but were slowed by the larger ones. Nick saw that Range and his men were accounted for, as were his and Ruskin's group. He could only hope that somehow Cord and his men were able to escape from the high point before the Thorns attacked.

Nick, Ruskin, and Range quickly sized up the situation and decided that they could take advantage of the difficulty the birds were having getting through the woods. They rounded up the men and ordered a slow retreat backwards while they continued to fire on the advancing Thorns. To further increase their effectiveness, Range and his men took a position to the side of the main advance so they could rake the Thorns with a deadly crossfire. Though they still had not seen Cord or any of his men, they couldn't wait any longer in the face of the advancing horde. With Range now in position off to one side, they sprang the trap.

The Thorns, which had met only limited opposition thus far, were suddenly shocked with a volley of arrows, followed rapidly by bolts streaking in from the side. For a moment, they seemed stunned and appeared to hesitate. In reality, it was only that their own dead and wounded slowed their advance. The rest of the Thorns continued to pour into the slowly retreating trap.

At short range, the shooting was easy. It was as simple as shooting barrels at Cord's place. Nick looked around and saw that Tara was just as busy loading and firing as everyone else. As he glanced at her, he caught her eye. She acknowledged him momentarily before bending over to reload her bow. For what seemed like a long time, they fought the birds while slowly retreating.

Despite the growing weariness of their hands and arms, they continued to fight effectively. How much longer could they hold out? How many more Thorns were there? As the afternoon sun dropped lower in the sky, the advance of the birds seemed to be slowing. Nick wondered if they had at last been able to kill the majority of them. During a temporary lull in the battle, he took a moment to look around. Then, he saw their mounts followed by the still loaded pack animals racing toward them. *The Thorns must have spooked them*, he thought. With a loud yell, he alerted the others. As they turned away from shooting the Thorns, toward the stampeding animals, they could see that behind the animals more Thorns were coming. They were in danger of being trapped. "Grab hold of our forcs as they come past!" yelled Range. "They'll take us out of here!" Nick hoped he was right.

Fortunately, the animals slowed as they realized that there were more Thorns ahead. This enabled the combatants to seize their reins, jump up, and hang on as the frightened beasts carried them away toward the only direction still open to them. Before long the exhausted forcs slowed again. They had reached the area beneath the cliff where they had last seen Cord. From this higher elevation, they could look to their right and see the rookery of the Thorns and the valley leading up to it. Only a few birds could be seen still flying near the nesting grounds. The men tried to keep out of their sight so they wouldn't alert the other Thorns of their presence.

Unfortunately, in order to move to the next wooded area, they needed to cross a treeless valley between two hills. By this time, the animals had settled down enough to go where directed, but Nick knew that it would be hard to make them climb up the embankment on the other side of the valley. They had to do something, as the Thorns behind them would soon be within striking distance. Nick hesitated. Then he heard Range's strong voice yell out, "Use the shields!" Nick circled back to join Range and Ruskin. They decided on a plan. It was a desperate scheme that might allow them to take advantage of the approaching nightfall.

Hurriedly, they unloaded the shields from the animals. Then they positioned themselves to form a shielded box protected on all sides and on top from the enemy. With Cord and his five unaccounted for, altogether eighteen combatants remained. Nick, Tara, and Ruskin, who each carried pulsars, and two others, stayed inside the rectangle of protective shields. Then, on signal, they hurried together across the valley as fast as they could with the heavy shields. They used a rope to hold together the reins of the animals that followed behind. As they continued across the valley unchallenged, they collectively breathed a sigh of relief. Either the birds didn't see them or else they didn't suspect that the moving phalanx of shields was the people they were chasing, even though their unprotected pack animals traveled behind them. The group soon came to a small rivulet that separated them from the forest on the other side of the valley.

"Careful now," said Range from the front, as he stepped into the water. The water was chilly but only a few feet across and less than a foot deep. Some of the rounded rocks in it were slippery. Suddenly Thad lost his balance and fell backward on top of his shield. He quickly got to his feet and rejoined the group at his place at the end of the phalanx. It was too late. The Thorns, catching sight of a human, began sweeping down toward them. "Shoot!" yelled Nick as the birds began landing a short distance away.

"I can hardly see them!" yelled Tara from the rear.

"Press your pulsar through a crack in the shields—you'll see them!" shouted Nick.

As she pushed the weapon through the rear shields, she could see them flocking outside.

"Nick, its really bad back here!"

"It's getting real crowded in front too!" said Ruskin.

"How much farther to the trees?" asked Nick.

"Fifty feet at most," Ruskin answered. "But there must be that many Thorns in our way!"

"OK," yelled Nick. "Everybody hold on to the shields. We're going to shoot our way through and make a run for the forest."

The phalanx picked up speed, and with pulsars blasting, Nick, Tara, and Ruskin cleared a path in front. As they crashed into the forest underbrush, half of them fell down as their momentum was stopped short. "Run for cover!" shouted Nick above the sound of the breaking branches and the flapping wings. He helped Tara to free herself from the undergrowth. Their panic stricken animals followed them into the woods.

"Look," said Tara pointing to a large crossbow half hidden in the bushes next to her. "Isn't that Cord's big crossbow?"

Without wasting any time, Nick grabbed it as they pushed through to the trees. Even in the dim twilight, he could see that it was stained with blood.

"Wait!" yelled Range from further inside the thick woods, calling to those who had kept on going. "Don't go too far. We have to regroup."

Nick, Ruskin, and several others hurried toward Range. Looking back, Nick could see that the advance of the Thorns continued though the trees and underbrush slowed it considerably. *We could turn around and kill them easily here*, he thought. *But how many more are there to kill and did they have enough arrows?*

When Nick and Ruskin reached Range's position, they spoke quickly. "I think we should make our stand here," said Range.

"They've slowed down but do we have enough arrows?" asked Ruskin.

"I have an idea," said Nick. "The Thorns are in two groups. I believe the one pursuing us is the smaller group. The Thorns we left behind on the other side of the woods is the other. Let's wipe out this first group before darkness if possible. Then go back and retrieve our arrows before the next wave comes."

"Will they stop at nightfall?" asked Range.

"I think they will," answered Ruskin.

"In any event, we don't have much choice," said Nick.

"I'm afraid the other men didn't make it," said Range. "I saw Dock's blood stained jacket when we came through."

"Yes, they may have got all of them," answered Nick. "This is Cord's crossbow," he added, picking it up to show them. There was a pause. Then Range said, "Let's get them! When they come a little farther we'll hit them hard!"

By the time the Thorns had advanced far enough for the waiting archers, everyone along the line knew that Cord and his men had probably been killed. Aware of the limited number of their arrows, they waited till the last moment to begin the counter attack. On signal, they let fly the first volley of arrows and the front row of Thorns fell shrieking to their deaths. Nevertheless, their charge continued unabated. Only the dense trees held them back long enough until the archers could reload, fire, and again dispatch their front line. Then suddenly, the melee stopped. For a moment, the men waited quietly, bows drawn and ready. But the Thorns were gone. Abruptly they broke into cheering. They had defeated the diabolical creatures. The cheering was short lived, however. They knew that tomorrow they might return.

"Retrieve your arrows men, but be careful. They might not all be dead. There's still another wave of them to get ready for," directed Range. For the next quarter hour, they all hurried among the Thorns, retrieving the blood soaked arrows as the last glimmer of daylight eked through the forest trees. Before long, it became too dark to see anything. Range called them back. What was left of the platoon regrouped in the darkness of the woods.

Range spoke to the tired fighters. "Men, we don't know how many there are or when they might attack again. We can rest and have something to eat but if they return tonight, we must retreat. We can't fight black birds in the dark. If we do have to retreat, we will have to keep moving through the night. We can't take a chance on them surrounding us. Do you understand?"

"What if they don't attack tonight?" someone said.

"If they don't it's to our advantage. We'll post guards in shifts and try to get some sleep. If they don't come tonight, I feel sure they will in the morning so we have to be ready. All right. We need three guards for the first three hours. Everyone else can get some sleep."

In the calm that came after the battle, Nick thought more about their situation. No one knew how many Thorns were still alive or if they had enough arrows left to kill them. They could keep retreating through the woods but chances were that eventually they would come to a clearing. That could be disastrous. Then he remembered the high hill overlooking the Thorn's nesting site. If they could reach it, they might be able to attack from above.

"Range," said Nick, picking him out from the men moving about in the darkness, "I've got an idea."

The two of them talked at length. Then they sought out Ruskin who also listened to Nick's plan.

"There are nineteen of us left," said Nick, "counting Tara. I'll take five men and we'll sneak around to the hill on the backside of the cliffs. Range, you position five men with the large bow at the spot where Cord was, and have the others be prepared to back them up. This time, if the Thorns come close, evacuate the position. When they go back to their nests tonight, as I hope and expect they will, we'll be in excellent position to deal them a fatal blow."

"And if they don't?" asked Ruskin.

"Then maybe they'll return to the nests if we can create enough commotion above them," said Nick incisively. "At this point, we don't have many options. I don't think we can handle another full scale assault like we had today."

They accepted the plan, and Nick asked five volunteers to go with him. He had no trouble getting them. He sought out Tara in the darkness and finding her, he told her what he was going to do.

She nodded, pleading him with her eyes not to go.

"It's our only hope, he told her.

"I would go with you, except. . ." she looked down at her stomach.

Nick looked steadily into his wife's eyes, glowing in the dim light of a small campfire. "I know. I will come back, for both of you. They embraced, and she whispered, "Be careful, Nick." As he left her arms and disappeared into the darkness, she held on to his words, "I will come back."

The six, Nick, Jon, Thad, Rolan, Noly, and Elan picked up their bows and arrows, and together set out from the camp. They moved to the rear, and then gradually proceeded downward toward the edge of the open valley, which was to the left of the final resting-place of the Thorns killed earlier. They skirted the glen, going through high brush and low trees, taking care that they remained out of sight from any Thorns that might be flying overhead. Then they began the long trek up the other side of the valley.

The going was slippery. In the darkness, they felt their way up the incline, and softly cursed at the briars that left them with lacerations on their face, hands and arms. When they reached a terrace preceding the main hill, they stopped to rest. They had hardly sat down when Thad whispered, "Listen. Do you hear that squawking?" They strained their ears and caught the faint sound of innumerable Thorns in commotion.

"I think we're at their level now," whispered Nick. "When we finish climbing we should be able to get a good view of them. Keep low and out of their sight."

They resumed climbing but the angle of the hill increased and it became rocky.

"Take it slow," Nick whispered to Thad who had gone on above him. "Be careful."

They proceeded slowly, quietly, trying hard not to loosen any rocks whose fall might attract the attention of the Thorns. Finally, they reached the top of the hill and found themselves in a meadowland of soft grasses with scattered small trees. They still couldn't see the lair of the Thorns but knew they couldn't be far away. As they rested from their steep climb, Nick told them what he hoped to do.

We can only guess how many there are," he said, catching his breath from the hard climb. "We hope they all went back to the nest after the today's battle. Our job is to kill as many as we can."

"But how?" asked Rolan, "There are only six of us."

"What I hope to do," Nick replied, "is to quietly loosen enough rocks before daybreak, so that we can start an avalanche."

"Good idea," said both Thad and Elan. Nick sensed a burst of enthusiasm in his team.

"What we need to do now is to move along under the trees, away from the rim, until we can reach a point right over their nests. Once we're there we'll see what we can find to drop on them."

They edged away from the rocky hilltop, and circled through the sparse trees toward the point that would lead them over the Thorns. Then they sat down again and reckoned the time by the stars. It appeared to be approximately four hours before daybreak. They had a lot to do in those few hours. Thad volunteered to sneak his way toward the edge to determine the exact spot over the

Thorns. Nick cautioned him to keep low in the tall grass. Soon he came back with good news.

"They're only about one hundred and fifty feet to the left of us, Nick. Judging from the sounds there has to be hundreds of them there, right beneath us."

"What's the terrain like? Is it mostly grassy or did you see many rocks as you neared the edge?"

"There was long grass until near the edge. Then there are some rocks."

"Good," said Nick. "OK men," he continued. "This grassy knoll appears to be only a covering over bedrock. Trees don't grow toward the edge because the soil is too shallow. If we dig down a few inches, I'm sure we'll find rock. What we need to do is to somehow dislodge enough rock to push down on those Thorns. Anybody got any ideas?"

"Where there are rocks we can see," said Noly, "there may be cracks in the bedrock. If we can locate some near the edge, we should be able to dig up more of them."

"Did you see much of that, Thad?" asked Jon.

"I can't be sure," he answered. "There were definitely some bumps and depressions."

"There has to be an easier way," said Elan, "Without shovels, it's going to be real hard to dig rocks out of the ground."

"Yes, if there's any other way to gather enough rock we should do it," agreed Nick, "If we don't find enough, we may have to dig. Let's start with what we can find on the surface."

"Basically what we want to do is collect enough stones and boulders to be able to start a landslide. Right?" asked Rolan.

"That's what I hope we can do," Nick answered. "We need to keep a low profile as we crawl over toward the edge, gathering smaller rocks and taking note of any larger ones we encounter as we make our way there. We have to move everything we can to the rim. Let's also try to notice as we get toward the edge, any dips or depressions that might be a source for loose rocks. We're going to be busy, men, and I know that none of us has had any sleep. At the same time, we have to stay down low in the grass and keep quiet so that the Thorns have no idea of what's going on above them." Nick reached out his hands to the men who formed a small circle around him and, for a short time, they held hands together in prayer. Then, in a quiet voice, Nick said, "Let's go."

It was hard work, crawling like snakes, looking for rocks, bringing them to the edge, and then going back by different routes in search of more. It could have been fun, like a game, had they been able to yell out to each other or laugh aloud at the craziness of it all. Surely, anyone who had been able to watch them would have thought so. Occasionally they bumped into each other, and had to hold themselves to a soft chuckle to prevent the Thorns below from hearing.

Time passed slowly. Nick saw, from the position of the stars, that there were only about two hours left before daybreak. He crawled up to the low wall of rocks they had gathered and assessed its size. He was disappointed. So far, they just hadn't collected enough to make a major impact. Furthermore, the stones didn't appear big enough to create an avalanche. If they could just find one or two really large stones it might be enough. But where could they find them? He tapped the man who had just pulled up along beside him. It turned out to be Thad. "We need to find some heavier rocks," he whispered.

"Where?" answered Thad, his hands gesturing his question.

"I don't know. Let's explore. Follow me." Nick led the way away from the edge until they were back again in the sparse tree area. There they felt safe enough to stand up under the protection of some low branches. Nick spoke. "Thad, let's look farther afield to see if we can find something bigger to throw down on them."

They moved back, further away from the cliff, guided only by the dim light of the stars. Not finding a boulder worth bringing back, they turned and went farther into the woods, and then circled back toward their starting point.

"Wait," said Thad. That may be a big rock over there"

Nick strained his eyes to see. The dim gray shape of a large boulder came into focus about thirty feet away. They quickly walked to it.

"It's huge," said Thad, "but can we move it?"

The light was so dim Nick couldn't see the bottom of the waist high rock. "A lot depends on how deeply it's imbedded. Let's go back and get the others."

When the six of them returned, Nick gave the signal and they all pushed at once from one side. The boulder didn't budge.

"We need a stout pole to dislodge it," said Noly.

"This slender tree might work if we can cut it down," replied Rolan.

"Let's try it," said Nick. They took turns carving the four-inch thick tree with a small knife till they finally cut through it. Then they cut off the upper branches and sharpened the bottom into a point. They pushed the sharpened edge of the pole into the ground next to the boulder. As they grasped the other end of the shaft, Nick counted. "One, two, three, pull!" The rock finally budged. Sweating and panting they were slowly able to move the huge rock to the edge of the drop-off. Fortunately, the Thorns didn't notice them. Next, they moved some of the rocks already there out of the way and positioned smaller rocks underneath the boulder so that it stood balanced at the edge of the cliff, ready to be pushed over.

"Now we're ready," gasped Nick, wiping the sweat from his brow. The exhausted men lay back in the tall grass catching their breath. Looking up, they could see that dawn was just beginning to lighten the sky. They wouldn't have to wait much longer.

As the first light of dawn began to spread over the cliff and valley, the men moved into position behind the rocks. Nick hoped that on the other side of the valley, Range and the archers were ready. He stood up. "OK, men, let's do it!" Together they pushed over the bolder and then raced to quickly push the other rocks over the cliff. In seconds, they had them all rolling down the hillside. The ground began shaking under their feet, and they ran back to safety as an avalanche of rock began thundering down on the unsuspecting Thorns. The noise of crashing boulders became mingled now with the din of screeching Thorns far below. The men stood up and began congratulating each other. Their rejoicing was short lived as they saw, coming from below, more Thorns flying up into the sky.

"We didn't get them," said Thad, standing near the edge, hardly believing his eyes.

"Get back, Thad!" yelled Noly, as he and the others grabbed their bows and arrows and hurried back toward the trees. Thad turned to run as across the valley, arrows shot by Range and his men began to whistle through the air. He stumbled forward a short distance and went down in the grass.

"They got me," he said, falling down in the grass.

Nick and Noly cautiously crept toward Thad and on reaching him they laid down in the grass next to him. Thad was writhing in pain with an arrow in his chest and another in his leg. "Don't struggle, Thad," said Nick. We'll get you out of here."

They watched the sky, waiting until the Thorns were almost gone. When they turned back to Thad, they saw that he had lost consciousness. Nick checked his pulse, and found it to be weak but regular. He and Noly picked him up and carried him back toward the trees. They set him down in a sheltered spot behind two tree trunks and then returned to the fight. The Thorns were more numerous now, seeming to be coming from every direction From behind the protection of the trees they fired arrow after arrow to try to bring them down, while from across the valley more arrows were flying. For the moment, it appeared that they were able to hold their own against them.

As time passed, there were fewer Thorns to be seen and soon they were able to reclaim the grassland on top of the cliff. They stayed low to the ground however, fearful of being struck, like Thad, by their own men.   Only a few birds remained in the air, and one by one, they shot them out of the sky. They waited and listened. Aside from an occasional screech from below, everything was quiet. Finally, they couldn't restrain themselves any longer.

Standing up, they yelled victoriously toward their friends on the other side of the valley. Their voices resonated across the rocky divide and then they saw and heard their compatriots yelling also. Could it really be, thought Nick, that the Thorns were finally vanquished? "Yes!" he screamed across the valley.

Chapter Fourteen

When they returned from the edge of the cliff to get Thad, they saw that he was still unconscious. Kneeling beside him, they could see that he was still breathing. Nick looked closely at the two arrows that passed through his side and upper leg. Taking out his knife, he cut the pant off Thad's wounded leg and examined where the arrow entered and exited. Rolan also bent down on one knee to look at it.

"How does it look to you?" Nick asked.

"The wound appears to be clean and it doesn't seem to be near an artery," he answered.

"I think we should remove it."

"If you hold the arrow tight, I'll cut off the head."

"OK. We should have a tourniquet ready in case it starts to bleed."

"Here," said Noly, handing him a short rope.

"Noly, hold Thad while I pull out the arrow." Nick drew out his pulsar and setting it at the heat only setting, he sterilized the wooden shaft of the arrow. Then, with one quick jerk, he removed it. Thad grimaced and jerked his leg up but surprisingly remained unconscious. As there was not a lot of blood, they bandaged his leg and wrapped it, but didn't apply the tourniquet.

Next, they looked at the arrow, which had penetrated his jacket at the lower right hand side of his chest. "I'm afraid to pull that one out," Nick said, speaking to Roland and Noly. "If it's in his lung it could be disastrous."

"Let's just cut off the arrow in back and carry him to the camp," said Noly. "Maybe Tara will know what to do."

They cut down two stout poles and used their jackets to make a stretcher to carry him. Then they picked up their weapons and carrying Thad slowly returned to the main party. The sun was now high in the sky, the air was breezy though not as cold, and small birds chirped and darted here and there in the bushes and trees. It had turned out to be a beautiful day.

When they arrived back at the camp, everybody there was in high spirits. Several of the party had left to scavenge and hunt for extra food. When those who remained saw Thad's lifeless form, the merriment suddenly stopped. Nick glanced across the clearing looking for Tara. When she saw him, she rushed and met him with a hug. Then she saw Thad's still form. "What happened?" she asked in a hushed voice.

"He was too close to the edge when the arrows started flying. We pulled one out of his leg already but this one is in a bad spot.

"Let me see," she said, holding one hand on Thad's forehead and checking his pulse with the other.

"Tara," said Thad weakly, opening his eyes.

"Thad," she said. "You're going to have to take it real easy now."

"Why?" he murmured.

"Oh Thad," she answered, tears in her eyes. "Don't you know you've got an arrow in your side?"

"Oh, yes." he said with faltering voice. "You'll take care of me, Tar..." His eyes closed.

"Of course I will," she said, looking down sadly at the handsome young man.

"What do you think?" asked Nick.

She looked up from Thad, and turned to face him. For a moment, she was silent. "I really don't know, Nick," she said at last. I don't think it's through his lung or he would have had a harder time speaking. What it is through inside I don't know. Oh, how I wish we were back at the Laboratory. But we can't leave it in that long. We're going to have to take a chance and just hope the internal bleeding isn't too bad. Help me Nick."

They removed his jacket and shirt, cleaned the arrow, and Tara rubbed some antibacterial herbs on the shaft. They prepared bandages and swabbed the area of the wound with a medicinal poultice. Then, Tara prepared a sleep inducing drink made from water and some powdered herbs she had taken from the medicine bag.

"What's that for?" Nick asked.

"Once we pull out that arrow he's going to wake up and be in a lot of pain. This will help with that and put him to sleep. He's going to need complete rest for at least two days so the internal wounds can start to heal. Are you ready?"

"Yes," he answered, bracing himself to remove the arrow.

"Noly, you hold on too," she added. "We need to keep him from moving after we pull out the arrow. OK. Ready? Quickly!"

With a strong, swift pull, Nick jerked out the arrow. Thad's body jumped and he uttered a brief cry of pain before slumping back down.

"That's it, Thad," said Tara, bending over his head while Noly held him down. "We got it out. You're going to be OK now."

Thad shuddered and clenched his teeth. His lips were compressed as if he was trying to keep from screaming.

"I know it hurts," said Tara, her long hair hanging over him as she lowered her head to face him. "Now just lift your head a little and sip this. It will make you feel a lot better." Thad raised his head slightly, the fear and pain obvious in his eyes, but he managed to sip some of the liquid. He caught his breath.

"Just try to drink a little more," she said softly, "and then you can go to sleep." Thad swallowed more of it and Tara let his head down gently. He closed his eyes and soon the strain in his face softened as sleep came over him. They finished bandaging his wounds and covered him with two blankets. Ruskin, who was just returning from foraging for food, approached them. "How's he doing, Tara?" he asked, putting his hand on her shoulder.

She shook her head and closed her eyes a moment before responding. "We don't know yet, Grandpa. We've done all we can for him. Now he needs to rest as much as possible. I've given him a sedative that should keep him asleep for awhile."

"You look tired," said Ruskin. "Let's move him into my tent where I can look after him. You and Nick can set up one of the extra ones."

"Are you sure you'd want to do that, grandpa?"

"Yes, it's no trouble."

"Well, thank you."

Range walked over and asked about Thad. Nick told him about his condition.

"He's young," Range said. "With his youth and Tara's care I bet he's going to turn out just fine." Then, changing the subject he added, "Nick, I want to tell you, you and your men did a terrific job on those Thorns up there. We were watching the whole thing from our high vantage point. The smaller rocks didn't do much but when you released the boulder, it started the whole hillside crashing down on them. That really caught them by surprise."

"Thanks Range. We were lucky to find that stone. Without the strenuous effort of every man on our team we would never have been able to move it to the edge."

"Yes, when it fell we could feel the reverberation all the way across the valley."

"Even with that," said Nick, "I don't think we could have handled the remaining Thorns without your sharpshooters knocking them down."

"That was the most fun we've had on the whole trip," Range answered, laughing. They deserved to die." Then Range spoke in a more confidential tone. "Nick, a lot of the men are anxious to start going back home. I understand that Thad can't move yet. How many men do you think should stay on to help with him?"

"He will need to be carried on a stretcher. That will take four of us, not counting Tara."

"Do you have any lined up so far?"

"Not yet, although I'm staying, and I think Noly and Rolan may also stay." While he was speaking, Tara joined them.

"That makes three right there," said Range. "Tara, I think you should consider leaving tomorrow also, I mean expecting your baby."

"Thanks Range. I'm sure I'll be OK. The baby may not come for six weeks and I'll be careful. Besides, I want to be able to do anything I can for Thad."

"I'll line up one or two more to help. Then the rest of us will set off early tomorrow morning. Except for the relatives of the men who died, I know the townspeople will be overjoyed. I'm sure they'll want to celebrate."

"If I know you, you'll be involved in that," replied Nick.

"It goes with being on the Council," said Range with a wink. "Here, let me give you a hand with Thad. Where is he going to stay overnight?"

"In Ruskin's tent," Nick answered.

They moved Thad in, and talked with Ruskin awhile before separating. After leaving the tent, Nick looked for Tara and found her applying a salve to the lacerations Jon got from the brambles they encountered climbing the hill. They had swelled up substantially. When she finished, Nick and Tara went to get Cord's tent and together they set it up a little apart from the others. It was not late in the evening, though after being up most of the night before, almost everyone was turning in early. The night had become rather cool and breezy but inside the tent, it was comfortable. Nick and Tara finished rolling out their individual bedding and by chance faced each other as they stood up. She looked into Nick's tired eyes and stepped forward to hold him. Nick sighed and lowered his head into her dark brown hair as he returned her embrace.

"Nick, I'm proud of what you did on that hill this morning," she said. "I'm sorry for what I said to you before."

What was that?" he asked, trying to remember what she had said.

"I mean about our being different because of your training to be brave and to fight for what you believe in."

"Oh, that," he said, remembering their conversation.

"Nick, I truly am sorry. I don't want anything to come between us."

"I have missed your cheerfulness and the little things you do that make me happy," Nick answered. "I don't like being distant from you."

"I don't either. These past several weeks were terrible for me. And, I was the one to blame for it all. How could I have been so stupid?"

"You weren't. You only wanted to protect me and others. He lowered his head to kiss her. For weeks, they hadn't kissed and now they kissed each other tenderly, lovingly, with feeling.

"Wait," said Tara, freeing her mouth to speak. "Do you smell something?"

"You."

"No, I mean food."

"Oh, yes. It must be suppertime. I'm hungry."

"Me, too," she said. "Let's eat supper and then come back to the tent."

"First things first." They smiled at each other. Tara led the way out of the tent and they walked hand in hand to the campfire.

The small party was in good spirits. They chatted and ate the hot, thick meat and vegetable soup, as well as the hard crust bread. The moon rose over the hill as they finished eating, and some of the men decided to clean up at the small, nearby stream. It was the first chance they had had to bathe in days. Nick and Tara went back to their tent, got soap, towels, and a change of clothes and went to a section of the stream away from the others. By the time they had finished bathing, the moon was covered by a cloud and they shivered and leaned into each other to avoid tripping on the undergrowth as they made their way back to their tent. Once inside Tara sat down and combed out her long, dark, still damp hair by the light of the single candle. Nick lay back on the other side of their bed, content to watch her. He saw how full she was with their child and when at last she came to bed, he put his hand on her stomach. He felt the tap of a small foot.

"He's active tonight," said Tara, smiling.

"He's not the only one," he said, reaching to draw her closer. Tara nestled in his arms still smiling.

"What are you smiling so much about tonight, my little mink," he asked.

"Because I love to be in your arms. Because I love you."

"Yes, I love you too, my sweet," he whispered.

"Does this tent lock?" she asked.

"No, not that I know of."

"Then let's blow out the candle, darling."

"I'd rather see you."

"I know."

"OK," he said, extinguishing the flame.

Chapter Fifteen

During the next two days, the small party of seven rested and made preparations while waiting for Thad to get strong enough to be moved. They fashioned a four-man stretcher out of two long, slender saplings to which they attached tent fabric. It was obvious that Thad was gradually getting better. His appetite was returning, though it was still quite painful for him to move. Tara and Ruskin administered various herbal remedies that gave some relief and they reminded him that the pain was nature's way of telling him to remain still so he would heal.

Early on the morning of the third day they decided to set out. Ruskin rode ahead, scouting to find the least difficult path through the rugged terrain, followed by the stretcher bearers, Nick, Roland, Noly, and Chard. After them rode Tara leading the extra forces, which were loaded with supplies. They went slowly so that Thad would be jarred as little as possible. By the next day, Thad began to feel better and began to grow restless at being carried everywhere. At one of their rest stops, he got up and said to Tara, "I appreciate everything you and everyone have done for me, but I'm stronger now and able to stand up just fine. See."

"Thad, I know you're feeling better and that's good. Your wounds are mending on the outside but we don't know about inside. Be patient and let the men carry you at least one more day."

"If you say so, Tara, but I don't want to be a burden on them and I sure don't want to be carried on a stretcher into town."

"Oh, is that what you're concerned about?" she replied with a knowing smile. "That certain townspeople might think you are permanently disabled?"

"Well, I don't care about the townspeople as a whole but I'd hate for Frecka to see me being carried into town like an invalid."

"Frecka? Oh yes, I think I know of her. She's about eighteen with lots of blond hair and a very pretty smile."

"Yes, that's her," Thad replied, unable to withhold a smile himself.

"Well then," she said, as she checked and removed the bandage from his leg. "Let's just make sure you're walking when we get there. On the other hand," she appeared reflective, "I bet she would just love to nurse you back to health."

"Maybe, but you do think I'll get over this soon, don't you?"

"Yes. To be honest, I was worried at first, but really, Thad, you seem to be making a nice recovery already. Try walking a little tomorrow if you feel like it, though only for a short time. "Don't over do it and stop when you feel tired or if anything hurts. You'll notice that you won't have the energy you had before and that's something that is just going to take time."

"OK. I will," Thad agreed. He hadn't known Tara long, but he knew already that he liked her in a big sister kind of way.

Three days later, they arrived at last at the outskirts of the town. It was very late at night but their desire to return home had kept them going through the day. Soon they passed by the first houses of the town. Chard said, "Well, there's my house. I'll be seeing you all."

As they continued into the town, they said goodbye to their companions as each left for home until at last Nick and Tara arrived dead tired at their own house.

The next morning, Tara was the first to awake. She quietly got up and stood, with her hands on her stomach in front of the mirror. *I think he's dropped some more,* she said to herself. *It won't be long now.* Nick stirred in bed, opened his eyes, and seeing her standing there he asked, "Did you say something?"

"No. I was just thinking Nick, that it can't be too long before our baby will be here. We better stop and see Madelin."

"Does she even know you're pregnant?"

"Of course. She's known for months. I haven't seen her for a while though. Maybe she can tell us when he or she will come. I do hope it's soon."

It was bright and chilly that morning as they walked to Madelin's house. On the way, they were greeted by townspeople who congratulated them for killing the Thorns. Some asked when the baby was due. At length they reached her house. A large boned, congenial woman opened the door.

"Tara, you're back," she said as she let them in. "I was so worried about you when I heard you were out there with the men. I congratulate you both. Say, you look just fine, Tara," she said, standing back to take a good look at her. "Maybe a little tired but in good shape. It's so nice to see you." The two women embraced. "And you too, Nick," she added, giving him a hug also.

"I know I should have come sooner but, well, you know what happened," said Tara.

"The whole town knows what happened and you are all heroes," she said with gusto. "You're going to be honored at a special town dance this Saturday night."

"Really?" said Tara, surprised.

"Oh yes." Madelin replied, clapping her big hands together. "They're already starting to make preparations at the town market. It's going to be a gala affair. Everyone will be there and I'm sure they'll have food, drinks, and music played by all the bands. The whole town is looking forward to it. My, my, and you just got into town and didn't know anything about it. I'm so glad to be the first to tell you."

Nick and Tara looked at each other and Nick sighed.

"Well, I guess we might as well enjoy it," said Tara cheerfully.

"We'll need to dress warm," Nick added.

"No need. No need for that," laughed Madelin. All the grills will be lit. It should be just as warm as a summer evening."

"Yes, Nick," said Tara. "You've never been there when it's heated and all set for a big dance. It's so nice."

"Let me look at you, girl," said Madelin. Just seeing you now, I do think your baby has dropped. Come with me, Tara. Excuse us a few minutes, Nick." Madelin escorted Tara into a small adjacent room and closed the door. After a few minutes Tara emerged first and was literally beaming. For a moment, she tried to hide her enthusiasm by putting her hand in front of her mouth. But she couldn't hold it in. "One week!" she said excitedly to Nick, "One week, or two at the most."

Nick got up from his chair, put his arms around his wife, and kissed her. Then he looked down sideways at his wife's bulging stomach and, addressing his child, added, "So you're not going to keep us waiting much longer are you, Rod."

"Or it might be little Tessa," added Tara demurely.

"Whatever," said Madelin. "I'll be ready for him or for her. Just let me know as soon as the contractions begin."

"Do you think we should even go to the dance, I mean it being this close?" asked Tara.

"Sure, sure," she enthusiastically replied. "You go along and have a good time. You can dance too if you like. Just don't jump around too much. I know you wouldn't be doing that. And, sit down if you're tired. Enjoy yourselves."

Tara thanked Madelin heartily as they went out. She looked into Nick's eyes. "Talking to her really makes me feel better," she said with a sigh. "She really knows about babies."

* * *

The days before the dance passed quickly. Tara spent her time at home or going shopping, buying supplies and little things she thought of for the baby, and Nick returned to work at the Lab. On the Saturday morning of the dance, Tara discovered that she really didn't have anything to wear. Try as she may, she couldn't fit into the only evening dress she owned.

"Nick, I don't know what I'm going to do. I can't get into this dress anymore, with the baby so big."

"Wear something more casual," Nick answered, looking up from the shelf he was making in the nursery.

"This is a special event, Nick. Everybody will be dressed up."

"Everybody knows, or will know, that you're going to have a baby soon, Tara. They won't care what you're wearing."

"But I like to look nice too."

"I know, honey, you do look nice. You look lovely."

"I know what," Tara said brightly. I'll see if Tes has anything I can borrow. She's a little bigger then I am and has nice clothes. I'll ride out to her house."

"Are you sure you want to go that far?"

"Sure, I'll be OK. I'll take it easy."

"OK, honey. Just don't stay too long. In your condition you really should get some rest before we go to the dance."

"Don't worry, I won't be long," she said, blowing him a kiss as she walked out the door.

Sometime later, when the sun had shifted lower in the sky, Tara came back. The bright look in her eye told Nick she had found what she was looking for..

"How was the ride?"

"Not bad," she answered, noncommittally.

"Well, let's see it," he said. "I can tell you got a dress you really like."

"Not yet. You'll see it on me tonight. Right now, I really do need to rest for a while. I know you're really going to like it."

Later that evening as they prepared for the dance, Nick got his first look at his wife in the borrowed dress. "Tara," he exclaimed, "you're beautiful!" The dark black dress was cinched beneath her bosom, accentuating her figure, and the brocaded fabric swirled elegantly downward to her ankles.

"Thank you. Tes has wonderful taste in clothes. Are you sure it doesn't look too elegant for me?"

"Tara, you are absolutely beautiful. You definitely should wear it."

"Thank you, darling. I'm so glad you like it. Really, it's almost too enchanting. Even with being so pregnant, I feel special in it."

* * *

It was only a few blocks to the town market, the site of the dance, and ordinarily they would have walked or taken their forcs. For the evening, however, Ruskin had obtained a carriage, and he invited them to come with him. Seeing him pull up, they exited their house and stepped into the carriage, noticing by the dim evening light that Ruskin was not alone.

"Tara, Nick, I'd like to introduce you to an old friend of mine, Silva. Silva, this is my granddaughter and her husband, Nick."

"Pleased to meet you," said Silva. She bowed slightly and offered her hand to them both. "Just call me Sil, like everyone else. My, my, Tara, you certainly have become a beautiful woman since last I saw you."

"Thank you," said Tara, taking her hand. She noticed a certain air of elegance about the older woman. Nick settled into the carriage and Tara added, "I'm surprised grandpa hasn't mentioned you."

"He hasn't?" she asked, looking over at Ruskin.

"What did you say, Sil?" asked Ruskin.

"Nothing," she replied, turning back with a reflective smile. Noting her smile, Tara felt warmth toward the older woman.

Ruskin started off and in no time, they were there. He dropped off Nick and Tara first and Silva stayed with him to park the carriage. The young couple walked together up the slight rise toward the entrance and through the stone wall enclosing the market area. When they reached the entrance, Nick was surprised. The Market Square had been transformed. Instead of vendor's stalls, the whole area was furnished with tables and chairs and lit with the soft light of at least forty unique fireplaces. As they walked past one, he noted its pyramidal shape and felt warmth radiating from the stone walls. He went closer and saw glowing embers near the bottom. Walking away from it to return to Tara he could feel how the banked fires effectively warmed the whole walled in area, which was open to the starlit sky above.

"Look," said Tara, walking gracefully by his side, "it looks like they have four bands playing tonight. Let's walk around and hear what they sound like before we sit down."

Their stroll around the market place was slow as they kept meeting friends and acquaintances, and was slowed some more when they stopped at one of the drink serving areas. Soon they both were feeling a delightful sense of conviviality. Tara was getting tired of walking and at last they found a table that was near a band playing stringed instruments and something akin to waltz music. On looking around, they saw Range standing up motioning to them. As they reached the table, Tes rose to meet them. "Tara," she exclaimed, "you look absolutely lovely. That dress is just stunning on you."

"Thank you, Tes." Tara answered, taking her seat. "It's such a beautiful dress. "Trila," she said, seeing that her young cousin was also at the table. "I'm so glad you've come."

"Tara, Nick, this is my friend, Burl," said Trila. Burl stood up and walked around the table to shake Nick's hand. Nick couldn't help but be impressed by his size and muscular build.

"Are you still in school, Burl?" he asked.

"Yes, sir, he answered. "I'll be starting my last year next month."

"He's going to be an agricultural chemist," said Trila, who had also walked around the table to join Burl.

"Good for you," said Nick.

The music started up again and many couples began leaving their tables to go to the dance floor.

"Let's dance," said Trila to Burl and they excused themselves and walked to the dance floor.

"Do you feel like dancing?" Nick asked Tara

"Let's wait a little if you don't mind."

Nick and Range began talking to each other across the table and Tes and Tara chatted. Nick moved over to Trila's vacant chair so he could hear Range above the music. From there, he also had a better view of the dance floor. "Look at Ruskin and Silva" he said, pointing them out.

The older couples, along with several others were doing a minuet, complete with pirouettes, rounds and bows. When the music was over Nick and Tara clapped, and Silva, noticing them, walked with Ruskin to their table.

"Why aren't you young folks dancing," she asked.

"Oh, we will," answered Tara. "You two look great out there."

"Thank you, darling," said Silva. "When we were young we could dance all night. Right Ruskin?"

"We did, as a matter of fact," he answered with a smile and a wink.

"Really, grandpa, you've known Sil that long?"

"A long time," he answered.

"We were neighbors," said Silva, "and we danced together at the old school house. Do you remember that, Ruskin?"

"Well, let's see," he answered, apparently trying hard to remember. "I know I danced with a lot of different girls back then. We were learning the steps. Do you remember it that well, Sil?"

"Oh, yes, I remember you," she said. "We were quite young then. Yes, I remember it well."

The band started a different song and Nick caught Tara's eye.

"Why don't you take our seats for awhile," suggested Tara. "Nick and I are going to dance."

Nick led Tara in front of him to the dance floor, savoring the scent of her long dark hair. "Well, what do you think about the young couple?" he asked Tara.

"You mean Trila and Burl?"

Tara looked over to see them dancing nearby and gave Trila a nod. "Oh yes, they dance very nicely together," she said.

"No, I mean do you think they'll get married?"

"Married? There are no plans for that. I think they've only really known each other for a couple of months."

"Look at them dance. He looks so protective of her and she just seems to melt into his arms."

"He is a lot bigger than her. A girl would surely feel safe with him."

A ringing sound came from the center of the Square. "Time to go up the dais," Tara said.

They walked toward the platform and were greeted by town officials.

"I don't really enjoy this," Tara whispered to Nick as they waited.

"Me neither, but I know they want to do something to show their appreciation." He held her waist and hand as they walked up the steps to the platform. At the top, the others who had fought the Thorns joined them. Nick felt camaraderie with them and they all shook hands, though it wasn't part of the program.

It seemed like they were there a long time, with the music, the speeches, and the awarding of the silver rings engraved with the town insignia. They all stood proudly as the town anthem was played and then walked solemnly off the stage to the grateful applause of over a thousand people. Nick was glad it was over. He could see that Tara was tired. He tried to clear a straight path back to their table but before they got there, she said, "Wait, Nick. I feel something."

"What is it?"

"It may be a contraction."

"I hope not tonight."

"It's gone," said Tara with relief."

"What do you think it was?"

"I don't know. It could have been a fake contraction. Madelin told me they sometimes come as much as a week before the real thing. She said they're very irregular. Not like the real thing. Time will tell which it is."

"So, if they come regularly, it's only a matter of hours?"

"I think so. Honey, you know I've never done this before."

"Want to go home?"

"No, let's just sit down awhile for now."

The rest of the evening passed uneventfully. They enjoyed the food and music, and spending time with their friends and relatives. When they were ready to leave, Ruskin took them home and left them off at their door. Nick escorted Tara into their house by the dim light of the candle on the table. He helped her with her shawl and asked how she felt. As she turned toward him, he could see her bright eyes glowing by the candlelight.

"I had a wonderful time, Nick," she said, turning to kiss him. They embraced and he felt her body quiver.

"Darling, you're trembling."

"Maybe I'm a little chilled. Hold me tight, Nick." Her eyes were bright as he held her tight and kissed her soft lips tenderly.

* * *

Very early the next morning Tara woke Nick up.

"Nick, I think it's time."

"You mean for the baby?"

"Yes. I've been awake for a while now and the contractions are regular, not like that one last night."

Nick sprang from the bed. "I'll run and get Madelin. Do you need anything right now, before I go?"

"I'd like a drink of water."

Nick got the water and then hurried to Madelin's house. He knocked loudly on her door. When it opened, Madelin appeared in her robe.

"The baby, it's coming!" he blurted out.

"OK, I'll be right over." Looking at him, she added, "Don't worry. Go back and warm up a kettle of water. I'll be over just as soon as I get dressed. Everything will be just fine."

Nick hurried back home, where he found Tara in the midst of a contraction. Tara sighed in relief as the contraction ended. "That was a hard one."

"Then maybe it won't be too long," Nick said optimistically. "I got Madelin up. She'll be right over."

Tara turned and smiled weakly at him. "We better finally decide on a name. I just have this feeling that it will be a boy."

"I like David," he said. "It's a strong name and means beloved one."

"But I like Ben, too, and Rob has. . ." she winced and took a deep breath.

There was a knock on the door, and before Nick could get there, Madelin burst in saying, "I'm here." As she removed her coat, she called out, "How's our new mother doing?"

"She's in pain right now." Nick answered from their bedroom.

"Oh, my, darling," said Madelin as she entered the bedroom. "Just hold on," she instructed Tara. "Don't fight it." Tara sighed as the contraction ended. "That's a girl," said Madelin, coming to her side. "Relax between contractions, that makes it easier. Nick, I want to see how far along she is. Would you go and check on the water? And please bring in some fresh towels."

Nick left the room and noticed that it was beginning to get lighter outside. Soon the sun would be up. He got the towels, checked on the water, and then went back to the bedroom. Tara appeared to be very intense. Nick went to her side.

"She still has more to do," said Madelin, "to push this baby out."

As she finished speaking, Tara shuddered as another contraction began. Nick held tightly onto her hand.

Another hour passed and the baby still hadn't come. Nick had left the bedroom frustrated because he felt he wasn't able to do anything to help. He paced back and forth in the front room of the house, worried, though Madelin had told him that things were going normally. He didn't know what to do so he just paced back and forth across the front room of the house. The waiting was getting to him. That, and knowing that by now Tara must be extremely exhausted. He heard a knock at the door, opened it, and Ruskin walked in. Nick was happy to see the older man.

"We're having a baby," he announced.

"I know that," Ruskin replied. "How does Tara feel today? Is she still asleep?"

"We're having a baby right now!" Nick said loudly.

Ruskin seemed startled for a moment, then turning, took Nick's hands and looked straight into his eyes. "You mean now, right now?"

"Yes, she's in the bedroom with Madelin.   "And is everything all right?" he asked, still holding his hands.

"I guess so. Madelin says she is doing fine."

"Oh, well then," he replied, seeming to immediately relax. "All we have to do is wait."

"That's not easy," Nick answered. "All the waiting and not being able to do anything."

"Oh, I know how you feel. We all go through it. Of course it's a lot harder on the women, but waiting is hard enough."

Just then, they heard an unmistakable cry from the back of the house. They exchanged glances and Nick ran into the bedroom. Tara was lying on the bed propped up with pillows and standing at her side was Madelin, cradling a beautiful child with one arm as she wiped him off with a towel.

"Nick," she said solemnly, "you have a son."

Nick looked at the baby and then down at his wife who smiled up at him. He knelt down beside her while Madelin with skilled hands cut and tied the cord and then returned the baby to his mother. Nick and Tara looked at the small new person, and with both their hands on him, they turned to smile at each other.

"Isn't he beautiful?" said Tara.

The baby squirmed and made sucking movements with his mouth, and Tara opened her robe and drew her son to her breast. The baby calmed.

Tara leaned her head gently on her baby's, grinned and said, "Our son." Nick reached around to embrace them both. At that moment, he couldn't even dream of the adventures the three of them would share.

Chapter Sixteen:

(Eight months later)

"Rock a bye baby,

cradle and all,

when the wind blows,

baby will fall."

Tara was kneeling, gently rocking the cradle to and fro. She saw the sated look on her baby's face and his little smile as his eyes began to shut in sleep. She rocked him a little longer, then buttoned her dress, blew out the candle, and stepped out of the room.

"He's asleep," she said softly to Nick who was in the next room reading by the light of two candles.

Nick glanced up from his reading, and looked at his wife. She wore only a simple one-piece dress, secured in front with leather loops and buttons, and to Nick, she was beautiful. Her long hair flowed down her back and the sparkle in her eyes still captivated him, now over a year since their marriage. "Come sit with me," he said, putting down the manuscript, and making room for her at the side of his chair. "Are you tired?"

"Yes, a little," she answered, snuggling against him within the narrow confines of the chair. "It's been a busy week."

"For me too," he said, putting an arm around her and rubbing her back with his other hand.

"That's nice," she said, turning a little and smiling contentedly at him. "Oh, don't stop," she added as he moved to put both arms around her. Nick continued to massage her back until Tara looked dreamily into his eyes and said softly, "That's enough." She turned to face him and they kissed.

* * *

The next morning Nick woke up feeling refreshed. He had plans for the day and was eager to get started. He quietly got out of bed and saw that Tara was still asleep. He realized that she had been up at sometime in the night nursing their baby. Getting his clothes, he put them on in the next room, and stopping only a moment for a quick bite to eat, he wrote a note to Tara and quietly closed the house door behind him. He hesitated a moment, and decided that since it was such a nice day he would walk rather than take the forc. He picked up a two-handled bag from above his workbench and soon was on his way.

The sun had risen and fresh scents of spring were borne by gentle breezes. Though cool at first, soon the sun and the briskness of his walk warmed him, and he unbuttoned his jacket. As he reached the heart of the little town he saw many people up and about, some he knew and waved to. He entered the wagon shop which was connected to the hard goods store operated by his friend, Range.

"Good to see you, Nick," said Range heartily. "Come, have some fresh guava with us."

Nick walked back to the workshop area. "Hi, Thad. How are you? Haven't seen you for quite a while."

"Yes, Mr. Bartok. I was in school till this month but now I'm working here full time. Range is adding a coopers shop and he's showing me the trade."

"Actually, I'm still it learning myself," said Range. "Soon, the way he's going, Thad will know more than me. Cord didn't leave many notes before he died on how he did things at his shop, but we can tell a lot by the workmanship he left behind. So, what are you and Tara doing now at your house?"

"Nothing much with the house anymore. We're satisfied with the inside, though Tara wants to put in some flowers and shrubbery in front. What I want to do now is make a crib. Rod is getting too big for the cradle already, so I'd like to make something for him until he's ready for his own bed."

"Why don't you just borrow one, or get one from someone whose children have grown up? I'd give you mine but Brad still needs it. I'm sure I could round one up for you."

"That's nice of you, Range, but I'd like to make my own. You see, I want to make it different from others I've seen."

"Really, how's that?" asked Range with obvious curiosity.

"Well, I want to make it low to the floor, with only three sides."

"Only three sides. Aren't you afraid he'll fall out?"

"No, that's the advantage of making it low. Another is that when Rod's tired he can just craw or walk in. Of course I'd want to have a fourth side to close it at night."

Range smiled broadly at his friend. "I hope your baby's as rational as you, Nick."

* * *

On the far outskirts of town, Rakel looked sympathetically at her husband, Peat, asleep in the easy chair. He had worked long and hard in the field today harvesting their crop of cartins, the potato-like crops they grew for the market. Although he was getting older now and had no sons to help him, Peat insisted on putting in a big crop every year. They didn't need the money. She and Peat lived simply, and they had a nice, comfortable house. For her part, she would have liked to live closer to the town and all it's activity but when she married Peat, a long time ago, she knew then that she would go anywhere he wanted to go. She knew him to be a good man. To others, he might appear to be gruff, and he never failed to say exactly what he thought. But she knew his tender side.

They had three daughters, all grown and married and six grandchildren with another on the way. How he loved those grandchildren. He would romp with them in the field and tell them stories that he made up in his head. The children loved him, especially the younger ones who were not old enough to become worldly wise. He was generous to a fault. Between his daughters, his grandchildren, the church, and her, he spent about all he earned. She could sense that the work was taking a toll on him, however, and she feared for his health. She resolved that tomorrow she would help him in the field.

* * *

That evening was one of the first warm nights of spring, and in town, people were taking advantage of the weather. Nick placed Rod in the baby carrier and lifted him onto his shoulders as He and Tara set out for a long walk. The redolence of numerous flowers and trees in bloom filled the evening air, and families and friends walked along together chatting and taking in the pleasant sights of the town. Nick and Tara greeted many people they knew along the way, and as they made their circuitous return, the stars in the sky gradually appeared. On reaching their own neighborhood, Nick saw something moving in the night sky, and he pointed it out to Tara. "Have you seen anything like that before?"

"No, never," she answered. "Do you have any idea what it might be?"

"Yes, I'm afraid I do," he said, as he opened the door to their house.

"What, Nick? Tell me."

"It may be an oil ball."

"What? An oil ball. What is that?"

"It's used to haul unprocessed fuel back to the refineries. If it is one, we'll have visitors very soon."

"But they'll be friendly, won't they?" she asked with concern. "I hope so."

That night Nick tried to answer all Tara's questions about what it meant for petroleum extractors to arrive on a planet. A lot depended, he told her, on the size of the operation and on the men in charge. The laws regulating the oil recovery process were spelled out clearly in the Galactic Charter. Unfortunately, they were not always adhered to, especially in the more remote areas of the galaxy. In the end, after all their talk, both Nick and Tara felt uneasy as they retired for the night.

Chapter Seventeen

Very early the next morning, while it was still dark, two large craft, one bigger than the other, descended quietly and landed on the outskirts of the town.

When Peat woke up early that morning, he could hardly believe his eyes. He went back to the bedroom to waken Rakel.

"Get up Rakel. Come, and look out the window."

As she gazed in amazement through the pane, she asked him, "What are they?"

"They're spaceships, Rakel. They're like what that man Nick came in."

"Well, I can hardly believe my eyes. There they are right on the edge of our land. What should we do?"

"I know what I'm going to do. I'm going right over there and see what they're up to."

"Don't you do that Peat. You don't know them and they don't know you. Besides, they might not be friendly."

"Well, I hear that Nick is friendly. Maybe they're friends of his."

"You don't know that, Peat. Please don't take any chances."

"Rakel, all I'm going to do is walk out on my own property and wave and maybe talk to them. Besides, I've got to go out there and keep digging up the cartins. You know if we leave them in the ground too long they start losing their flavor."

"OK, Peat, but don't get too close. Give me a minute to get dressed. I'm going out with you. I'll help with the cartins."

"Rakel, you don't need to do that. I can handle it."

"You hush now and wait for me. I'll just be a minute."

Peat waited, and they walked out of their house together into the early morning sunshine. The dew on the grass glistened in the sunlight and they walked quietly, awed by the size of the steel blue craft that loomed larger and larger before them.

"Let's not go any further," Rakel cautioned.

"I'll just go to the little hill there and wave," he answered, leaving her side to climb the small mound. As he reached it, he suddenly fell forward and cried out in pain.

"Peat! What's the matter?" she yelled as she hurried to his side. When she reached him, she screamed and fell on top of him.

* * *

In town, the morning dawned clear and bright, and gradually the people started to waken. A few, who lived on the outskirts, saw an unexpected sight. In fear, they hurried into town and spread the word. Now, several people hurried toward Nick and Tara's house.

"Nick!" said Range, as he knocked loudly on the door.

"Come on in, Range," Nick answered from the back of the house. "What brings you here so early?"

Range and the three other townspeople entered. They explained to Nick what they had seen and asked him what he might know about it.

"I think they're after oil," said Nick. "What that means for us, I'm not sure. We need to talk to them to find out how big an operation it is. Two ships, if that's all, may not be a major problem."

"Then you'll talk to them?" the others want to know.

"Yes, I'll go out there today."

Tara came in from the bedroom. "I heard what you said, Nick. You don't expect any trouble do you?"

"No, I wouldn't think so."

"Then I'd like to go too, to see what other Earth people are like. Besides, it's not that far. I'll get Rod ready and we can go right away."

Soon, four men, a woman, and a baby traveled the green road toward the two spaceships. As they drew near, one of the men said, "Look, they're practically on Peat and Rakel's land."

They left the road and entered the farm, taking care to stay on the path that led between the fields of cartins. Then they saw the bodies.

"Oh, no!" said Nick, as they all immediately stopped. "Don't go any closer!"

"But we have to help them," exclaimed Tara as she continued toward them.

Nick rushed to her and held her tight. "Stop! Tara, don't try to go any further!"

"Why? We can't just leave them there."

"I think they have an energy field surrounding the ship. If so, it would kill us just as fast as it has probably killed them."

"Then what are we going to do?"

Before he could answer, Range asked, "Nick, is there anything we can do to see if the force field is still in place?"

"Yes, it will be easy to tell. All we need to do is throw something in the direction of the ship."

"Here's a branch," said Kaid, one of the two townsmen who had traveled with them.

"Nick took it, drew back, and threw it toward the ship. It flew through the air and suddenly there was a sharp crack as it stopped in mid air and dropped to the ground, smoking.

"Look at that," marveled Sarkin.

"It's impenetrable!" Range exclaimed.

"Well, we could tunnel underneath it," said Nick, "but I'd rather try to hail someone on the other side."

"Wouldn't that be dangerous?" asked Range.

"It could be, if they really mean to kill. I suspect this force field is up for protection against unknown animals. I doubt if they even know there are humans in the area. Matt and I didn't know either, when we first landed."

"Just then, they saw a man walking on the other side of the force field. In his hand, he carried a pulsar. "Take cover behind those bushes," said Nick, motioning for the others to get out of sight. He moved behind a tree. Then he called out to the man on the other side of the force field. "Hey, there. Do you speak English?"

The man turned, and saw Nick, who had stepped from behind the tree. "What are *you* doing here?" he asked, obviously surprised.

"I live here," answered Nick.

"Really? I was not told there were humans on this planet."

"They probably didn't know. But there are, as you can see. I'd like to talk to your captain. Can you arrange that?"

"It's possible. Are you alone?"

"For the moment, yes."

"No weapons?"

Nick held up his arms to show he had none.

"OK. I can open this force field a little if you want to come through."

"Which way?"

"Here, walk between these two small trees."

"So, where are you from?" Nick asked as they walked toward the ship.

"Algernon."

"Algernon? You mean you're not from Earth? That's a surprise."

"Why is that a surprise?"

Nick didn't want to give anything away so he said, "Somehow I just thought any ship coming here would be from earth." The guard either let it pass or didn't think anything of Nick's reply. When they reached the ship, the door opened and the sentry escorted him inside.

Nick was impressed with the spaciousness of the cabin and with its state of the art equipment, but there was no one to be seen. Then a door slid open and a broad shouldered man in relaxed attire came toward him.

"So, there is human life on this planet," he said, extending his hand. "My name is Orson."

"Pleased to meet you," answered Nick, shaking his broad fleshy hand. "My name is Nick Bartok."

"We were completely unaware there were people on this planet," continued Orson. "Our sensors didn't pick it up either. Are there many of you?"

"Yes, and you're just on the outskirts of our town. Unfortunately your protective shield killed two of our townspeople this morning."

"Oh, my God!" said Orson, with what appeared to be genuine concern. "We had no idea. What a terrible tragedy! Is there anything we can do to help the family?"

"They are an older couple, whose children are already grown up and married. Money wouldn't help, as we don't use galaxy currency. You definitely need to express your sorrow to the family. Besides that, I'm sure flowers would be appreciated."

"Oh yes, yes. We will do that," he said peremptorily. "But tell me, Nick," he spoke with concern, "how are the natives taking it? I mean is there likely to be a problem?"

"It's possible," answered Nick, carefully choosing his words. People are upset and fearful—wondering if they could be next."

Orson withdrew slightly, seeming to think to himself for a moment. Then he said, "Can't you just tell them the truth that our shields were up to protect ourselves from any dangerous animals?"

"I can tell them that. Were there any in particular that you had reason to fear?"

"To tell you the truth, Nick, we had heard that there were huge birds here that are not afraid to attack people and even spaceships."

"That's true. Our people will understand that. We eradicated them several months ago."

"You did? I don't believe it. Are you serious? Come, sit down. We need to talk. Can I get you a drink?"

The two men spent the next half-hour in conversation. Nick explained how he came to be on the planet and he learned that Orson's home, Algernon, was an industrialized planet of the star Perseus. Orson didn't admit it, but Nick was able to infer that he wasn't authorized by the galaxy to extract oil. Nick also suspected that he had somehow obtained information on his and Matt's own oil findings over a year ago. Basically, he knew that Orson was an unlicensed brigand who was taking matters into his own hands in order to obtain oil for his colony on Algernon. Nevertheless, he appeared on the surface to be a cultured man who traveled with his wife, stepdaughter, engineers and a number of guards. As they finished talking, Orson invited him to bring Tara and visit them. He apologized that his wife, Sabrina, was "under the weather," not being used to the unpolluted air, he explained. As Nick was about ready to leave, he asked him, "Nick, don't you miss the larger universe."

"Not really," he answered. "I'm happy here. My only regret, and it's a small one, is not being able to see Olanda and some day take my family there.

"Olanda. We have it here! Of course, you couldn't have known. Uni Studios made a virtual of it last year. It's already the biggest hit of the century. They call it *Paradise*, or, *A Day in Paradise*, but it's really Olanda. We bought the system and installed it right here in the ship. You won't believe it. You and Tara will be my guests, and there's even room for two more."

"That's amazing," said Nick, incredulous.

"Yes, I know it's hard to believe, Nick. But it's just like being there. I've been to the real Olanda twice, but I won't be going back. This virtual is just as beautiful, even better in some ways. You really have to experience it. Just let me know when you, your wife, and a couple of friends can come for a few hours and we'll have it ready for you. The show is so big in the galaxy now that some newlyweds are doing the extended virtual rather than actually going on a trip. It *is* like paradise."

After leaving the ship, Nick returned to the area where he had left Tara. He found her alone, curled up next to some bushes, with Rod asleep on her lap. The midmorning sun danced on her face through the overhanging foliage, and she appeared to be asleep. As he approached, she opened her eyes.

"Were you asleep?" he asked softly.

"No, I was praying for your safety," she replied.

"Where are Range and the others?"

"They went back for reinforcements."

"That won't be necessary. I've met them, they've taken down the shield, and we are invited to a movie, a virtual movie."

"Really?" she said, gathering Rod in her arms and then standing up. "What are they like?"

Nick proceeded to tell her about Orson and all that he had
learned as they rode their forcs back into town. After passing the
word in town that reinforcements would not be necessary, they
stopped before going home to order flowers, "a lot of flowers," as
Orson had directed, for Peat and Rakel's funeral.

"Hi, Tara. Hi, Mr. Bartok," Frecka greeted them as they
entered the store. (Nick had long since given up trying to be called
Nick without the Mr. in front of his name.) "What can I do for
you?"

"We need flowers, Frecka, for Peat and Rakel's funeral."

"Oh, yes, I heard. How dreadful! Mr. Peat came quite often
to buy flowers for his wife or one of his daughters. I'm so sorry to
hear they were killed."

"It was a terrible mistake," said Nick. "They've already
removed the electrical barrier that caused their death. They had it
up because they had heard about the Thorns. When I told them
what happened they were extremely sorry and asked what they
could do for the family. I didn't know what to say except that
flowers would be appropriate. So they asked me to buy plenty of
flowers."

"Oh," said Frecka, "I could see how they would be worried
about the Thorns. Didn't they know that there were people
nearby?"

"Apparently not," said Tara. "That's what they told Nick
when he went to talk to them this morning."

"I'll make up some really nice arrangements for them. They
were such a fine old couple. Mr. Peat always had a way of saying
something that made me smile."

"We didn't know them ourselves, but people are saying so
many nice things about them," added Tara. "I'm glad their
children are all grown up."

"Speaking of the spaceship," said Nick," They have a special
video presentation there called *Paradise* that they say is quite a
heavenly experience. It features islands floating in a warm ocean

with trees you can actually pluck fruit from with the most wonderful tastes you can imagine."

"That is hard to imagine," replied Frecka. "How could they do something like that within a hard, metallic ship?"

"Well, it's not real, that's true. Nevertheless, they create the sensations that make you feel that it's genuine."

Frecka reflected a moment and added, "Then it has to be terribly expensive."

"Orson's showing it to Tara and I, and he said there's room for two more. Would you like to go?"

"Oh, I'd love to," she answered, her excitement obvious. "Do you think Thad could go too?"

"I think that would be wonderful," said Tara. "We'd love to have you both come with us."

"I can't wait to tell him," she said.

On their way back from the florist shop, they saw Range and told him about Nick's visit to the spaceship, and then they returned home. The next week passed without any more trouble. Although the townspeople were initially alarmed by the presence of the two spaceships, as the days passed and nothing happened, they lost some of their concern. After what happened to Peat and Rakel few wanted to go anywhere near the ship. Most were glad that the visitors on the edge of town stayed where they were.

Frecka, however, was anxious to see "Paradise." After leaving work, on the third day of the week, she rode over to Nick and Tara's house to ask them if they had made any plans yet for going to the show. As nothing had been decided so far, they agreed to go on the first day of the week, and Nick said he would ride out the next day to make arrangements. As he was leaving to go there on the afternoon of the next day, Tara asked him to notice Orson's wife and stepdaughter, in particular what they were wearing.

Nick returned later that evening from the trip.

Hi, darling," said Tara as he stepped inside. "Can I fix you something to eat?"

"Yes, I'd like some coloon soup if we have any left."

"We do. I'll get it from the cellar."

She brought it up and adding a few wood chips to the embers of the fire, heated it for him.

"Ah, that's good," he said after swallowing a large spoonful.

"Tell, me, did you see anyone else besides Orson?" she asked, taking a seat next to him at the table.

"Yes." I met his wife, Sabrina and his stepdaughter, Colleen. They came in while Orson and I were talking."

"Well, what are they like?" she asked, anxious to know more about them.

"They were nice," he answered between sips of soup.

"But what were they like, Nick? What were they wearing?"

"Let's see. Sabrina was wearing an airy white spun top with black pants and a lot of gold jewelry."

"What color is her hair?"

"Blond, platinum blonde, with orange and red highlights in it. None of it may be her real hair coloring."

"What was Colleen like?"

"She was there for only a short time while Sabrina introduced her. She's fifteen years old, pretty, with lovely green eyes and very light skin."

"What was she wearing?"

"Let me think." he closed his eyes a moment. "She was wearing an unbuttoned medium green sweater with half sleeves. Then under that, she wore a white blouse with the cuffs partially rolled up and light tan pants. I don't believe she had any jewelry or make up on."

"I'm so anxious to meet other people from space, Nick. Do you think Sabrina and Colleen will be around when we go for the movie?"

"Yes, the VM is set for Sunday afternoon and I think they'll all be there to meet us."

"Wonderful," she said with a big smile. Immediately her smile faded as she added, "I don't know what to wear."

"Darling, you look very nice in what you are wearing now."

She smiled momentarily and then seemed reflective. He knew she was thinking of what she was going to wear for the occasion.

Chapter Eighteen

Early the next Sunday afternoon the four of them set off on their forcs to see *Paradise*. They were in high spirits. Tara had left Rod with her sister, Shari, and felt a sense of freedom and adventure she hadn't experienced since Rod was born. She rode ahead with Frecka while Thad and Nick brought up the rear. When they reached the area of the ship they were met by one of the guards, whose name was Tyrone.

"Well there you are," he said. "We've been expecting you. Come along, and I'll let them know you're here." He spoke briefly into his communicator and led toward the ship, chatting as he did so, apparently glad to have visitors. He escorted them to the entrance where they could see that Orson, Sabrina, and Colleen were waiting for them.

"Well, do come in," said Sabrina. "It's nice to see you folks. I'm Sabrina, this is my stepdaughter, Colleen, and of course, my husband, Orson."

Colleen bowed slightly as she was introduced, and Orson said, "You folks sure look human enough to me. "Come right in," he added, holding the door open for them.

"This is my wife, Tara," said Nick, and these are friends of ours, Thad, and Frecka."

They shook hands and there was a bit of confusion over the Crystal way of shaking back and forth and the earth way of shaking up and down.

As they entered the ship and were led up to the spacious living room, Orson said, "Make yourselves comfortable and we'll get drinks for everyone."

"Yes," said Sabrina, still standing as everyone else was seated. "What would you like? We have or can make most anything."

"Nothing for me," said Nick quickly. "I'm just looking forward to the show."

"Same goes for me," said Thad.

"Well, then," said Sabrina, I know you're probably all anxious to see it, especially since it's you're first time. We can talk afterwards."

"That would be nice," said Tara. "I do look forward to getting to know you."

Sabrina looked at Tara and said, "Yes, dear, I'm sure we have a lot to talk about."

"So, let the show begin," intoned Orson. "Come, follow me into the theater." He led the way down.

The room was large and open, and in it was some strange looking equipment. In the center were four big, comfortable looking armchairs, which were fully reclined.

"Nick, I'm sure you've done VM before but I bet you haven't seen anything like this," said Orson proudly.

"No, I can't say that I have," answered Nick, as he looked around the room.

"It's all state of the art. Not many places outside of earth have it, and this is the only one that's been built into a spaceship," continued Orson.

"Where are the head monitors?" Nick asked.

"That's the real beauty of it," answered Orson. "There are none. The sensors and monitors are all built into the chairs and in the surrounding equipment. It tracks your pupils and ears allowing almost unlimited movement without confining you in headgear. You'll be surprised at its technical realism."

"One thing that's really special about this VM," said Sabrina, "is that it comes with different settings."

"Yes," affirmed Orson. "Even paradise can get boring after awhile if it's always the same."

"The settings," continued Sabrina, "add excitement to the VM. Of course, since this is your first time, Orson will adjust it to low level variation."

"Now if you each take one of the four chairs, we can dim the lights and you should be ready for quite an adventure," said Orson, rubbing his hands together with enthusiasm. "By the way, I should have asked you, how do you want to go?"

"What do you mean?" asked Nick.

"Do you prefer to go nude, with bathing suits, or totally clothed?"

Nick looked at Tara and back at Orson. "We would like to go in bathing suits," he said, walking toward Orson.

"No, no, you don't have to do anything," Orson explained. "It's just in how we program it. After all, the equipment sees through clothes anyway."

"We will go in bathing suits also," Thad said. "That's OK with you, isn't it Frecka?"

"Oh, I guess so," she answered. If that's what everyone else is wearing."

"OK, it's set. You'll all be wearing bathing suits this trip."

"Here, Tara, sit in this chair next to me," Nick said. They sat down, reclined, and held hands. Thad and Frecka took the chairs behind them.

"Lights, camera, action!" exclaimed Orson as he switched on the circuitry that would take them to paradise.

* * *

Nick woke up. It was twilight. He sensed the gentle undulations of the floating island and felt the soft coral breezes bringing wonderful fragrances of flowers and springtime. He saw Tara sleeping next to him and he reached for her. Her eyes opened at his touch.

"Good morning, my darling. Welcome to paradise."

"It's so beautiful, Nick."

"And you are so beautiful too," he said, caressing her. As they kissed, they heard the quiet call of a bird, announcing the beginning of the day. From a distance, another bird answered. They began kissing again, long and slowly, until Tara lifted her head. "Nick, we can't. We're at a movie."

"OK," he murmured. "It *is* possible that someone could be watching. I wonder where Thad and Frecka are?" he asked, turning to look around. "Are you ready to get up?"

"Yes." She took his hand.

Standing, they could see that light was just breaking on the horizon. Under their feet, they could feel the soft grass and the gentle current that ran beneath it. Not used to the soft sponginess, they held hands as they took their first steps in paradise.

Nick explained it to her. "This is what I was telling you about several months ago. What they've done is recreated the island world of Olanda in the star system of Pegasus. It's the planet I told you about where most of the land consists of floating islands on a tranquil sea. The islands are held together by interlocking plant fibers and buoyed up by an extensive root system with air filled tubercles.

"Yes, I remember you said it was the one place in the galaxy that you would like to be able to take me to. It's something like the vegetation in the lagoon where we collected medicinal plants, but on a much larger scale."

"Yes." Something soft bumped his ankle.

"Look," said Tara, bending down to pick up one of several little furry creatures that had just appeared. "It's a cute black ball of fur. I think it likes being held." She raised it up in front of her with both hands to try to get a better look at it in the hazy morning light. "Nick, have you ever seen anything like it?"

"No, not really, though it reminds me of a miniature bear cub, without the claws and powerful teeth. This one appears to be a vegetable eater, judging from the molars. The little animal seemed to be in a quiver of motion even while being held, and Tara moved the furry ball to her shoulder. There it seemed calmer and less agitated.

"I think that's what it wanted," she said. "To be on something. It's settled down now. I can feel a gentle vibrating sensation. It's very pleasant. You should try it."

Nick picked up one of the creatures and perched it on his shoulder. "Ah, that *is* nice."

Tara sat down, carefully so as not to sit on one of them, and several of the little furry balls climbed on her. "This is so delightful, Nick. Come, sit by me." Nick sat down next to her and several more of them climbed on him too.

"We should name them something," said Nick.

"How about 'Carebears,' suggested Tara.

"Yes, that's perfect."

For quite a few minutes, they relaxed together, letting the carebears do their gentle massage. As the daylight increased, they could see that they were near the edge of a sparse forest. The lacy low growing palm trees and other varieties of vegetation formed an airy canopy that allowed light to filter through the greenery. Nick turned to look in the other direction. "Look," he said, "now you can see the water." He quickly got to his feet, leaving four carebears scrambling to get off. Tara, too, stood up to face the sea. The newly risen sun played colorfully on the gentle waves and breakers giving them an amber cast, while a few white clouds hung suspended in the distance. "It's so beautiful, Nick," she said in a hushed voice. Toward their right, another floating island was just coming into view, and they watched as it slowly drifted across their vista.

"I wonder where Thad and Frecka are?" said Tara.

"They're probably somewhere on this same island. If we look, we can probably find them. I think it would be fun to go swimming with them later. Right now, I'm getting hungry. Let's try the fruit. You know," taking a good look at his wife, "you look delicious yourself in that bathing suit."

Tara looked down at herself. "Thanks. Do they really wear ones like this on earth?"

"Oh yes. With even less fabric in the past, but styles are always changing."

They walked together over the soft grass to the canopy of trees. Once underneath they could see luscious looking fruit hanging down from the branches. They looked just right for eating. Surprisingly, there didn't seem to be any on the ground. There were different colors and sizes, from bright rose colored and yellow to russet brown, orange and green.

"What a nice selection," said Nick as he selected a yellow pear-sized fruit and gave it to Tara. She took it in her hands and brought it up to her face.

"It smells wonderful. Should I bite into it?"

"Sure, but taste it first before swallowing to be sure you like it," he answered. He reached up higher for a russet colored fruit the size of a large orange. It too smelled wonderful and he took a big bite out of it. It was delicious.

"This is really good," said Tara, savoring the yellow fruit Nick had given her. "I would like to let Frecka and Thad know about this."

"Thad. Frecka." Nick called out loudly. There was no answer. "Maybe they are on another island," he conjectured. The carebears, who had scurried away at the sound of Nick's loud voice, came closer again.

"Let's take some of the fruit and eat it by the sea," suggested Tara.

"OK," Nick answered, reaching up toward a large white soccer ball sized fruit. When he touched it the fruit suddenly opened up and sprayed them both with its fragrant contents.

"Oh," said Tara, "this is delightful."

Nick gently set the fruit he was holding down and put his arms around Tara, who held several pieces of fruit in her arms. He held her as they enjoyed the last of the perfumed spray from the opened fruit.

"Wonderful," they said with one voice as the shower ended. The air was still filled with the aromatic scent as Nick picked up the fruit he had set down. Together they walked the short distance to the sea, and Tara picked out a spot where a small tree stood at the edge of the water. They set down their assortment of fruit and sat right on the edge of the island, legs suspended into the warm water and lapped by the gentle waves.

"What a place," said Tara, as she leaned back in the grass to lay next to Nick.

"Yes," he agreed. "Uni has done a wonderful job. I see no way to tell that we're not really on Olanda." As he reclined next to Tara, a carebear jumped on his stomach. "Shoo!" The carebear scampered away.

"I can see why honeymooners would like to come here," said Tara, contentedly resting beside Nick. He pulled a small yellow wildflower from the grass and teased it on Tara's face and mouth.

"That tickles," she smiled up at him. He turned, and kissed her lips softly.

Suddenly there was a loud clap of thunder. "What? Thunder in paradise? How could that be?" said Nick.

"Didn't Sabrina say something about adding excitement?" asked Tara, sitting up.

"Yes, that's right. She said that otherwise even paradise can get boring."

"Well, then. This must be part of the excitement. You know, I think the winds are starting to pick up too," said Tara.

"I wish we could tell them to leave off the enhancements. I was enjoying it as it was."

"Me, too," echoed Tara. "Maybe it will quickly pass."

There was another crack of thunder and the clear daylight they had been experiencing dimmed as gray clouds began to obscure the sun. As they watched, the water became choppier, and looking out, they saw that another island was floating past them. Something moving on the island caught their attention. It was a person. Peering more closely across the distance, they realized that it was Thad and Frecka. They were running quickly—running away from something.

Nick and Tara hailed them. Across the distance, they saw them stop for a moment. Nick and Tara continued to wave and shout at them, trying to get their attention. Finally, Thad and Frecka saw them and when they did they jumped into the water and began swimming toward their island. The thunderclaps began increasing in volume and frequency. One after another, the loud booming went on, and the sea roiled as the distant figures of Thad, and Frecka continued to swim toward them.

Now the winds were blowing harder, and the waves were increasing in size. They heard then the first tearing sound of electricity, followed by a sharp crack of thunder. A jagged bolt of lightning crashed into the sea. Thad and Frecka continued swimming toward them but their progress was slowed, hampered by the surging waters. As they came closer, they could see that Thad was in front, followed by Frecka. Then they saw that there was something else in the water with them. Watching helplessly from shore, Nick stared in disbelief at what he saw. A huge coiling green snake swam in the water behind them and appeared to be gaining on Frecka. "Hurry!" he heard Thad cry out to her. Frecka appeared to be tiring.

"Nick, it's a huge snake!" exclaimed Tara. "It's gaining on them!"

Nick turned around, looking frantically for something he could use against the writhing creature. Finally, he spotted a large branch that might make a good club. He tried breaking it against the side of a tree to shorten it and when that didn't work, he told Tara to take one side of it while he held the other side. Pointing to the nearby tree, they ran toward it. They struck the middle of the branch against the tree trunk and as it broke in two they both fell to the ground. Nick picked up the smaller side and so armed, jumped into the water and swam toward Thad and Frecka. He heard Frecka's shriek of horror as the snake coiled around her.

"Help! Help! screamed Thad, as he turned back to save her. Nick swam hurriedly toward them. He could see the huge size and length of the glassy green snake encircling Frecka's torso. Then he saw that Thad, too, was becoming enmeshed in another of the snake's coils as he tried to extricate her. As Nick neared them, the green monster reared its grisly head to strike. Nick slammed the club on it with all the force he could muster. The snake shuddered and its head dropped beneath the surface of the water but it didn't release its grip. Instead, it appeared to be trying to drag Thad and Frecka under. Thad was yelling as he fought the coil around him and he kicked to try to stay above water but Frecka appeared to have lost consciousness and was going under. Nick circled closer to them, cudgel ready, trying to locate the snake's head beneath the water to give it another blow. From the shore, he heard Tara scream.

"It's behind you!"

Nick turned in time to raise his club, and the snake lashed out, seized the club in its mouth, and disappeared again under the water. "Hold on, Thad!" Nick yelled as Thad valiantly fought to keep himself and Frecka from being pulled under. The club bobbed up in the water on the other side of the monster. Nick swam quickly toward the club, but just as he reached it, the coil of the long snake squeezed around his legs and he was pulled sideways in the water. Fear seized him, but he held on to the cudgel and prepared to try to give one last blow to the creature's head. Then he saw Tara swimming toward them.

"Go back! he yelled. "Go back!" She kept coming. The snake tightened around him and he fought to stay above water. As Tara reached them, he saw the snake raise its head once more, this time to strike Tara. With all his might he reached out and slammed the club down on it. At last, he felt the coil around his legs go limp and then he and Thad were able to free themselves.

"You got it, Nick!" said Tara.

"Thanks to you. Can you help me get Frecka back to the island? Thad, can you make it on your own?"

"Yes," said Thad weakly, still pale from fighting for air. "If you and Tara can get Frecka."

The four of them slowly made it back to shore. As they reached land and pulled their weary bodies onto the grass the sun came out and the wind died down. Frecka opened her eyes and looked up to see Thad watching over her. She smiled wearily as her eyes met his and he smiled too, and breathed a sigh of relief.

Nick and Tara saw that Frecka was awake and was apparently going to be all right. Taking a deep breath, Nick got up and went to Tara's side, putting his arm around her. Her hair was wet and her breathing was still deep from the exertion of bringing Frecka to shore. She sat up, and taking his free hand in her lap she regarded him proudly. A welcome sun reappeared from behind a cloud, warming them as they rested from their perilous adventure.

"Bravo! Bravissimo!" came a voice from above. Then they heard clapping as the bright lights of the studio flicked on. The four of them looked up in awe. They were suddenly back in the theater. Above they saw Orson and Sabrina looking down at them and clapping.

"What's the meaning of this!" said Nick as he stared at Orson and Sabrina. "Don't you realize you nearly killed us all!" He saw Sabrina whisper something to Orson.

"It was only virtual reality," said Orson with a laugh. "You were in no real danger. But you didn't know that did you? All the more impressive. You, Tara and Thad are heroes of first rank. I salute you. Wait a moment and we will join you down there."

The four left the central area of the theater and were met by Orson and Sabrina at its entrance. Although Nick tried to suppress his anger, he was in no mood for light conversation over drinks, and he sensed that all four of them felt the same. He quickly excused himself and the others from Orson and Sabrina's company. Sabrina was quite disappointed that they weren't going to stay, but she seemed to appreciate Nick's state of mind better than Orson. As they were leaving, she asked if it was all right for them to come to the Deplinth Festival, scheduled for the following weekend. She appeared to be so genuinely interested in going, that Nick said to her, "Of course, come as you are or in costume. Either way, you're welcome."

They exited from the ship, got back on their forcs, and waved good-by as they left the perimeter of the spaceship. When they were out of sight of the ship, Tara rode up alongside Nick andsaid, "I don't understand how they can act like friends and yet treat people the way they did in the theater."

"I know what you mean. I didn't expect it and definitely didn't like it either."

"Is that the way people are on Earth?"

"Most are not but some are. There are people on Earth who will do almost anything for excitement"

"That kind of excitement I don't need," said Tara emphatically.

Nick turned to face her, and reached for her hand. She returned his gaze and smiled, realizing that they were in complete agreement.

Riding quietly along together, they noticed that ahead of them Thad and Frecka were engaged in animated conversation. Darkness fell as they reached the center of town where the two couples separated. Nick and Tara went on to pick up their baby at Shari's house and after a short ride from there, they were glad to be at their own front door. Tara put Rod to bed, made her husband a warm drink, and after the intense excitement of the day, was content to be held in his arms.

Chapter Nineteen

It was Deplinth Day. A day the town eagerly looked forward to because it marked the beginning of spring and the return of warmer weather. The deplinth blossoms were right on schedule and their fragrance filled the air. Otherwise, it was a far from an ideal day. "Unusually cold for Deplinth," people were saying to one another as they hurried about doing their last minute preparations. Shops closed at noon, and they would remain closed the next day. However, with the weather cool and windy, and the sky overcast and dark, it didn't look good for the Deplinth Day dance that evening. It might even rain.

Like so many of the townspeople, Nick and Tara were getting ready for the dance. Nick was concerned about how the evening would go with their new visitors. They were coming, he knew, but whether it would be only Orson and Sabrina or if it would be the entire crew, he didn't know. He hoped young Colleen would come, because she, at least, seemed genuine and friendly. He especially hated the thought of having Orson's guards standing around. Knowing Orson, he didn't think he would come without them.

Though it was a costume dance, people could come however they wanted. At first, Nick thought he wouldn't wear one, but Tara had talked him into it, so he decided to go as a hunter. He used old clothes to make deerskin breeches and a jacket, cut a gun stock out of wood, added a dowel for the barrel, and made a cap that at least resembled coonskin. Tara had decided to go as a princess, something she remembered seeing on DV back at his spaceship. She looked just like one too, Nick observed, as he took an appreciative look at her in her costume.

"You look great," he said as they got ready to leave.

"Thank you, sir," she replied, curtseying a little in his direction. "I hope it won't be too cold for bare shoulders tonight."

"With the way that wind is blowing, it might be. Why don't you take a shawl?"

"Good idea. I can take it off when we're dancing."

They arrived later that evening at the fest, and looked for a table where they could be with their friends. Glancing around they saw Range and Tes seated at a large table with her mother, along with Thad and Frecka and his mother. Nick and Tara greeted their friends and were introduced to the two older women, who were sitting next to each other on the other side of the table.

"So nice to meet you," said Tara, taking each of the ladies hands in turn as they were introduced.

Before Nick and Tara had had a chance to talk with anyone else, a horn sounded, and Orson and Sabrina were ushered in, coming directly to their table. They were escorted by guards and crewmembers who were dressed as Roman soldiers, wearing leather cuirasses and carrying short Roman swords. Orson was himself outfitted as a Roman senator with a gleaming white toga and an honorary garland circling his dark hair. Sabrina wore a long, flowing décolleté gown with a gold chain around her neck, and a golden filigree crown woven into her platinum hair. She looked stunning. Following several steps behind them, as if wanting to remain inconspicuous, was Colleen. She wore a simple, but attractive kelly-green dress that accentuated her narrow waist and pale skin.

Orson wasted no time in settling down at their table. He introduced himself, Sabrina, and Colleen with a flourish to those there he didn't know, and Nick thought to himself that Orson probably would have liked for them to bow in his direction. Sabrina, too, held a regal bearing, but she at least looked at those around the table as if she would like to get to know them. Nick noticed that Colleen seemed embarrassed by her stepfather's display of pomposity.

Sabrina was quite interested in the tradition of the celebration, and Range and Tes explained to her the local customs relating to the event. Orson, on the other hand, though he knew nothing about it, spoke officiously about "native customs," "rites of spring," and other generalities that nevertheless seemed to impress Sabrina. The conversation was beginning to bore Nick and he was glad when the music started so that he could leave the table to dance. It was a slow cadence, similar to a waltz, and taking Tara's hand, they walked onto the dance floor. "What so you think of our guests from Algernon?" he asked.

"I think it's nice that they are interested in our traditions. Sabrina, especially, impresses me that way. I think Orson tries to act interested, but I get the feeling he's not, really."

"Yes, that's my perception, too. Isn't Colleen nice? Such a pretty young girl."

"Yes, but I sense that she's sad about something. I really would like to get to know her better."

More people were arriving on the dance floor, including Range and Tes, who chose a spot near them. "Tara, I've been meaning to tell you how lovely you look tonight," said Tes, as they passed while dancing.

"Thank you. I just love that dress on you," said Tara. "Is it made of linen?"

"Yes it is," answered Tes. "I'm so pleased with the color."

Orson and Sabrina, who had been dancing nearby, came over. Orson left Sabrina and said to Tes in a rather commanding voice, "May I have this dance?"

Range was startled by the request to cut in, which was not a local custom in Crystal. He looked at Tes who out of politeness was willing, then shrugged his shoulders and said, "Go ahead." He stood for a moment on the floor and started to go back when Sabrina said, "Range, why don't you dance with me?"

Range turned, and said with a smile, "Why not?"

The evening passed that way, with Orson apparently feeling that he could dance with whomever he wanted to at any time. As the night went on, however, it was apparent that he was helping himself to quite a few glasses of wine, and his step was becoming unsteady. Furthermore, he seemed to be increasingly interested in Tes, so much so that she and Range tried to hide by dancing on the other side of the floor.

With Range and Tes gone so much, Nick and Tara spent more time talking with Colleen and with Thad and Frecka as well as their mothers. However, whenever Orson came back he tended to monopolize the conversations due to his loudness and his habit of breaking into any discourse. The more he drank the more there was a noticeable slur in his speech and the less civilized he became. Sabrina tried to tell him to slow down his drinking, but he wouldn't listen to her and instead made fun of her efforts. Nick looked at Tara in silent acknowledgment that things were starting to get out of hand. Orson got up from the table, still holding his wineglass in his hand and left, saying he would find her. Nick, realizing that he probably meant Tes, went around the dance floor in the other direction to try to find her first. He was too late.

Orson was arguing with Range, insisting that Tes dance with him. Range, however, had had enough and furthermore could see that Orson was badly drunk. When Orson tried to take her from him Range pushed him back and Orson, tipsy as he was, fell to the floor. Then, the guards Orson had brought sprang into action. Pulsars drawn, they pushed through the crowd. Fortunately, Sabrina, who had followed her husband, came on the scene. She motioned the guards back, and taking Orson's hand, helped him off the floor. By that time, Range and Tes had disappeared. Sabrina didn't want to make any more of a scene and she tried talking softly to her husband to get him to settle down. When that didn't work, she raised her voice and began to yell at him. That got his attention. At long last, Orson waved his arm to signal his men that he was ready to go back to the ship.

With things starting to settle down again, Nick left to go back to his table. On his return, he saw that Colleen was engaged in animated conversation with Thad and Frecka. Tara was smiling as she listened to them talk. No one at the table apparently knew what had happened on the other side of the dance floor. Soon, Sabrina came back. Eyeing Nick, she said that she was sorry for everything. She started to leave, motioning for Colleen to come with her, and when she didn't follow, she said, "Colleen, we have to go now."

"Why, mom? I'm having such a good time. No one else is leaving yet."

"Just come with me now, honey. I'll explain it to you later."

"Please, mom, can't we stay a little longer?"

"Just say good-by, Colleen. We really have to go now."

Colleen reluctantly obeyed her mother and as they went off together, she turned and waved goodbye to them at the table. She had a sad expression on her face, as if she would never see them again.

"It's too bad she couldn't stay," Tara said to Nick. "She was beginning to enjoy herself. It's probably very lonely for her not to have anyone near her age on the spaceship."

"I'm sure it is," answered Nick rather cryptically.

Chapter Twenty

It didn't take long for word to spread about how crudely Orson had acted on Deplinth Day. The fact that armed guards were almost unleashed on the townspeople caused everyone uneasiness at having such dangerous and unwelcome neighbors on the edge of town. From mild apprehension before the incident, the tenor of the local sentiment went to outright fear and justifiable anger at the intruders. No one, however, knew what to do about it. Since there had been no injuries, most of the townspeople seemed willing to wait, in hope that the problem would go away. Others prepared for self-defense, and there were some that wanted to mount an attack.

Nick and Tara, having enjoyed the company of Sabrina and her daughter, Colleen, were less predisposed to see the "aliens," as many were now calling them, as all bad. Nevertheless, Nick knew that it was Orson who was in charge, and Nick didn't trust him. It was clear to him that Orson was there for one reason, and he felt that he would be very dangerous if crossed. Nick hoped that nothing would happen that would force Orson to choose between the townspeople and his precious oil, because Nick didn't have any doubt which way it would go.

After a time, things settled down in the town. People for the most part tried to ignore the presence of the spaceship at the edge of town. The aliens kept to themselves, went about the business of extracting oil, and didn't mingle with the citizenry. The only exception was Colleen. She had become a friend of Frecka's, and sometimes she could be seen driving her little rover car to her house.

The peaceful interlude did not last long, however. The first family to be affected directly by the oil operations was that of Jon Edars. Jon and Macy lived near the drilling area, and one day they noticed that their front porch was beginning to slant downward. Jon didn't think too much about it until the next day when he saw that his whole house was slanting in the same direction. Worried, he talked with everyone he could think of about what could be done. By the next day, it was already too late. Their whole house had subsided five feet into the ground and its walls were caving in. Theirs was only the first, as within three days two others began sinking. By this time, the townspeople were incensed. They could see that the homes were sinking in the area closest to the drilling, and those who lived nearby realized their houses could be next. Things were happening too fast. Before anything was decided on, thirteen more houses were affected, six of them so badly that they couldn't be lived in. The victims had had enough. Seventeen men, carrying an assortment of bows and arrows, clubs, shovels, etc., marched on the spaceship. They wanted to be heard, to demand that the drilling be stopped, before going back to repairing their houses. The weapons they carried were for self defense. They never made it to the ship. To a man, they were electrocuted at the charged perimeter boundary.

Now, the formerly peaceful inhabitants of Crystal were outraged. Everyone wanted to do something to avenge the deaths, but no one knew what to do against such power. The local officials called on Nick, as much out of helplessness as anything else. Nick confirmed their worst suspicions as to the strength of the ship and its firepower. As town representatives could think of no way to overcome their enemy, they asked Nick to talk to Orson about drilling in other areas. Nick agreed reluctantly to try to talk to him, although he didn't really think that Orson would move the drilling sites away from the town.

The next morning he set out, against the wishes and fears of Tara, to visit the spaceship. He had thought of bringing his old pulsar, which he still kept in a locked box, but decided it would look too warlike, and wouldn't help anyway against his well-armed enemy. His friend, Range, was going with him and the two met at an agreed upon place and continued together to the site. Range often encouraged Nick to speak with him in English and he was becoming somewhat proficient in using it himself.

When the two of them reached a point where they could see the spaceship, they dismounted from their forcs, tied them to a tree, and walked cautiously on, being careful to keep to open areas where they could easily be seen. They didn't want to be mistaken for combatants. They hoped that by coming obviously unarmed, they would be admitted. Nevertheless, they advanced cautiously, and Nick repeatedly threw pebbles ahead of them to determine if the invisible electric shield was still up. It was probably a needless precaution, since they should be able to see singed vegetation at the power point, but he didn't want to take any chances.

They continued walking, and stepping right up to the spaceship door, they quietly congratulated themselves for getting this far without any problem. The door slid open, and Sabrina stood at the entrance.

"Come on in, gentlemen," she said.

"Thank you," they replied. Then Nick said, "Sabrina, it's good that we can talk with you."

"Why's that?" she asked, preening her hair with one hand.

"Because I have the feeling that you have an appreciation for sensitive situations"

"Well, I feel somewhat flattered, but I really don't know what you're talking about."

"It's about the awful incident outside your ship last week."

"Yes, I know about that. I'm very sorry it happened. They were carrying weapons and just walked into the shield. Had they come in peace it wouldn't have happened. I hope you can understand that."

"We can try," said Range.

"Really," she said. "What did they expect of us? Just to let them come right up to the door? They were a mob, a very dangerous mob."

"But you didn't have to kill them!" Nick blurted out.

Range put his hand on Nick's arm for a moment as he began speaking to Sabrina. "People in town are very upset; now we know your side of things."

"I hope you will tell them for me," said Sabrina, wiping a tear from her eye.

"We will do that, Sabrina," said Nick. There is something else we want to say.

"Yes. What is it?"

"People are angry because their homes have been sinking into the ground. It's because of the drilling. We want to ask Orson to drill further away from the town."

"Of course I will ask him. He's sleeping or I would do it now. Orson doesn't want to hurt anybody. He's been working so hard to get on with this project that I doubt if he's even aware of any damage. I'll tell him later when he's awake. By the way, Colleen, you know, has taken quite a liking to you're little town. She tells me about it. She really seems to enjoy Frecka's company."

"Colleen seems to be a very nice girl," Nick replied. "I'm sure she enjoys having someone nearby who's closer to her age."

"Oh, yes, she does. I'm afraid she's going to miss Frecka when we leave. But, that can't be helped, so there's no sense being concerned about it now."

Nick and Range talked a little more with Sabrina before saying goodbye and leaving the ship. When they were out of sight of it, they talked.

"What do you think the chances are that what was said there will make any difference?" asked Range.

"Not good. I'm sure she will tell Orson, if it's necessary."

"In other words you think that Orson really was awake."

"Yes, I think he was, and if not, I feel sure everything was recorded. My guess is that he's fully awake. He is probably just letting Sabrina take care of negotiations. Not that she's just acting a part. She, at least, really does seem to care what happens to people. Anyway, I think he lets her represent his good side. She obviously thinks he has one."

"That's an acute observation, Nick, one I wouldn't have thought of."

"Fortunately, I don't think you have to deal with such complex people here in Crystal. But then, I'm only speculating about her. I could be completely wrong."

"Well, I definitely think you're right about the problem," said Range. "I don't think it's going to go away because of our talk with Sabrina."

"No, and unless it does we're going to have to do something."

"Speaking of that," Range added, "did you know that the Town Council is making plans right now?"

"Yes, though I'm surprised they didn't contact me. Not that I'm important to them, but I thought they might at least want to get more specific information on their weaponry, etc. from me."

"To be honest, I think they're a little bit paranoid in your regard. I'm sure they know you'd be the most knowledgeable about it, but they may be afraid that you'd choose the wrong side."

"So that's it. They are actually fearful that I would leave our beautiful town, my wife and child to side with them!"

"Don't let it upset you, Nick. They don't know you, so they're just being cautious. But speaking of taking action, I was just talking with Hall. You know, the well digger. He wants to talk to you about what we can do against Orson. I believe he thinks that you would know more than the Town Council when it comes to dealing with Orson, and I, for one, agree."

"Calm said something to me about the same thing the last time I was at his shop," Nick said. "Maybe the four of us can work together and come up with a plan."

"That's a great idea. We could meet at my house or yours and try to determine if Orson has a weakness we can exploit."

The two parted to go to their homes. When Nick opened his front door, he was still deep in thought.

"Darling, I'm glad that you're back," said Tara as she met him at the door. "I was worried about you. Is everything all-right?"

"Nothing has been settled so far. We could only talk with Sabrina. She said she would talk to Orson, but frankly, I'm not very optimistic."

"You mean Orson wasn't there?"

"She said he was sleeping."

"Sleeping?"

"That's what she said. I don't believe it either. That's why I don't really think anything is going to change. Range and I, and probably Hall and Calm are going to meet here in two days to talk about what we might be able to do."

"Please don't, Nick," she said, embracing him and lowering her head on his shoulder. Then she lifted her head and faced him, entreating, "Nick, please give it more time. Don't do anything dangerous. Let someone else take the lead in this. The Council is making plans. Let them be in charge."

"Darling," he said, his arms around her waist, "we're just going to talk about it. If the Council comes up with a good plan, we will stand behind it. Only if we think of something less dangerous or more likely to succeed would we bring it forward. So, don't worry.

Tara looked into his eyes and managed a smile. "That's right, honey. We both know what a poor planner you are." Before Nick could reply, she kissed him . Just then, the baby cried. She glanced back again at her husband as she went toward Rod's bedroom.

Nick watched her leave. This was another one of those times when he couldn't quite figure her out.

* * *

Two evenings later, four men occupied the chairs around the table at Nick's house. They looked closely at a map showing the town of Crystal and its environs.

"As best I can determine, the specific location of the spaceship is here," said Range, pointing to the site on the map.

"The oil drilling sites are to the left, here" said Nick, pointing, "and then they continue to this area behind the ship."

"The neighborhood where the houses are sinking extends from Peat's land to Vinnie's place." said Calm, showing the location on the map.

"We know that so far there have been no problems at all on the side east of the river," stated Hall. "It may be that they are being careful not to get too close to it."

"Yes," said Nick. "They probably don't want to get any water in the oil, especially since the oil is so close to the surface."

"Nick, you said they can be expected to have enough firepower to turn back a small army. What kind of weapons are they likely to have?"

"To start off, each person there, excluding possibly Colleen and Sabrina, would have two pulsars. You already know about the protective electrical shield. That barrier can be moved somewhat closer or further from the ship. At a greater distance, it wouldn't be as strong but it still would be powerful enough to kill us. Besides those weapons, the ship itself has a powerful laser which can burn right through an object as large as a tree."

"Well, so much for an all out attack," declared Hall.

"It would have to be a surprise to have any chance of success at all," affirmed Calm.

"Personally, I don't like the idea of killing them or of getting killed," said Range. "There must be some way we can drive them off "

"It's very likely they would fight if we tried to make them leave," Nick predicted. "Unless we could come up with some way to take away their defenses."

"What is the source of the power for their pulsars and perimeter defense?" asked Range.

"It's all electrical," Nick answered. "If we could somehow get in and disengage their transformers it would disable the laser and the perimeter defense but that would have no effect at all on their pulsars."

"Assuming we could get in to disconnect the transformers, is there anything you know of that would neutralize the pulsars?" asked Range.

"Nothing that we have here," Nick answered. "If we had a powerful electromagnetic wave generator we could jam them"

"That technology is beyond us right now," said Calm somberly. The four of them sat at the table, quiet now, with heads bent, trying to think of what they could do. Tara walked in from the baby's room. "Can I get anyone some fresh guava"

They all said yes, and soon she had a glass for each of them. As they took a break from the problem at hand, she took the opportunity to catch up with them about their families. Soon they were in better spirits. As it was already getting late, they decided to break up for the night and come back again in two days, hopefully with a fresh outlook on the situation.

After seeing the last man out the door, Nick and Tara turned to each other. Nick sighed. "It's very difficult to do anything at all against such power."

"I understand how you feel, Nick. I know somehow there will be an answer."

Two nights later when they met a lot had changed.

Twelve more killed," stated Hall, with bitterness in his voice.

"And seven more houses in ruins," added Calm. "They're putting up some of the families at the church hall for the time being."

"The townspeople are up in arms," continued Hall. "It's the only thing anyone is talking about. Everyone wants to know what can be done to make them leave."

"How were the people killed?" asked Nick

"They were an expedition organized by the Council," answered Range. They were sent to the shield to try to break through it. The idea was to put some large logs, etc. at the shield to drain its power."

"They came to the shop to get some scrap iron to use for it," added Calm.

"Anyway, it could have worked," said Hall, "but then Orson moved the shield a little further out and they were all killed."

"Now, I'm convinced he will stop at nothing," asserted Nick, angrily.

"The Council has been recruiting more people," stated Calm. "They're having no trouble getting together a lot of young men who are anxious to fight. I hate to see it because we are so defenseless against their weapons."

"They feel they have to do something," said Hall.

"We've got to figure out some way to overcome their defenses." Nick declared. "Calm, you have a lot of iron at your shop, don't you?"

"Yes, plenty."

"One thing we may be able to do is to make shields for the men. The iron will give some protection from pulsar power, especially if it is attached to wood so that it's insulated."

"How big, and how thick does it need to be to stop a pulsar?" asked Calm.

"Ideally man size, but that would be too heavy to carry so we'll need to compromise. At about an eighth of an inch thick, a shield should withstand pulsar power for up to a minute. More than that would probably be too heavy to carry. I think that a size three feet from top to bottom and two feet wide would offer some protection without being too heavy.

"I'll try making one that size and see how it turns out," said Calm.

"That may help if we can break through the perimeter shield, but we still don't know how to do that," said Range.

"I have an idea," said Hall. He stood up and began pointing on the map. "See, the river runs near where they are drilling on the plain. The spaceship is situated in a low lying area, opposite the river's bank and beneath this small hill," he pointed out the exact location on the map. "With enough manpower, why couldn't we dig a trench across the bank and channel through the hill, letting the river through to flood them out?"

The other three men looked at each other with skepticism.

"Do you really think we could do that?" asked Calm. "It sounds like a massive undertaking."

"It is to be sure," answered Hall. "I know the lay of the land there and have no doubt that it's feasible. With enough people digging, I think we could do it."

"It's the best idea we've had yet," said Range.

"Yes," agreed Nick. "And what is very important to us is that they can't run a force field over water."

"We should take this right to the Council," said Range. "Better to have all those volunteers digging rather than being killed."

"We will need to be very careful so that Orson doesn't find out what we're doing," said Nick.

"Hall, that's a terrific idea," said Calm, giving Hall a big pat on the back.

"It sure looks workable," said Range. "I think the Council will approve it and supply us with the manpower."

"I'll get right to work making shields and shovels too, if needed," said Calm. "Nick, if you can come over to the shop sometime tomorrow, I'd like you to check out the design for the shields."

"I'll be there early," said Nick.

Chapter Twenty-One

Over the next several days, there was a lot of activity in the town. The Council approved the plan, and the volunteers were deployed to work with the "Team," as the four planners came to be known. One group was sent to Calm's foundry to make shields. Another went with Hall to map out the area that would be submerged and to create barriers where necessary to contain the water within the targeted area. The largest group was assigned to work on the extensive tunneling that was necessary to divert the river, named Sorber, toward the spaceship.

Everything had to be done with utmost secrecy for the trap to be successfully sprung. The leaders decided that it would be safest to start an initial tunnel in the woods where it couldn't be seen from the spaceship. That tunnel would lead to where they would start a larger one that would carry river water toward the ship. The Sorber was not a major stream, and in most places, was no more than four or five feet deep and about forty feet across. The trench across the river's bank, as planned, would lead the water directly toward the side of the hill, which once tunneled through, would open directly onto the plain where Orson's spaceship stood.

After Hall returned from surreptitiously surveying and topographically mapping out the area, it was time to begin the digging. This was going to be the hard part of the job. Nick took a crew of five. Their task was to dig underground to where the main tunnel would begin. Range took five more volunteers to start a second entrance on the other side. Both tunnels were begun in woods where the dirt could be brought out and yet not be seen from the ship. The plan was that they would dig toward each other, meet in the middle, and then proceed together carving out the main tunnel leading toward the river. Once they neared its bank, they could employ more manpower to finally connect the tunnel to the hillside leading toward the ship.

* * *

"This isn't easy," said Tain, as he lifted his shovel for the four hundredth plus time.

"It sure isn't," agreed Carlt, who was working alongside him. "Ready," he called to the men standing above the hole. The three of them pulled the heavy bag of soil up to the top.

"We've already got enough soil on this side," said Nick. "Let's start a new pile over there." They dragged the burlap over and dumped it. Returning to the hole, Nick asked, "Are you guys ready for a change yet?"

"Sure," they replied.

"I'll go down this time," said Nick. "One of you guys can take a break."

"I'm OK," said Tain. "Don't really need a break yet."

"Me too," spoke up Carlt.

"Colbert and I can relieve them when they're ready," said Darr. "Why don't you stay on top and tell us where to put it."

Nick grinned. Did these young men, barely twenty, think that he, at twenty-nine was too old for heavy digging? "OK," he answered.

The work of excavating the two entrance tunnels continued until the next day. At last, they were joined, and from there the tunnel was enlarged as it led toward the river. It was then that they were able to utilize a large team of workers. Hall directed the digging so that it kept going in the right direction and so that it didn't get too shallow or too deep. He showed the team of men working with him how to make reinforcements wherever the earth was too loose in order to prevent cave-ins. Besides the shoveling, the other difficult job was removing all the soil. They couldn't take the chance of placing it anywhere where it could be spotted from the ship. It all had to be hauled back through the smaller tunnels and disposed of in the woods. There it was building up so much that they had to spread it out over larger and larger areas so that it didn't get too high.

At last, they finished the main sections of the tunnel. Now, before opening it to the river, it was time to make the final preparations for the attack.

The Team met at Range's house. Hall, Calm, and Nick were there along with Storch, who represented the Town Council.

"The problem," said Calm, "is that we don't know what they're going to do once the water hits them."

"It will quickly disable the perimeter defense," said Nick. "We won't have to worry about that."

Hall reported his calculations. "If my figures are correct, the water level around the ship should be approximately six feet deep. It will be several inches above their entrance door and it should also submerge just about all the places where they have been drilling."

"After we flood the plain a rational person would cut his losses and leave," said Nick. "I'm sure he has collected a large quantity of oil by now, and the water will make further extraction difficult. Unfortunately, Orson doesn't impress me as being a levelheaded engineer or mathematician. I think he will try to do what it takes to win a battle even if he loses financially."

"I get that impression of him too," agreed Range.

"That means that we'll need to be prepared to fight," Hall asserted.

"That's true, though if we can discourage him enough he may go home without an all out battle," Nick replied.

"Do you have any ideas on how to do that?" asked Range.

"Nothing definite," Nick admitted. "Just a feeling that if we can keep pressure on him without igniting his ire, he will give up."

"The shields are ready, all thirty-six of them including three full body extra thick ones," said Calm with some pride.

"We have eighty-two bows now and are making more. There are over two thousand arrows left from the battle with the Thorns," said Range.

"I've rounded up twelve boats, and most of their owners," added Hall.

"The town also has four you can use," said Storch.

"That makes sixteen," said Nick. "As for their manpower, I estimate they have eight guards, most of who double as oil field workers, and three engineers."

"That's not a lot, compared to the over a hundred that we can easily field against them," said Storch.

"Remember that all of their men will have pulsars, which are not only more destructive but can shoot at least ten times as fast as bows," said Nick. "We will need to make sure our men are well protected."

"Nick, I think it would be instructive for you to demonstrate the power of the pulsar to the men before we engage the enemy," remarked Range.

"Good idea," Nick answered.

The meeting broke up late that evening. They knew they would need another day to make the final preparations. Then, on signal, they would unleash the water to flood the plain.

* * *

It was dark and breezy on the day of the attack. The sky was filled with clouds and a cool dampness seemed to penetrate everything. Over a hundred men were up and moving about before the light of day while most of the townspeople were still sleeping. Since secrecy was critical, there had been no announcement, though everyone in town had known it would be soon.

The troops were dispatched to the chosen locations, while underground at the small hill near the ship half dozen men shoveled carefully. They were removing just enough soil to permit the water to sweep through without giving any notice to the enemy of what was being done. On the other side of the tunnel, at the river's edge, another dozen men waited for word to break through the remaining soil that would carry the water through the tunnel into the plain.

When those nearest the ship finished their digging, they hurried back through the two entrance tunnels and hastily caved them in before emerging from the woods. A signal was given, and the troops at the river easily broke through the wall of sandy loam that remained. They laughed aloud as the river found the opening, gushed through it and rushed through the tunnel toward the ship. It slowed for a moment when it hit the remaining soil on the other side of the hill, then quickly pushed through and flowed onto the plain.

Water quickly reached the invisible electrical barrier, and for a moment it stopped as the electricity vaporized it into a cloud of steam. The force field couldn't withstand the tumult of water for long, and as it broke down, the volunteers, stationed behind trees at the edge of the plain, could hardly hold back their excitement.

Although they couldn't talk, so as not to give away their positions, they saluted each other exuberantly as they saw the widening stream sweep forward to surround the ship. Nick was watching as the lights of the ship turned on. He saw shades open and figures moving inside. Ruskin stood alongside him in the underbrush and the two of them saw the ship's door open as the crew tried to assess what was happening outside. Then, they could see that depth measurements were being taken. Suddenly, a pulsar blast hummed out from the ship and then another and another.

A pained scream was heard above the sound of the gurgling, swirling waters, and Ruskin moved quickly toward the wounded man. "Get down!" yelled Nick. "Use your shields!"

The deadly humming of the pulsars continued awhile longer and then there was silence. Nick had a premonition that inside they were planning something. The water had already reached a level a foot over the entrance of the ships door where it remained and rose no further. Most of the window shades had been closed, and he could no longer see what was going on inside. All he and the others could do was wait. Time passed slowly.

"There you are," said Tara, finding him behind a boulder that was perched near the edge of the newly created lake.

"Tara! It's great to see you, but it's not safe here."

"We're bringing lunch. Aren't you hungry?"

"Yes, I sure am. Keep low. They've been shooting with their pulsars."

"I will," she said, handing him a wrapped lunch. "I have some more to pass out and then I'll come back."

"Tain, Carlt, Darr, and Colbert are a little farther to the right. You probably know that the main force is to the left."

"Yes. My sister and Tes are there, bringing lunch to them now."

She disappeared through the brush. In a little while, he saw the branches moving again and Tara stepped out and sat down next to him. Nick felt she looked at him with pride, and he took her hands in his. They didn't speak. She snuggled next to him, and he was glad to be near her for this short time. "You're quite a wonderful creature," he said softly, running his free hand along her hip. She looked into his eyes and wordlessly mouthed "I love you," in her native language. Then, she got up to leave. "Be careful, Nick."

Time passed slowly along the front. Very little movement could be seen at the ship or along the shore. Eventually the last light of dusk gradually faded into darkness. The rain they had been expecting had not materialized, though the sky remained overcast and bleak. The Team of Nick, Hall, Calm and Range kept in contact with each other via messengers and now that the darkness was settling, they grew wary, knowing that the enemy might try something under cover of night. They alerted their men to be on the lookout for any activity from the ship. In the dark, the lights of the ship took on a brighter appearance.

Then, inexplicably, all the lights were switched off. Nick knew that it was not normal for a spaceship to extinguish all its lights, and he alerted the others. Night came over the land bringing a darkness unrelieved by moon or stars. Nevertheless, they could still make out the tall spaceship outlined against the dark clouds, and the water could still be seen as a dark, silvery sheen in front of them. The wind had died down, and that was to their advantage, for it would be hard for the enemy to launch boats without disturbing its surface. Except for the sound of a wild bird that occasionally cried out from the forest, there was silence.

Time crawled as they waited. Nick decided to try an experiment. Reaching into his pocket he drew out a small, flayed piece of wood tipped with flint. Striking it on the rock in front of him, it began to smolder. He blew on it and it caught fire. Then he attached it to a thin reed that grew near the rock. He lifted the burning reed above the rock. A flash of light burst over him and he heard the hum of the pulsar in the distance. The undergrowth behind him steamed from the heat. Nick grinned wryly at the success of his ploy. The enemy was obviously in a high state of watchfulness. It was likely that they would soon make their next move. He contacted a messenger and sent word to the others to be ready.

Then he heard a faint movement in the bushes. He wondered if it was an animal. As the sounds came closer, his hair stood on end and he withdrew his pulsar from its holster and waited, listening. Whatever it was, it was coming toward him. He got up and crouched on his feet. He knew that it was now very near. Then Tara stepped out from the bushes.

"Tara! What are you doing here?"

"I heard in town that you and the men would be on guard overnight. I came to bring you a blanket so you'll be warm."

"Tara," he said, trying to calm himself, "Get down here by this rock. Thank you for the blanket. I appreciate it. But please don't come here any more than necessary. It's just too dangerous. They're shooting at anything they see that moves. I suspect that soon they're going to try to break through our defenses."

"Honey, I can't stop thinking about you. Knowing you're out here with your life in danger, I can't just sit and do nothing. Please don't tell me you don't want me to come."

"Darling, you know I don't mean that. I just don't want you to be hurt." He took her in his arms and held her close. She turned in his arms to face him. They kissed, and sensing her fear for him, he told her, "Don't worry, Tara. They're not going to be able to break through our defense."

She combed back her hair with her fingers and rose to leave, blowing him one last kiss as she did so. Across the distance, Nick heard the hum of a pulsar and he turned toward it. Then he heard Tara fall to the ground. As he jumped up to go to her, another pulsar hummed and grazed his arm near the elbow. He grimaced in pain and crawled toward his wife, falling at her side. "Tara," he whispered, but she didn't answer and didn't move. Getting to his knees, he bent down, lifted her lifeless form, and held her tight. He could see the ugly burns on the side of her neck and face and with numb hope he pressed his fingers on her pulse, beseeching God, "Please, let her live."

Suddenly, from all around him he heard men yelling. "They're coming! They're coming toward us!" He quickly wrapped the blanket around Tara and turned to look out from behind the rock. He saw eddies in the water and could just make out the outlines of men in small pontoons. There were seven boats coming in their direction. He gritted his teeth and fought back the rage he felt at what they had done to his wife. He passed the word, to wait until they were closer before firing. Stoically, he watched as they came into range. Finally, he shouted. "Fire! Sink their boats!" Saving his pulsar, as he had no way to charge it, he grabbed a handful of arrows and began shooting. In the distance, he could hear the havoc he and his men were wreaking. He heard the enemy yell, "Help, we're sinking!" and he heard at least two of them cry out in pain. He felt a hot glow of satisfaction, as he watched the vessels turn back carrying their wounded. Finally, he called out, "hold you're fire, men. We've got them on the run."

Chapter Twenty-Two

Morning dawned cool and crisp. The skies were clear and the brightness of the dawn promised that soon the sun would appear, spreading its warmth over the land. But the night's victory and the weather meant nothing to Nick. He knelt down beside his wife and wept, praying that somehow she would survive. Then he heard Ruskin's deep voice calling out.

"Anyone hurt over here?"

"Yes," he called out, "This way."

Ruskin turned the wagon toward them, and stepped down, as did Thack. They walked the few paces through the bush to them.

"Oh my God!" he said, as he looked down at Tara, his granddaughter. He knelt at her side and saw the terrible burns on her neck and face. "How did it happen, Nick," he asked with faltering voice.

"They shot her," he answered without looking at him. "They just shot her."

"She needs attention right away. We need to take her to the Lab immediately. It's been a long time since I've seen burns this bad. Has she been unconscious long?"

"Since early this morning."

Ruskin bent his head down over his granddaughter. "At least her breathing is steady and she has a weak pulse. Once she wakes up, she's going to be in a lot of pain. We can give her something to help with that. Very gently, Thack. That's the way," They carefully lifted her into the wagon. Ruskin nodded to Nick and turning the wagon around, began driving back to town.

Nick sat down and became immersed in thought. He realized the mortal danger of burn wounds, and knew that Tara's best chances of recovery lay with the resources of the ship. Pulsar burns were a commonality in the galaxy since colonists had pushed outward from earth. Even when they didn't kill, they caused terrible burns, which were never easy to deal with. Nevertheless, those who lived past the first two critical weeks could often be saved.

Nick considered his limited options. Knowing Orson, he couldn't count on any compassion from him, especially in the present situation. Did he dare try to sneak in and steal some of the ship's medical equipment? No, that would be almost impossible, and there wouldn't be anyone at the lab who would know how to use it anyway. The best he could realistically hope for was that there could be a truce. Even then, he didn't know if Orson would allow his medical specialist to do what needed to be done. For now, there was not much he could do for Tara. Just hope and pray that she could overcome the trauma and that her body could regenerate damaged tissue.

As for the situation out there in front of him, the next move appeared to be Orson's. The staging area and the oil drilling sites were now underwater. Orson was not accomplishing anything now, and unless he was planning to fight, there was no reason for him to stay. Yet, there he was in the spaceship across the water, not budging. His first attempt to break the defense had not succeeded. Nick didn't know for sure, but he suspected that Orson's oil ball was two thirds full. If he were right about that, the rational thing for Orson to do would be to leave. Why endanger his wife, stepdaughter and men for limited further gains. That was the way Nick looked at it, and that was the idea behind the strategy of flooding the oil fields. Now, it appeared that everything had backfired. Orson, his wife, daughter, and his men were safe within the spaceship, while Tara and at least one other defender lay near death.

Range wanted a meeting. The four Team members met at a halfway point among some trees adjacent to a sunny meadow.

"I'm very sorry, Nick" said Range, laying a hand on his friend's shoulder. "I know the Lab will do everything possible for her."

"Thank you," Nick murmured.

Calm and Hall also expressed their condolence.

"What do you think they're doing now, Nick?" asked Range.

"I don't know. I just don't know. They may be planning something. Otherwise there's nothing, including the water, that is preventing them from leaving."

"That's what's so unnerving about it," spoke Calm.

"Yes," said Hall. "We think we have them stymied, but maybe not."

"It's not that it's so hard on them," said Nick. "They have all the conveniences right there. They could wait a long time. Doing that wouldn't necessarily help them, however. That is, unless they thought we would go away. In the meantime their colony isn't getting any oil."

"There must be something we can do to change their mind," said Range emphatically.

"An attack on the ship would be suicidal," declared Hall.

"I just thought of something," said Calm. Why don't we put something in the water that would make it a lot less pleasant for them to stay?"

"If you mean something rotten smelling, I don't think it would work," said Nick. "They don't need to breathe our air. If necessary, they can go back to recycling their own."

"I have an idea," Range announced.

"What is it?" they asked.

"It's a little crazy, so don't hesitate to tell me what you think."

"Go ahead."

Range spent the next several minutes explaining his plan to them. At first, the others were doubtful, but as he answered their misgivings one by one, they began chuckling. Their somber mood was broken. Getting up from the makeshift table, they congratulated Range.

"So you guys don't see any drawbacks?" Range asked.

"Not at all. A brilliant idea. Simple, and yet effective," Nick answered. "I'm just wondering if we should give Orson a chance to surrender before we do it. It wouldn't be right to sink him without warning."

"He won't surrender until he sees his ship go down," Hall predicted.

"I'm going back to the forge to start working on the pierce points," said Calm. "It will be my pleasure to do this job."

"Choose a couple volunteers and let them help you," said Range.

"Yes," added Nick. "It would be safer if you also make two more of the full body shields."

"And two shields to place our best archers behind, in case they try using pulsars to separate the points from the poles," Hall suggested.

"In that case I *will* get a couple of volunteers," Calm replied.

"We'll need to get a lot of the men working on the logs," stated Nick.

"Let's get Lingo to handle that," said Range. "He'll know the most about it, and he will know the best way to dovetail the logs together."

"Anything else that we need to do right now?" asked Range. "Then let's get back to our posts. Nick, why don't you delegate someone to take your place for awhile so you can be with Tara."

"OK, Range, I'll do that. See you guys later," he said as he walked away. Immediately his upbeat feeling disappeared. He had actually forgotten about Tara for a while in the enthusiasm they all felt for the new plan. Somberly, he went back to his position. After asking one of the men to take his place until he returned, he began walking with long strides toward town and the Lab.

He was not overly optimistic. He had seen burn victims and the sight of scorched flesh was never pretty. Even with the advances in medicine, there was still not much that could be done for the victim for the first two weeks other than damage control, and protecting against infection. They had better painkillers than in the old days, and that was helpful, but recovery was still far from easy. Besides that, sometimes burn patients just died, despite the best medical treatment, often in an unanticipated and quick spiral to death at times when recovery seemed immanent. Definite progress had been made in the grafting process and it was no longer necessary to implement the primitive procedure of removing large patches of epidermis from areas less visible to graft onto areas that are more visible. Did they have that type of technology here, at Crystal? He doubted it. He had never seen anyone come into the Lab with more than a small burn. He would be surprised if the Lab did skin growths. If only he could get to the resources on the ship. Maybe he could, he suddenly realized. If the new plan worked as they hoped, it was definitely in the realm of possibility. His spirits lifted a little. Then he thought of his wife lying pale white and silent in the grass. His heart sank and he increased his pace to be near her sooner. He lifted his eyes to the heavens and asked for help. He didn't care, even if she was disfigured, as long she lived. That is what he prayed for. That she live.

* * *

He walked up the two steps to the Lab and opened the door. A clerk saw him and immediately said, "Come, Nick, I'll show you to her room."

She preceded him into the room and then exited quietly, leaving them alone. The room was darkened, illuminated only by one window covered with a semitransparent curtain. He came closer and saw that she was asleep. Loose bandages covered much of the left side of her face and neck. There was a strong, sweet smell pervading the room that he couldn't identify. Then he noticed two small candles burning within glass vials on opposite sides of the room. He didn't know what they were there for, though they were the source of the aroma. He took one of the two chairs near the bed, moved it next to her, and sat down.

He watched her sleep, saw her shallow but steady breathing, and after a time he closed his eyes. His mind wandered back, back to the time he had first seen her. How he had dreamed about her even then. It hadn't been that long ago and already they had shared so much. They had so much more to share. He thought of their son, whom he hadn't seen for three days. He opened his eyes, looked down at his sleeping wife, and gently placed his hand on her side. She stirred slightly, opened her eyes, and looked up at him. He stroked her shoulder. She tried to move her head to face him better and winced in pain at the attempt. He saw it and leaned over the bed so he could better meet her eyes. "My darling," he whispered.

"Nick." she said, her voice barely audible.

"Darling, don't try to move if it's painful for you."

"Oh, Nick, it hurts so much. I can hardly stand it."

"Hold on darling, I'll get some help." He turned, rising from the chair just as Doctor Gefert stepped in.

"Doctor, she's in terrible pain. Is there something you can give her?"

"I understand," he said, placing his hand on Nick's shoulder. "I was just coming for that. If you like, you can give it to her. In this covered glass is her medicine as well as her food. So as not to move her more than necessary we've been giving her food via a straw. I'll get her started and then you can take over. Nick, could I talk to you when she goes back to sleep?"

"Of course."

Dr. Gefert gently helped Tara to take the straw into her mouth and then when Nick was again seated he gave him the glass to hold for her. The two exchanged glances, but said nothing, and Dr. Gefert exited the room. Nick, for the first time, felt a bonding with the doctor, something that he had never felt before. He watched Tara and gently stroked her body. She stopped drinking and for a fleeting moment smiled at him. He was so glad he saw it because immediately it changed to pain. Even smiling caused her pain, Nick realized. The thought tore at his heart.

"Don't try to smile now, my sweet. There will be plenty of time when you're better. Just know that I love you very much and that we're all praying for you. When you get better, we're going to be able to do all kinds of things again. Just take it slowly now and do all you can to get well."

Tara closed and then opened her eyes, saying, "Yes," without words. She finished her drink and gradually appeared to be getting sleepier. She moved her hand slightly and Nick took it in his. Soon she was asleep. He held her hand for a long time before letting go. When he got up from the chair, he bent over and whispered in her ear, "I love you." Then he left the room.

He found Dr. Gefert in his office looking over some papers and charts.

"Nick, come in and sit down. Can I get you a cup of guava?"

"No thank you, Doctor."

"Nick, when Tara was brought here she was in shock. We were able to strengthen her heart's pumping action with massage and medication. It's fortunate that Ruskin was there in time with the wagon. She's stabilized somewhat now, but we can't say she's out of danger. Quite the contrary. The next ten days are critical."

"I know something about burns, Doctor, and understand what you are saying."

"Good. Believe me Nick, she will have the best care possible. After two weeks, we will need to begin the process of grafting skin. You probably know that it is not an easy process. We are not as advanced in this as you may be on earth. To do it we have to remove skin from other parts of her body. The alternative, however, is worse. Face disfiguring scars that she will carry the rest of her life.

"Doctor, just pull her through. If you can do that I will be eternally grateful."

"Nick, you know we all will do the best that we can. I think you know Trila. She is a highly responsible young woman. I'm glad to tell you that Trila has taken it upon herself to give Tara the best personal care possible."

"Thank you, doctor. I'm glad to know that."

"I should tell you that Carn, one of our soldiers, is also here. He is also being treated for burns. Fortunately, he was lightly scathed in comparison. In fact we will probably send him home tomorrow."

"That is good news."

"Those pulsars are terrible things, Nick. I can tell from the shape of the wound, that Tara was partially protected by a branch or something. A direct hit would have been fatal."

"I know. We are doing everything possible to inform and protect the men. We are also taking steps which I am hopeful will end this stalemate very soon."

"Nick, in that respect I have every confidence in you."

They shook hands warmly, and Nick went in to take a last look at his sleeping wife before leaving the Lab. As he walked down the steps, he saw Shari riding on her forc coming toward him. She waved as she approached.

"Hi, war hero," she said as she pulled up. "Here's someone I bet you'd like to see."

Nick watched as she removed the blanket covering his son. She handed him to him.

"Hey, big boy," he said as he enfolded his son in his arms. "How are you?"

Rod squirmed in his arms and showed his big, toothless grin. Nick looked back at Shari.

"He sure doesn't look like he missed any meals."

"He's a handful, so active, and yes, he's definitely a good eater," said Shari, bending down and making eyes at Rod as he settled into Nick's arms. At the moment, Rod was actively playing a game of peek-a-boo with Shari, closing his eyes, then opening them again and flashing a smile at her. Nick lifted him from his chest up into the air, and brought him back down. Rod giggled in delight, so he did it twice again.

"He likes that," affirmed Shari.

"He sure does," Nick said, holding Rod up in front of his face. "Hey guy, we're going to be doing a lot together, aren't we?" Rod looked somewhat doubtfully at him before giving him a little smile. "Yes, son," Nick continued. "Just you wait and you'll see how much fun we're going to have." He handed him back to Shari. "Shari, I really appreciate all you've done for Rod and Tara. I have to go back to the front now but all of us are looking forward to the time when this is over. Thank you so much for all your help."

"I'm glad I can help, Nick. Just be safe and take care. All our hopes and prayers go with you." They embraced, and he turned to start the long walk back. Before he got very far a wagon pulled up to him and a familiar voice said, "Could you use a ride?"

Nick turned to see the welcome sight of Ruskin sitting atop the wagon beckoning him to come aboard. "It's really good to see you," he said as he climbed aboard.

"Yes, you too, young man," said Ruskin as he flipped the reins to start them off.

Soon they were back at the lake. "I certainly hope that no one else has been shot since we've been gone," said Ruskin.

"Yes, for sure. Thank you for the ride," said Nick as he jumped off the wagon. "Take care, Ruskin."

"You too, son."

Nick thought about Ruskin's words as he walked the short distance from the trail back to his men. He had never called him son before. He was actually his grandson-in-law, of course. Still, there was something special about being called "son."

Returning to the battle area, Nick greeted and checked on the men assigned to him in his sector of the battle area. They were mostly young, these volunteers, some as much as ten or more years younger than him. They were high-spirited youth, fearless, it seemed, and he felt personally responsible to them and to their families. He didn't want to lose any of them if he could help it. Some of them were gone now, working with Lingo felling logs, cutting off branches, and sawing out the joint notches at each end that would link the logs together.

After meeting with those remaining and ascertaining that nothing had changed much in his absence, Nick decided to see for himself how the plan was taking shape. He circled back from the lake, planning to try to meet up with Range, when he heard the sound of sawing in the woods ahead of him. Following the sound, he saw Lingo and a dozen men working on two large trees.

"Lingo, how's it going?"

Lingo straightened up from his work. "Nick! Good to see you." He set down his saw and walked through the felled branches toward him. "Keep with it boys," he said turning back to his crew.

"Hey, Nick. This is quite a project making poles out of all these trees. Do you really think this is going to work?"

"Well, it's the best idea we've been able to come up with."

"Yeah. They've got all the power and resources. It just seems kind of crude, coming at them with wooden poles. Not that I'm knocking it, Nick. I work with wood, it's my job. It just seems like we could come up with something more sophisticated when dealing with an enemy like that."

"I hear you, Lingo. At first, we laughed at the idea ourselves. And yet, when we thought about it, we realized that it is actually a good plan, simple as it is."

"Well, I sure hope you guys are right about that," said Lingo, looking back at the tree his crew was working on. "You know, they never really told me the whole plan. If you don't mind my asking, how are these logs supposed to work?"

Nick proceeded to tell him how the logs would be joined together to form a long, straight shaft that would be floated across the water at a high rate of speed and directed at the enemy spaceship. He explained how the ends of the tree trunks were to be vertically cut to link them together, permitting flexibility while keeping the shaft straight as it speeds toward the target. Lingo said, "Hey, I see what you mean. In that case, we should save some of the upper branches on each of the last few logs for pushers, to give the boys something to hold onto.

"Good idea," said Nick. "We will use rope handholds as well. If you already have forty-six done, we really don't have to fell many more."

"Yeah, we're moving right along. Soon we'll clear a straight path for the logs and then move them into position. After that, we can start working on the end notching to link them together. That's heavy work and will take some time."

"I'm surprised you've done so much already," said Nick.

"They're a good crew, the boys that volunteered for this. I just show them what to do and they do it."

"I'm going on to talk to Range and I'll let him know how far along you are. We want to be ready to go when you're done. I'll see you later, Lingo."

"So long, Nick," he replied, and went back to oversee his crew.

Nick continued toward where he expected to find Range, and soon met up with him.

"Hi, Nick. How is Tara?"

"Not good right now. She's in a lot of pain. The medication helps but it makes her very sleepy. Dr. Gefert says it's going to be at least ten days before she's past the critical stage. He's doing all he can."

"He's a good doctor, Nick, and I know Tara has a lot of determination."

"I happened to see Lingo on my way here. He's moving right along with the logs. Soon he'll be ready to notch them."

"Glad to hear that. Calm is about finished making the points. In fact, they're already formed. Now he's sharpening and tempering them to make them harder."

"Good. Looks like we'll soon be ready to get everything in position."

"Yes. I'll have my men start clearing a path and get with Lingo so he can lay the logs along it. When ready, he can start cutting the joints."

"I'll do the same from my position and send some men over to help Lingo transport them when he's ready."

"Then we can give Orson the ultimatum. I'm looking forward to that."

"Me too. But I doubt if that will be enough for him. We'll see."

Everyone kept busy the next two days with the clearing of two straight paths and then hauling the logs, and finally making the joints that would link the timber together. When that was done, they cut enough wood away from the two front logs to securely fit the sharpened ram points onto them. The points were very heavy, which not only made them strong, but would also help to keep them lower in the water. Toward the end of the second day, after much hard work, they were ready. Nick looked with satisfaction down the long line of logs. He sent word to Range that his side was finished and that when Range was ready he could use the megaphone to announce the ultimatum to Orson. As it happened, Range had sent his courier to Nick at almost the same time, so the two of them exchanged messages and in only a few minutes both sides were ready to attack.

Nick smiled as he heard Range's voice in the distance. Range had done a remarkable job of learning English, but he still had an accent that sounded like the ancient Norwegian he had heard in an old movie.

"You are under attack. Surrender now or your ship will be destroyed. You have very little time left before the assault begins. You must surrender or you will be destroyed."

In the increasing darkness of nightfall, as every man looked toward the space ship, a light appeared in its upper window. Then Orson's amplified voice boomed across the dark waters.

"Ha, ha, ha, ha, ha, ha, ha, ha, ha, ha, ha, ha, ha, you mindless creatures." Don't you know I can destroy you all with the flip of a switch? There's nothing you can do to harm our ship, but if you even so much as try, you will pay dearly. I don't really want to hurt you poor, ignorant creatures, but I am losing my patience with you. Open up the levees or you will taste the bitterness of my wrath!"

"It doesn't sound like he's ready to give up," said Nick to one of his men. Then he sent a message to Range and Hall to prepare for the assault and another to Calm and his men to join him in launching the second projectile. When Calm arrived with reinforcements, they directed their men to take their positions along the line of tree trunks. Then they stationed two stalwart men near the shoreline to handle the large shields. The two stood a little apart so that the log projectile could enter the water between them.

The signal was given to begin. At first, the long line of tree trunks didn't budge, but as the men braced themselves, it started to move into the water, slowly at first, and then with increasing speed toward the ship. Suddenly, shafts of pulsar beams burst from the ship. The beams struck the thick shields, which withstood the blasts long enough for Nick to hastily order those in the front line to move back out of danger. For a time the two shield bearers held their ground. Then one of them yelled, "It's getting hot! I can't hold out much longer!" Nick rushed to him and poured the contents of his water flask on his hands and shield handles, splashing what was left on the smoldering wood that backed the metal plate.

"More water!" Nick yelled. Then, the pulsar fire stopped, and as he watched, a beam of light from the ship flooded over the water, appearing to track the position of the poles. The long shaft was still moving toward its target and was already about two thirds of the way to the ship. As it continued to pick up speed, the pulsars started blasting in unison at the logs, causing them to steam in the water. Then Nick realized what the enemy was doing. They were trying to cut the shaft in two! He had hoped that the water would protect the timber, but now he was afraid that the power of several pulsars directed at one spot might vaporize the adjacent water, leaving the wood vulnerable. It was hard to see clearly from his vantage point what was going on. He backed away from the long shaft of logs, in case they started firing toward shore again, and climbed a nearby tree to try to see how the wood was holding up to their firepower. Once he got a good look, he quickly hurried down. "Bring back the logs!" he shouted down the line. "Pull it back! Quickly! They've just cut through one of them!"

The men groaned as they shifted positions and pulled the heavy logs back, back, back, until finally they heard the signal to stop. They let the weight down and dropped exhausted along the logs gasping for air. Nick went down the line and said, "Good job, men. That's enough for tonight." Then he went back to the front with Calm and, by candlelight, they looked closely at the charred log. "Look at that," he said to Calm. "They almost cut through it."

"A good thing you saw what was happening in time," said Calm on seeing the huge hole in the log. "Not more than one fourth of the wood left."

"I hadn't figured that they would mass fire their pulsars at one point like that. If there was just some way to get it under the water instead of floating it on top."

"I know a way," said Calm.

"Really?"

"Yes. We can tie heavy steel balls with chains at the ends of each log. That way the logs will stay underwater and will rise up to the ends of the chains."

"I can see how that might work, but the pole would be that much heavier to move with all that extra weight attached."

"That's true."

"We need to find out what happened on Range's side. I just realized we haven't heard a thing."

"We haven't notified him either," stated Calm.

About ten minutes later, word came back. Range had launched the projectile, but it was stopped when the pulsars caused the shields to become so hot they couldn't be held. Once the pulsars were directed at the logs, Range had likewise pulled back the pole. Nick sat down to digest the sobering news that neither of them had succeeded. Yet, as he thought it over, an idea came to him. He stood up and looked for Calm, whom he found in conversation with some of the men. He caught his attention and they stepped aside to talk.

"Calm, I just thought of something. We don't need to increase the weight of the logs. We just need to increase their speed through the water. We came close to striking the ship and I think Orson must realize that. All we really need to do is to replace the damaged logs, attach the points onto new logs, and provide extra protection for the shields so nothing slows the speed of the shafts. Then they will reach and penetrate the spaceship before they have time to cut through the wood."

"It might work but what can we do to prevent the shields from getting too hot?"

"The first thing we should do is to soak the wood on the inside of the shield. Then we need to provide thick protective coverings for the shield bearer's hands and arms. Lastly, we need to have buckets of water handy that we can use to help dissipate the heat if necessary."

"I think that would do it," said Calm.

"OK. Let's meet with Range and Hall to go over the plan so that each team knows exactly what to do so we can act in tandem."

Leaving two others in charge, Nick and Calm walked together through the trees and underbrush until they reached the far side of the lake. There they made out the shapes of Range and Hall sitting on opposite sides of a large tree stump.

"Good to see you guys," said Range as they approached. "Pull up a clod and join us."

"Thank you," answered Nick as he and Calm did just that.

"Could I interest you fellows in a little caboola tea," asked Range, putting his hand on a small kettle resting on the tree trunk. "It goes down real easy, I might add."

"Why not," answered Calm, "Pour me a cup."

"I'll try it," said Nick.

"Add a little more to my cup while you're at it," said Hall.

After dispensing the drinks, Range sat back, and stretched. Then, as casually as if they were friends just dropping by, he asked, "So what brings you gentlemen here tonight?"

"The caboola is excellent," said Nick

"We think we know how to get by their defenses," answered Calm, leaning toward Range.

Nick explained. "The only thing that prevented both of us from impacting the ship was the heating up of the shields. When that happened, we had to slow down the thrust of the shaft to protect the men in front."

"All we have to do is to take steps to prevent the shields from overheating and we can quickly send the point tipped logs directly to the target," added Calm.

"You definitely have a point there," said Range, much too nonchalantly, thought Nick.

"So, you're saying, we can do just what we've done, only faster?" asked Hall.

"Exactly," agreed Nick. The real point is, we almost won the battle tonight, and with some refinements we will be ready to win tomorrow."

"I'll drink to that," said Range, holding up his cup.

"Range, I think you've already drank too much," said Hall as he reached up to pull Range's arm down. "So tell us, how you think we can keep the shields from getting so hot."

They discussed a way they could protect the shields, and settled on the precise time when they would renew the attack the next day. Then they went over some details and decided that they would again give the ship a chance to surrender.

By the next evening, all the preparations had been made and the armed camp stood in readiness, waiting until Range again gave the enemy a chance to surrender. Time crept slowly until finally, the evening sun disappeared and darkness settled over them. Then, at last, they heard Range's voice call out over the waters.

"Listen, you invaders from another land. This is your last chance to save yourselves from attack. Do not be foolish or delay, for there will be no further warning. We will give you a few minutes to deliberate your course of action. After that, there will be no turning back. We will wait only a short time for your decision."

As Range's last words ended, there was silence both from the ship and from the shore. Those on the land surrounding the man made lake waited quietly for Orson's reply. When no answer seemed to be forthcoming, the stillness was broken by footsteps and quiet voices which gradually gave way to more activity and louder voices. Then, unexpectedly, a loud, booming voice echoed across the water.

"I am Orson, powerful ruler from a far distant land. We are here on a peaceful mission to bring energy back to a depleted world. To warm the home fires so children can play and mothers can prepare food for their families. We come not to take from people in need, but to provide for our own. We are on a mission, a mission to save a world far away from your knowledge. Now you stand before us with you're weapons of war and threaten us on every side. Do you expect us to back down? No, my friends, my enemy, we will not back down. We will fight to the bitter end. Let the testing begin!"

Nick shook his head, and could only say to Calm, who stood beside him, "What a conniver." Then, to the men who waited at the logs he said, "Prepare to launch! Ready with the shields! This time let's give it everything we've got! Get ready, lift up, go!"

The long shaft of the logs went with increasing rapidity over the water toward the ship. The searing rays of multiple pulsars blasted at the shields, which were angled away at the bottom so the logs could go through them. This time the pulsars targeted the shields for only a short time before being redirected toward the speeding shafts that surged through the water toward the spaceship. A veritable light show of pulsar beams lit up the darkness, allowing Nick to see that the second shaft was rapidly closing in on the ship from Range's position. His elation grew, as it appeared that they were both on target.

Then they all heard a loud CLANG as the projectile struck home, followed quickly by another. The spaceship shook visibly and it's lights dimmed and went out. Soon, however, the emergency lights came on, providing a partial glow. The ship remained upright. A door opened, and a large man stood at the entrance and appeared to look at the point where the metal tipped logs entered the ship. Then he stepped onto the log and started walking along it toward Nick and his men. A woman's voice from inside cried out, "Orson, come back!" The man turned his head back toward the ship, then abruptly turned away and continued walking toward them. He didn't look up, but concentrated on keeping his footing on the logs. As he got closer, Nick saw that in each hand he carried a pulsar.

"Stop, Orson!" he yelled. Orson halted, and lifting his pulsars, he fired in Nick's direction. The shot sizzled harmlessly in the woods. He continued hurrying along the logs, and was struck by an arrow. He cried out in pain, apparently wounded in the leg, because now he seemed to be hobbling. He stopped and raised his pulsars to fire again. Another arrow struck him, and he went down with a loud cry, falling sprawled out across the log. From inside the ship a woman screamed. Nick knew that it was Sabrina. Then she came out of the ship and began crawling along the logs toward Orson. When she reached him, they could hear her talking to him.

"Orson! Orson. My dear Orson. Talk to me Orson! Orson, please talk to me." Then she screamed. She covered his body with hers, laid her head down and wept bitterly. "Orson, I loved you. Why did you always have to be so stubborn? Why couldn't you ever be satisfied?" She laid her head on his body and wept.

At the ship, a small boat appeared. On it flew two large white flags, the universal sign of surrender. The craft was quietly rowed until it stood alongside Orson and Sabrina. Sabrina was helped in, and then they got Orson. Quietly, they rowed back to the spaceship. Those watching on shore heard only the dip of the oars and Sabrina's continued sobbing. The small group entered the ship, closed the door and then there was silence.

Chapter Twenty-Three

Day broke bright and clear. Across the water, the spaceship ports were decorated with white flags. Nick had not taken much part in the spontaneous festivities that broke out after the surrender. His heart wasn't in it. Now that it was morning, he wanted to finish the job so he could go back to Tara.

He was one of the first to awaken, and when he looked toward the ship, he saw that a boat was already being outfitted with white flags. He roused a courier and sent word to the team. They would need to establish the terms of surrender. In a hastily convened parley, he, Range, Hall and Calm decided among themselves what they would require from their foe. A short time later, the boat from the ship made it to shore, landing not far from where the long pole still spanned the water to its target.

"Good morning, sirs," spoke an older, bearded man. "My name is Jason Engels, and this is William Sanders, our geological engineer. Believe me sirs, neither of us wanted any part of this conflict."

"My name is Nick, and this is Range, Hall and Calm. Yes, we are very sorry that it reached this point. Accompany us to that small table there where we can talk. The six of them walked the short distance to the table and sat down in the rustic chairs placed around it. Nick began the discussion. "I don't know if you have been informed of the extent of the damages. Twenty-eight of our people have been killed, one of them a child who died when her parent's house caved in. Two others, one a civilian, have been injured by your pulsars, and twenty-four homes have been destroyed due to your drilling.

"We are very sorry about that sir," answered Sanders. Orson had not told us the extent of the fatalities or of the damaged houses."

Nick continued. "We have no desire for retaliation, for we are a peace loving people. However, in terms of a surrender agreement, we must insist on some conditions. We require that you give up your arms, as collateral and as positive protection for our people against any renewal of hostilities. Our main demand, however, is that you leave, as soon as your ship can be repaired, and that you never return within one hundred kilometers of Crystal."

"Let us talk briefly among ourselves, sirs," said Jason. He and Sanders stepped away from the table and for several minutes. They appeared to be immersed in intense conversation. Then they returned.

"Nick, may I call you Nick?" asked Jason. "We have every intention of leaving as soon as possible. Believe me, had it been up to us, we would have left long before damage had been done. As for our pulsars, we are willing to give you all our pulsars except two. The world being what it is, we ask only that you allow the two women, Sabrina and Colleen to retain theirs, with your kind understanding."

Nick and Range nodded to each other in agreement. Nick stated, "We accept your proposal with one condition. That is, that you allow us to inspect your ship for weapons initially, and then once a day until you are gone. Our inclination is to trust you gentlemen, but in our position we need to take precautions."

Sanders and Jason exchanged glances, and then Jason laid his hands on the table and said, "We accept."

Nick exhaled with relief, the terms were written down, and the six of them shook hands.

Jason and Sanders got into the boat and paddled back to the ship. In a short time later, two other men rowed back and turned over twenty-four pulsars. Nick picked two of them up and fired each at a nearby tree to make sure they were live. They were. Nick, Hall, Range and Calm decided that they could send most of the volunteers home. Out of approximately one hundred men, they determined that they would keep one fourth there to remain on guard. They drew straws to see which of the leaders would take the first day and Hall lost. However, Hall, and some of his men were needed to fill in the tunnel, which had created the lake, and to open the dikes. Consequently, Range, who had drawn the next shortest straw took the first day of guard duty.

The Team shook hands before parting company, and Nick gathered his things and started walking back along with a large number of the others. When they approached the main square, they saw a crowd of townspeople there, which had gathered to welcome back their heroes. Nick separated from the main group of those returning and made his way to the Lab. As he did so, his excitement increased at the thought of seeing Tara. He prayed that he would find her better. On reaching the medical facility, he realized that it was almost deserted; only a couple of forcs were to be seen outside the building. He walked through the main door, and not seeing anyone, went directly to Tara's room. Opening the door, he saw her sitting at the window ledge, leaning against its side. The bright daylight outside illuminated her figure in the otherwise darkened room. She turned and saw him and he hastened to her side.

"Darling," he said, his heart going out to her.

" Nick, I'm so glad to see you."

"We won."

"Somehow I knew we would."

"I'm so glad to see you up. I bet you're going to be home in no time."

"I hope so, Nick. Dr. Gefert says it's a day-to-day thing. He'll be here soon to do my face and neck again."

"What do you mean?"

"At least once a day he takes the gauze off, cleans everything and then puts new bandages on. It's painful but he says it's very important."

"I'll be with you then, when he comes."

"No, Nick. Please wait outside while he does it."

"But why? I won't be in the way."

"It hurts a lot."

"I'll hold you."

"No, Nick, please. Not yet."

"I don't understand. OK," he said, puzzled.

"Thank you, Nick. I think you really do love me."

"Of course I love you. I love you more than ever," Nick answered, becoming even more perplexed.

"Will you wait outside?"

"Yes, in fact I'll do that now, if you think Dr. Gefert is coming soon."

Nick kissed her gently on the forehead before leaving, and Tara held on to him as if she didn't want to let him go. He became aware of that, as he left the room. *She seems afraid of something*, he thought, but he couldn't think of what it might be. He looked for Dr. Gefert and soon found him walking down the short hallway looking at a book he held in his hand. "Dr. Gefert."

He looked up from his notebook. "Nick, good to see you. Congratulations, in defeating Orson and his crew."

"Thank you. Dr. Gefert. I'm concerned about Tara. How do you think she is doing?"

"Oh, then you haven't yet been to her room. She is much better. Not quite out of danger yet but getting there."

"I did see her. She said you're coming in for some kind of treatment."

"Oh, yes. She's doing well but with a severe burn like that, things can change without notice. That's why we have to be so careful. Another week or so and she'll be out of danger."

"Thank you doctor," he said, grabbing his hand to shake it. "I'll be outside her room when you're finished."

When Dr. Gefert returned twenty minutes later, Nick went back in. Tara was lying down on the bed, seeming more strained than when he had at first seen her. "Is everything OK?" he asked.

"Yes, I'm alright now." A slight smile came to her face as she added, "It's so nice to have you near."

Nick sat down on the edge of her bed, and moved his hand gently on her side and back. "That feels good," she said closing her eyes for a moment and then reopening them as Nick continued to stroke her.

"I sure will be glad when you're back home again."

She smiled wearily. "Sorry, Nick. I'm afraid I'm going to go to sleep again. It's the medication."

"It's OK. When you fall asleep just think of me here loving you."

"M'mmm, that's nice," she said closing her eyes.

Nick stayed there with her for the next hour and caressed her before getting up to leave. He had yet to see his son, and after that he needed to return to the ship for the initial inspection.

Unfortunately, since he was the only one in town who knew what to look for in a spaceship, it was necessary that he be there.

* * *

They met together at the bank of the lake as planned. He, Range, Hall and Calm stepped into two boats and rowed the short distance to the ship. The water had already receded more than a foot. One of the guards opened the door for them, and when they stepped in, Jason greeted them.

"Good afternoon, gentlemen. Can I interest you in some tea before you begin?"

"Not for me." answered Nick, "Thank you." The others also declined.

"Well, then, if I can't get you some tea, I'll give you the tour so that you'll know where everything is. Then you can take as much time as you need with the inspection. I assure you, we have nothing to hide."

Jason took them up to the different floors, showed them all the common rooms, and pointed out the private ones. Then he left them saying, "I'll be downstairs in the library. Just call me if you have any questions."

The four of them divided the ship into areas and went to make their inspections. It fell to Nick to enter most of the private quarters, since he was fluent in the language. As it happened, the first was that of Sabrina and Colleen. He knocked on the door.

"Who is it?" answered Sabrina.

"Nick. For the inspection."

"Come in," she answered, resignation registering in her voice.

"I'm sorry," he said, on entering.

"You've found everything you want here, haven't you, Nick?" she said, looking up at him from where she was sitting.

Nick turned from checking the room to face her. "Yes, Sabrina, I have."

"You're young, you've got your Tara. I envy you."

Nick continued to look through the room, not knowing how to answer her. Colleen entered from an adjacent room.

"I'm sorry about you're father, Colleen," Nick said.

"He wasn't my father, only my stepfather."

"She never did like him," said Sabrina, without looking up.

"Mother," Colleen said, coming over to hug her. "I love you."

"Why couldn't you even try to like him?"

"Mom, please don't try to make me feel bad." Colleen stood behind her mother and began massaging her neck and shoulders.

Nick finished in the main room and then went into the bedroom area, saying, "I just have to check in here and then I'll be done."

"Take you're time," Sabrina answered. "One thing we've got is time."

Nick finished the inspection and went to the door saying, "Well, that's all for today."

"If you see Frecka or Thad, please tell them I said hi," said Colleen.

"Sure will," said Nick, as he exited.

Nick went more quickly through the other rooms, until he came to one that was occupied by Brian Armando. Brian, he learned was the ship's nurse. He was a partially balding man in his forties who seemed to care little about appearances and spoke direct and to the point.

"So, did you sustain many injuries?" he asked.

"More deaths than injuries, due to electrocution from the perimeter shield." We did have two pulsar burn victims, one of them my wife."

"How are they doing?"

"The young man is going to be all-right but my wife is still in the Lab—hospital, you would call it. She's improved, although the doctor tells me she's not out of danger yet. Do you have much in the way of laboratory facilities aboard ship?"

"Yes, much better than most. Orson didn't spare money, in whatever project he was involved. I think I know where you're leading to, Nick. That is your name isn't it?"

"Yes, that's my name. I don't know if you would want to help or if you would be able to."

"How does it look?"

"I don't really know. I haven't been able to be with her very much due to being here and haven't seen her without the bandages."

"Were you the mastermind behind all this?" he asked sweeping his arm outward.

"What do you mean?" Nick asked.

"I mean the idea of diverting the river and using your homemade log shafts to disable the ship. That's what I mean."

"I had a hand in it, if that's what you want to know," said Nick, puzzled by all the questions.

"Well, I've got to hand it to you and your men. Defeating Orson with your Stone Age tools."

"You act like you don't even care."

"If you mean Orson, you're right. I have no allegiance to Orson, but I like the money, and he paid well. I just hope you haven't ruined the ship so much that it delays our departure."

"So, you do have a lab here. That means you should be able to grow skin. But would you?"

"Good question. I'm not totally devoid of humanity despite losing the ones I used to love. However, you are the enemy."

"What do you want? Oil, money, or just a safe trip home."

"Don't threaten me with that, Nick. I'm too experienced with human nature for that. You need something which you think I can help you with, but you have too many principles to kill for it."

"All-right. In the name of those you say you used to love, I ask you to take a look at the one I do love, to see if you can help her."

Brian hesitated a moment, then said, "I'm just interested enough in you and your town to do that. But no promises."

Nick finished his part of the inspection of the ship and then he and Brian got a pontoon and paddled it across the water. Once on land they mounted forcs and rode to the Lab.

"Now I remember why I gave up horseback riding," Brian remarked, as he ungracefully dismounted and rubbed his sore crotch. They walked into the Lab and once inside were met by the receptionist. After asking to see Dr. Gefert, they sat down and waited a short time until he approached, wearing, as usual, his crisp white Laboratory coat.

"Good afternoon, gentlemen, Nick," he said, extending his hand.

"Good afternoon, doctor," Nick replied. Doctor, I'd like you to meet Brian Armando, a nurse from the spaceship." The two men shook hands and Nick continued. "Dr. Gefert, on Earth they have developed some procedures for burn treatment that greatly improve the healing process. I learned today they have some of the technology on board the ship, and that Brian is knowledgeable in those procedures."

"I see," said Dr. Gefert. "Very interesting."

"I told Nick, that I'm not promising anything, but I did agree to take a look at the patient."

"Certainly, if there's something more that you can do for her. The main problem, as I'm sure you know, for burn patients, is that after the critical stage scars inevitably develop in and around the burn sites. I'm afraid our technology is limited in addressing that concern."

"Not that we have all the answers, doctor. Can we go now to see the patient?"

"Of course, come this way."

They followed him to Tara's room, where she lay sleeping peacefully on her side. Fresh gauze bandages covered the side of her neck and face.

"I need more light," said Brian.

Dr. Gefert opened the shades of the windows on both sides of the room and returned.

"The bandages need to be removed for me to see the extent of her wounds," stated Brian.

Dr. Gefert looked at Nick, who nodded his OK, and then he went to a drawer on one side of the room and returned with a long, thin pair of scissors. He gently cut off the bandages, exposing the red, oozing burns on the left side of her face and neck. Nick winced at the sight and turned to Dr. Gefert. "I didn't know it was that bad."

Brian drew closer, and for what seemed like a long time, he examined the wound. Then he turned, and looking at both of them said, "She's ready." Turning back to Tara, he opened his little black bag, and spoke to them while still facing her. "I'm going to take a small sample of skin from her neck beneath the wound. She probably won't even feel it. He used a small instrument, positioned it on her neck, and then withdrew it. "There, that's all I need. In fact, that's it for today." He returned the equipment to his bag and turned toward the door, obviously ready to go. The two followed his lead as he walked out of the room.

"Don't you have anything else besides those damn forcs, to get me back to the ship?"

"Yes, but aren't you going to do anything for her?" asked Nick.

"Of course," replied Brian. "Just get me that wagon, if that's the best you have. "To answer your question, I'm going to grow her some skin. Now, can we get a wagon or something besides a forc to get me back?"

"Use the Lab wagon," said Dr. Gefert. "I'll have Tore hitch up the forcs. How soon will you be back with this new skin you're going to grow, Mr. Armando?"

"Brian's the name. In two days. Can I count on your assistance?"

"Of course," Dr. Gefert replied.

Brian strode out, followed by Nick. Nick wanted to tell Brian how much he valued his help, but felt that Brian wouldn't appreciate any thanks. So, he only said, "I'll check to see if the wagon's ready."

The two of them drove quietly back, and Brian seemed to be engrossed with taking in the scenery and occasional houses along the way. When they reached the lake, he said, matter-of-factly, "You seem to have found a rather nice place here, Nick."

"Yes, I like it very much."

Brian got in the boat to row himself back to the boat, and as he started to pull away from the shore Nick asked, "When should I pick you up?"

"In two days, same time," he answered. Then, surprising Nick, he waved goodbye. Nick returned the gesture and turned to climb back up on the wagon. He didn't understand Brian, but he was grateful for his help.

Two days later, as scheduled, Nick came with the wagon to pick up Brian. This time, besides his small black bag, he carried a tube wrapped in plastic. When they reached the Lab, Nick parked the wagon, and they went inside where they met Dr. Gefert.

Tara was awake when they entered her room. Nick had informed her of the procedure that Brian would be doing, and she was ready. Dr. Gefert gingerly removed the bandages while Brian gently removed the covering of the tube. Then he unpacked surgical gloves, snuggled them on, and unscrewed the top of the canister. He added a white facemask, and then removed the contents of the cylinder. He looked closely at the burned area on Tara's face and neck, told her to close her eyes, and sprayed a strong smelling mist over the wounds. Then he said, "Tara, you can open your eyes now. I'm going to put a new skin over the burn area. It's your own skin; grown from a tiny piece I removed two days ago. You may want to close your eyes while I do this, though it won't hurt much. Just hold steady as I position it and cut off the edges. OK?"

Tara nodded her assent and Brian unrolled the package, opened it, and held up the sheet of fresh skin and placed it on her. "Now, lean back a little," he instructed her as with deft fingers he pulled at the edges until it smoothly covered the burn. Then he took a small pair of scissors and cut the excess off. The new skin overlapped a little on the edges. "That's all there is to it," he said. "I know the edges look unusual, but in a day or two the unneeded skin will shrivel up and drop off, leaving only that adhering to the wound. "Doctor," he said, turning from Tara toward Gefert, "treat this new skin with care for a couple days until it knits completely. If there should be any eruptions, they can be lanced. Within one to two weeks she and her skin should be almost as good as new."

"You mean that's all there is to it?" Dr. Gefert asked, obviously impressed.

"Yep, that's it," Brian answered, taking off his gloves, and zipping his bag. "Now if you'll get that wagon, I'm ready to leave."

"I can't thank you enough," said Nick.

"Just get that wagon and please don't get emotional. We do this a lot in my line of work and it's nothing state of the art. It's simple technology really. We happen to have it, you don't. He walked toward the door. "Let's go."

They drove in silence back to the ship. Nick wondered about the man who sat next to him. What could have turned him off from people, from feelings? Reaching the water's edge, he said goodbye, and watched him paddle across. The water level had dropped considerably in the last two days. Soon it would be gone completely. He turned the wagon around.

Chapter Twenty-Four

Nick was glad to be home with Tara and their son. At last, things were returning back to normal. Tara looked and felt good, and aside from a small discoloration on her neck, there was no evidence that she had been burned. Even that, he was told, would probably go away in time. It made him happy to hear her again sing lullabies to Rod, and to see her doing the ordinary things around the house that he had taken for granted. Soon it would be her birthday, her twenty-fourth, and it was going to be special. As for the spaceship, most of the repairs had been made, and soon it would return to the planet Algernon. He, and all the townspeople, would be glad to see it go.

The following Saturday Nick and Tara rode toward Range's house. In the carrier on Nick's shoulder, their baby was sound asleep.

"It's great to be going out again," said Tara, "and I can't think of a better place to go. A relaxed evening with Range, Tess, and their cute little kids."

"Yes," Nick replied, "I'm looking forward to it."

They arrived at Range's large house, dismounted, and walked to the doorway. Tara knocked on the door, and Tes opened it for them.

"Tara, Nick, it's so good to see you." She gave Tara a big hug and then hugged Nick. "Range, they're here!" she called out. "Come, let's go to the living room."

They followed her toward the living room, which was unlit, although it was already getting dark outside.

"Surprise!" they heard as they entered the room. "Happy birthday!" Sconces were quickly lit, and Nick and Tara saw their friends smiling at them. The music started, and Tara turned to Nick. "So, honey, a quiet night with Range and Tes."

She turned from him to look at all the people in the large room and to greet the guests who waited to wish her a happy birthday. It seemed to her that everyone she knew was there. "How wonderful," she said to Tes and Range.

Range gave her a big hug, saying, "Happy birthday, Tara. It sure is nice to see you healthy again. We were worried about you."

"Thank you for your concern and your prayers," answered Tara. "Without them I'd be lucky to be here today."

Nick and Tara visited with their friends and later she began talking with some friends from school. Nick went into another room to talk with Range and Ruskin. The three musicians began playing a very sprightly song and some of the young people began dancing in the middle of the room. Among them, were Thad, Frecka and Colleen. Nick casually looked around the room. Mrs. Marferti was talking to the midwife, Madelin, and Tara's sister; Shari was getting a drink for her daughter, Neena, who was holding hands with Tes' daughter, Rimmi. Trila, the pretty, young Lab assistant, was holding their son, Rod, and making eyes at the toddler, and Rod was grinning back at her. Dr. Gefert talked with Tes, who held a glass in her hand, and was probably getting all the information on Tara's care at the Lab. Something he said must have struck her as funny because she suddenly laughed out loud and shook her head as if she couldn't believe it. Nick smiled, not at anyone in particular, but because he enjoyed seeing everyone having a good time. He looked through the doorway at Tara, the prettiest woman there. She was engrossed in animated conversation with two of her friends. The music stopped momentarily, and he heard quite a few conversations going on at the same time.

He rejoined Ruskin and Range. They were talking about the warming weather and their plans for extensive vegetable gardens, complete with herbs. Before he knew it, it was time for a toast to Tara, and to sing the birthday song, so different from the English version, and to cut the Frango pie.

Then came the gifts. Nick watched as Tara reveled in them, some simple, but thoughtful, a few beautiful, and some that they could really use in their house. At the end of the gift giving, he stood up and put his arms around her and both of them thanked everyone for their kindness. The musicians began playing soft music and many got up to dance.

Much later in the evening, people began saying goodbye, telling Range and Tess how they enjoyed the party. Soon, only a few remained. Nick and Tara, carrying Rod who was sound asleep, warmly hugged their hosts as they, too, said goodbye. The night air was chill, and Tara wrapped Rod in a blanket as they set off for home. When they returned to their house, Nick lit a candle and they quietly put the baby to bed.

"You looked so beautiful, tonight, darling. I could hardly keep my eyes off you."

"You probably didn't notice that I was stealing glances at you all night."

"Really? I only saw you look at me a couple of times."

"Well, you know I don't always want to give away what I'm thinking" she said, coming to sit in his lap.

"This is where I like you," he said, putting his arm around her.

"This is where I like to be," she said, turning to kiss him.

"It doesn't hurt, does it?" he asked.

"Not at all," she answered, pressing her lips on his.

* * *

The next morning was a special day for the citizens of Crystal. It was the day the spaceship was scheduled to leave their world, forever they hoped. Hundreds of people lined the edges of the former lake, waiting to see it take off. Further away, in town, others kept looking in the direction of the ship, hoping to catch sight of it leaving. Nick had ridden out to the site, while Tara stayed home. At last, he heard the hiss of the steam that told him that soon it would lift off. He looked up to the port windows and thought he could see Colleen. She was waving. He lifted his hand. There was someone behind her; that would be Sabrina. The ship quivered a moment and then quietly lifted. The people around him yelled, and he waved goodbye to Colleen and Sabrina. He stood and watched the craft as it slowly disappeared from sight.

Then, he mounted his forc and rode home.

Map of the Regions
Not drawn to scale in order to show all the major sites

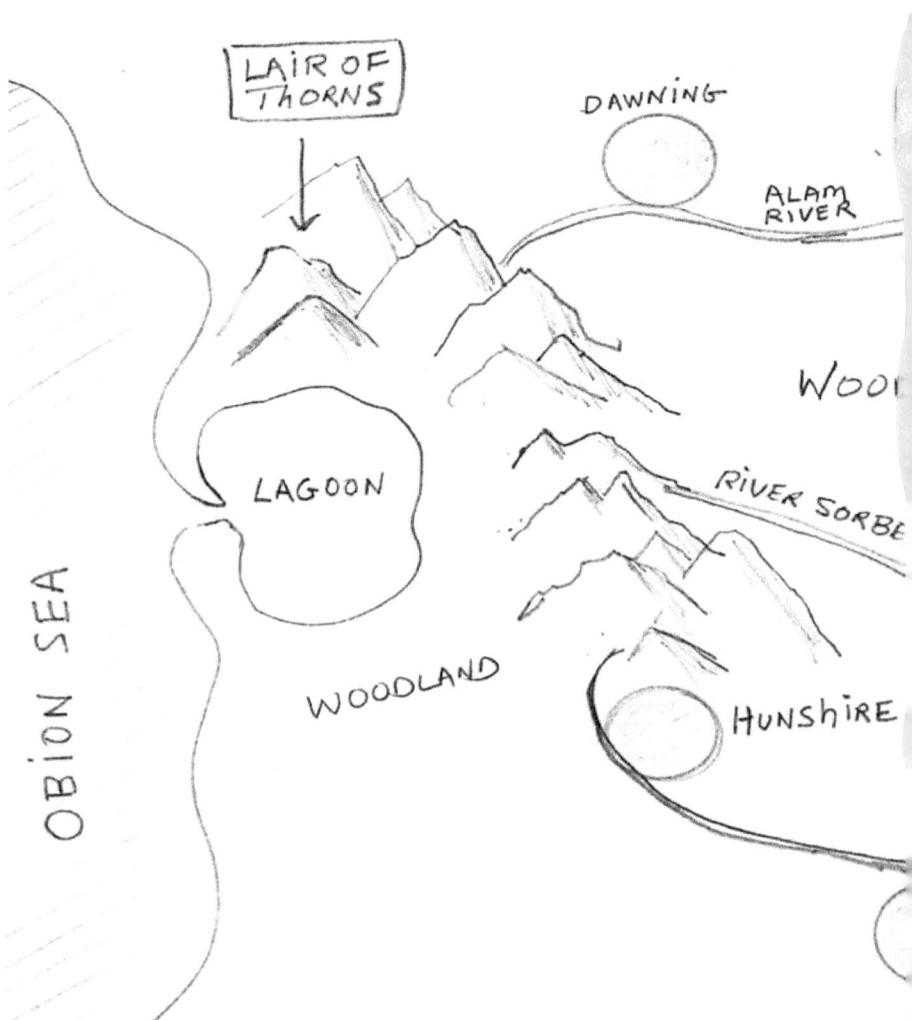

LAIR OF THORNS

DAWNING

ALAM RIVER

WOOI

RIVER SORBE

LAGOON

OBION SEA

WOODLAND

HUNSHIRE

The map includes sites for book two

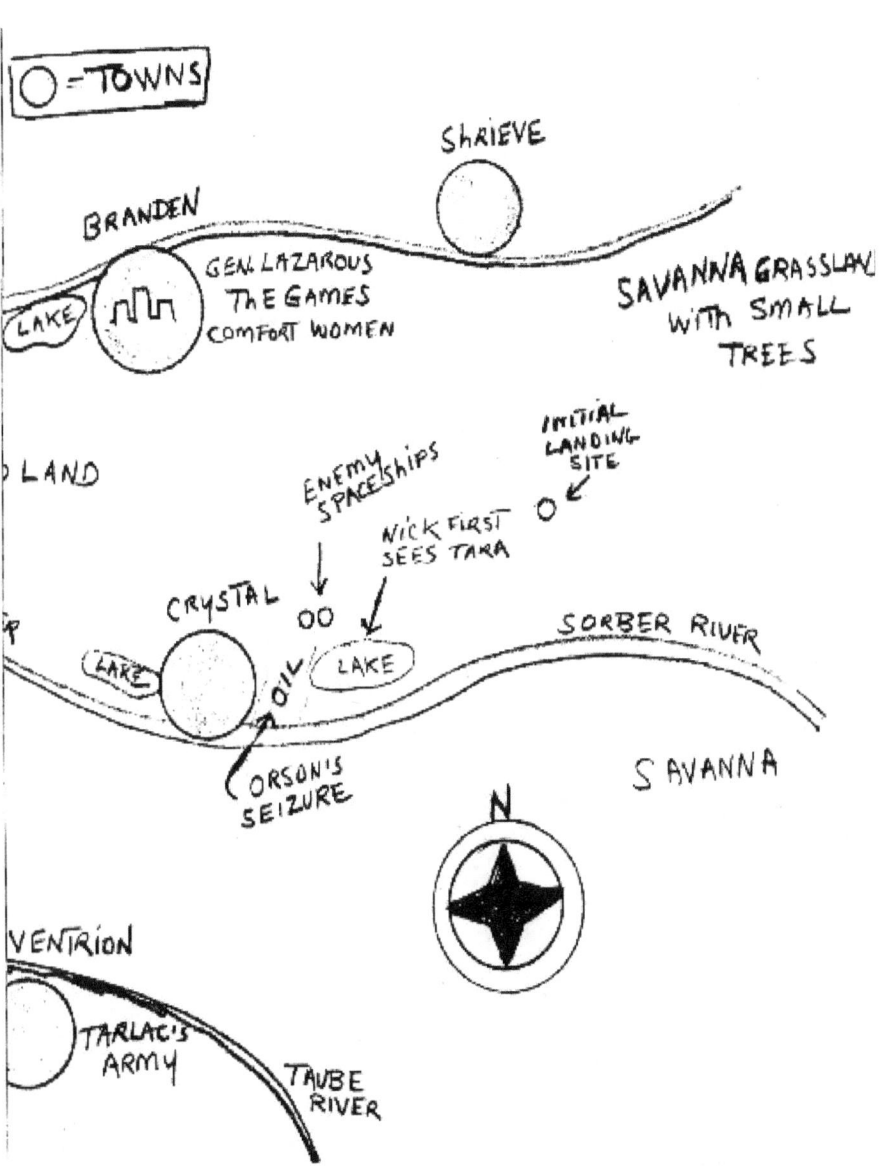

www.ingramcontent.com/pod-product-compliance
Lightning Source LLC
Chambersburg PA
CBHW071146170626
46809CB00002B/796